THE CHILDREN OF FREEDOM

On est tous l'etranger de quelqu'un

Also by Marc Levy

Just Like Heaven

MARC LEVY

The Children of Freedom

Translated from the French
by Sue Dyson

HARPER

Harper
An imprint of HarperCollins*Publishers*
77–85 Fulham Palace Road,
Hammersmith, London W6 8JB

www.harpercollins.co.uk

A Paperback Original 2008
1

Copyright © Marc Levy 2008
Translation copyright © Sue Dyson 2008
First published in French as *Les Enfants de la Liberté*

Marc Levy asserts the moral right to
be identified as the author of this work

A catalogue record for this book
is available from the British Library

ISBN: 978-0-00-727495-6

Set in Sabon by Palimpsest Book Production Limited,
Grangemouth, Stirlinghire

Printed and bound in Great Britain by
Clays Ltd, St Ives plc

Mixed Sources
Product group from well-managed
forests and other controlled sources
www.fsc.org Cert no. SW-COC-1806
© 1996 Forest Stewardship Council
FSC

FSC is a non-profit international organisation established
to promote the responsible management of the world's forests.
Products carrying the FSC label are independently certified
to assure consumers that they come from forests that are managed
to meet the social, economic and ecological needs
of present and future generations.

Find out more about HarperCollins and the environment at
www.harpercollins.co.uk/green

I am very fond of that verb, 'to resist'. To resist what imprisons us, to resist prejudices, hasty judgements, the desire to judge, everything that is bad in us and cries out to be expressed, the desire to abandon, the need to make people feel sorry for us, the need to talk about ourselves to the detriment of others, fashions, unhealthy ambitions, prevailing confusion.

To resist, and . . . to smile.

Emma Dancourt

For my father
for his brother Claude,
for all the children of freedom.

For my son
and for you my love.

Tomorrow I shall love you; today I don't yet know you. I began by walking down the staircase of the old apartment building where I lived, a little hurriedly, I confess. On the ground floor, my hand gripped the handrail and felt the beeswax that the concierge applied methodically as far as the bend on the second-floor landing on Mondays, and then up to the other floors on Thursdays. Although light was gilding the fronts of the buildings, the pavement was still glistening from the dawn rain. Just think: as I walked along lightly, I as yet knew nothing, nothing at all about you, you who would one day assuredly give me the most beautiful gift that life gives to human beings.

I went into the little café on rue Saint-Paul; I had time on my hands. There were only three people at the counter – not many of us had an abundance of leisure on that spring morning. And then, hands behind his raincoat, my father came in. He rested his elbows on the bar-top as if he hadn't seen me, an elegant mannerism that was all his own. He ordered a strong coffee and I caught

1

sight of the smile he was hiding from me as well as he could, which wasn't that good. He tapped on the counter, signalling to me that 'all was quiet' and I could at last approach. As I brushed against his jacket, I felt his strength, the weight of the sadness crushing his shoulders. He asked me if I was 'still sure'. I wasn't sure of anything, but I nodded. Then he pushed his cup towards me very discreetly. Underneath the saucer was a fifty-franc note. I refused it, but he set his jaw very firmly and muttered that in order to make war, one had to have a full belly. I took the banknote and, from the look he gave me, I realised that it was time for me to leave. I adjusted my cap, opened the café door and walked back up the street.

Walking past the window, I looked at my father inside the bar, a little stolen glance, that's all; and he gave me his final smile, to indicate to me that my collar wasn't on straight.

There was a look of urgency in his eyes that it took me years to understand, but all I have to do today is close mine and think of him for his last expression to come back to me, intact. I know that my father was sad that I was leaving, and I guess also that he sensed that we would never see each other again. It wasn't his death he was envisaging, but mine.

I think back to that moment in the Café des Tourneurs. It must demand a lot of courage on the part of a man to bury his son while standing right next to him, drinking

2

a chicory-blend coffee, to remain silent and not say to him, 'Go home right now and do your homework'.

One year earlier, my mother had gone to fetch our yellow stars from the police station. This was the signal for our exodus and we left for Toulouse. My father was a tailor and he would never sew that filth on a piece of fabric.

On that day, 21 March 1943, I was eighteen years old. I caught the tram and I left for a station that doesn't feature on any map: I went to seek out the Maquis.

Ten minutes ago I was still called Raymond; since I got off at the terminus of line 12, my name is Jeannot. Nameless Jeannot. At that still-gentle time of day, many people in my world have no idea what is going to happen to them. Dad and Mum don't know that soon a number is going to be tattooed on their arms; Mum doesn't know that on a railway platform, she will be separated from this man whom she loves almost more than us.

As for me, I don't know yet either that in ten years' time, I will recognise, in a heap of pairs of spectacles almost five metres high at the Auschwitz Memorial, the frames that my father slipped into the top pocket of his jacket, the last time I saw him at the Café des Tourneurs. My little brother Claude doesn't know that soon I will come looking for him, and that if he hadn't said yes, if we hadn't faced those years together, neither of us would have survived. My seven friends, Jacques, Boris, Rosine, Ernest, François, Marius, Enzo, don't know that they are

3

going to die shouting 'Vive la France', and almost all of them with a foreign accent.

I strongly suspect that my thoughts are confused, that the words will tumble over each other in my head, but from that Monday noon onwards and for the next two years, my heart is going to thump ceaselessly in my chest to the rhythm imposed by fear; I was afraid for two years, and sometimes I still wake up in the night with that same bloody feeling. But you are sleeping beside me, my love, even if I don't know it yet. Anyway, here is a little of the story of Charles, Claude, Alonso, Catherine, Sophie, Rosine, Marc, Emile, Robert, my Spanish, Italian, Polish, Hungarian and Romanian friends, the children of freedom.

PART ONE

1

You must understand the context within which we were living; context is important, as in the case of a sentence, for example. Once removed from its context it often changes its meaning, and during the years to come, so many sentences will be removed from their context in order to judge in a partial way and to condemn more easily. It's a habit that won't be lost.

In the first days of September, Hitler's armies had invaded Poland; France had declared war and nobody here or there doubted that our troops would drive back the enemy at the borders. Then the flood of German armoured divisions had swept through Belgium, and in a few weeks a hundred thousand of our soldiers would die on the battlefields of the North and the Somme.

Marshal Pétain was appointed to head the government; two days later, a general who refused to accept defeat launched an appeal for resistance from London. Pétain chose to sign the surrender of all our hopes. We had lost the war so quickly.

By swearing allegiance to Nazi Germany, Marshal Pétain led France into one of the darkest periods of her history. The Republic was abolished in favour of what would henceforth be called the French State. The map was divided by a horizontal line and the nation separated into two zones, one in the north, which was occupied, and the other in the south, which was allegedly free. But freedom there was entirely relative. Each day saw its share of decrees published, driving back into danger two million foreign men, women and children who now lived in France without rights: the right to carry out their professions, to go to school, to move around freely and soon, very soon, the very right to exist.

The nation had become amnesiac about the foreigners who came from Poland, Romania, Hungary, these Spanish or Italian refugees, and yet it had desperate need of them. It had been vitally necessary to repopulate a France that, twenty-five years earlier, had been deprived of a million and a half men who had died in the trenches of the Great War. Almost all my friends were foreigners, and they had all experienced the repression and abuses of power already perpetrated in their country for several years. German democrats knew who Hitler was, combatants in the Spanish Civil War knew about Franco's dictatorship, and those from Italy knew about Mussolini's Fascism. They had been the first witnesses of all the hatred, all the intolerance, of this pandemic that was infesting Europe, with its terrible funeral cortège of deaths and misery. Everyone already knew that defeat was only a foretaste; the worst was yet to come. But who would have wanted to listen to the bearers of bad news? France now no longer needed them. So, whether they had come from the East or the South, these exiles were arrested and interned in camps.

Marshal Pétain had not only given up, he was going to collude with Europe's dictators, and in our country, which was falling asleep around this old man, they were all already crowding around: the head of the government, ministers, prefects, judges, the police, and the Militia; each more eager than the last to carry out their terrible work.

2

Everything began like a children's game, three years earlier, on 10 November 1940. The unimpressive French Marshal, surrounded by a few prefects with silver laurels, came to Toulouse to start a tour of the *free zone* of a country that was in fact a prisoner of his defeat.

Those directionless crowds were a strange paradox, filled with wonder as they watched the Marshal raise his baton, the sceptre of a former leader who had returned to power, bringing a new order with him. But Pétain's new order would be an order of misery, segregation, denunciations, exclusions, murders and barbarity.

Some of those who would soon form our brigade knew about the internment camps, where the French government had locked up all those who had made the mistake of being foreigners, Jews or Communists. And in these camps in the South West, whether at Gurs, Argelès, Noé or Rivesaltes, life was abominable. Suffice to say that for anyone who had friends or family members who were prisoners, the arrival of the Marshal felt like a final assault on the small amount of freedom we had left.

Since the population was preparing to acclaim this very Marshal, we had to sound our alarm bell, awake people from this terribly dangerous fear, this fear that overcomes crowds and leads them to throw in the towel, to accept anything; to keep silent, with the sole, cowardly excuse that their neighbours are doing the same and that if their neighbours are doing the same, then that's what they should do.

For Caussat, one of my little brother's best friends, for Bertrand, Clouet or Delacourt, there's no question of throwing in the towel, no question of keeping silent, and the sinister parade that is about to take place in the streets of Toulouse will be the setting for a committed declaration.

What matters today is that words of truth, a few words of courage and dignity, rain down upon the procession. A text that is clumsily written, but that nonetheless denounces what ought to be denounced; and after that, what does it matter what the text says or doesn't say? Then we still have to work out how to make the tracts as broadly balanced as possible, without getting ourselves arrested on the spot by the forces of order.

But my friends have it all worked out. A few hours before the procession, they cross Esquirol Square with armfuls of parcels. The police are on duty, but who cares about these innocent-looking adolescents? Here they are at the right spot, a building at the corner of rue de Metz. So, all four slip into the stairwell and climb up to the roof, hoping that there won't be any observer up there. The horizon is empty and the city stretched out at their feet.

Caussat assembles the mechanism that he and his friends have devised. At the edge of the roof, a small board lies on a small trestle, ready to tip up like a swing. On one side they lay the pile of tracts that they have typed out, on the other side a can full of water. There is a small hole in the bottom of the vessel. Look: the water is trickling out into the guttering while they are already running off towards the street.

The Marshal's car is approaching; Caussat lifts his head and smiles. The limousine, a convertible, moves slowly up the street. On the roof, the can is almost empty and no longer weighs anything; so the plank tips up and the tracts flutter down. Today, 10 November 1940, will be the felonious Marshal's first autumn. Look at the sky: the sheets of paper pirouette and, to the supreme delight of these street urchins with their improvised courage, a few of them land on Marshal Pétain's peaked cap. People in the crowd bend down and pick up the leaflets. There is total confusion, the police are running about in all directions, and those who think they seek these kids cheering the procession like all the others don't realise

12

that it's their own first victory that they're celebrating.

They have dispersed and are now going their separate ways. As he goes home this evening, Caussat cannot have any idea that three days later he'll be denounced and arrested, and will spend two years in the municipal jails of Nîmes. Delacourt doesn't know that in a few months he will be killed by French police officers in a church in Agen, after being pursued and taking refuge there; Clouet is unaware that, next year, he will be executed by firing squad in Lyon; as for Bertrand, nobody will find the corner of a field beneath which he lies. On leaving prison, his lungs eaten away by tuberculosis, Caussat will rejoin the Maquis. Arrested once again, this time he will be deported. He was twenty-two years old when he died at Buchenwald.

You see, for our friends, everything began like a children's game, a game played by children who will never have time to become adults.

Those are the people I must talk to you about: Marcel Langer, Jan Gerhard, Jacques Insel, Charles Michalak, José Linarez Diaz, Stefan Barsony, and all those who will join them during the ensuing months. They are the first children of freedom, the ones who founded the 35th brigade. Why? In order to resist! It's their story that matters, not mine, and forgive me if sometimes my memory fails me, if I'm confused or get a name wrong.

What do names matter, my friend Urman said one day; there were few of us but we were all one. We lived

13

in fear, in secrecy, we didn't know what the next day would bring, and it is still difficult now to reopen the memory of just one of those days.

3

Believe me, I give you my word, the war was never like a film; none of my friends had the face of Robert Mitchum, and if Odette had had even the legs of Lauren Bacall, I would probably have tried to kiss her instead of hesitating like a bloody fool outside the cinema. Particularly since it was shortly before the afternoon when two Nazis killed her at the corner of rue des Acacias. Since that day, I've never liked acacias.

The hardest thing, and I know it's difficult to believe, was finding the Resistance.

Since the disappearance of Caussat and his friends, my little brother and I had been brooding. At high school, between the anti-Semitic comments of the teacher of history and geography, and the sarcastic remarks of the sixth-form boys we fought with, life wasn't much fun. I spent my evenings next to the wireless set, listening for news from London. On our return to school for the autumn term, we found small leaflets on our desks entitled 'Combat'. I saw the boy slip out of the classroom; he was an Alsatian refugee called Bergholtz. I ran at top speed to join him in the schoolyard, to tell him that I wanted to do what he did, distribute tracts for the Resistance. He laughed at me when I said that, but nonetheless I became his second-in-command. And in the days that followed, when school was over, I waited for him on the pavement. As soon as he reached the corner of the street I started walking, and he speeded up to join me. Together, we slid Gaullist newspapers into letterboxes; sometimes we threw them from the platforms of tramcars before jumping off while they were in motion and running away.

One evening, Bergholtz didn't appear when school ended; or the next day, either . . .

From then on, when school ended I and my little brother Claude would take the little train that ran along beside the Moissac road. In secret, we went to the 'Manor'. This was a large house where around thirty children were living in hiding – children whose parents had been deported: Girl Guides and Scouts had gathered them together and were taking care of them. Claude and I went there to hoe the vegetable garden, and sometimes gave lessons in maths and French to the youngest children. I took advantage of each day I spent at the Manor, to beg Josette, the woman in charge, to give me a lead that would enable me to join the Resistance, and each time, she looked at me, raised her eyes to the heavens, and pretended not to know what I was talking about.

But one day, Josette took me to one side in her office.

'I think I have something for you. Go and stand outside number 25, rue Bayard, at two o'clock in the afternoon. A passer-by will ask you the time. You will tell him that your watch isn't working. If he says to you "You're not Jeannot, are you?" It's the right man.'

And that's exactly how it happened . . .

I took my little brother and we met Jacques outside 25, rue Bayard, in Toulouse.

He entered the street wearing a grey overcoat and felt hat, with a pipe in the corner of his mouth. He threw his newspaper into the bin fixed to the lamp-post; I didn't pick it up because that wasn't the instruction. The instruction was to wait until he asked me the time. He stopped beside us, looked us up and down and when I answered that my watch wasn't working, he said he was called Jacques and asked which of us two was Jeannot. I immediately took a step forward, since the name was definitely mine.

Jacques recruited the partisans himself. He trusted no one and he was right. I know it's not very generous to say that, but you have to see it in context.

17

At that moment, I did not know that in a few days' time, a partisan called Marcel Langer would be sentenced to death because of a French prosecutor who had demanded his head and obtained it. And nobody in France, whether in the free zone or not, doubted that after one of our people had brought down that prosecutor outside his home, one Sunday on his way to mass, no court of law would dare to demand the head of an arrested partisan again.

Also, I did not know that I would kill a bastard, a senior official in the Militia, a denunciator and murderer of so many young resistors. The militiaman in question never knew that his death had hung by a thread. That I was so afraid of firing that I could have wet myself over it, that I almost dropped my weapon and that if that filth hadn't said, 'Have mercy,' this man who'd never had any for anyone, I wouldn't have been angry enough to bring him down with five bullets in the belly.

We killed people. I've spent years saying it: you never forget the face of someone you're about to shoot. But we never killed an innocent, not even an imbecile. I know it, and my children will know it too. That's what matters.

At the moment, Jacques is looking at me, weighing me up, sniffing me almost like an animal, trusting his instinct, and then he plants himself in front of me: what he will say in two minutes will change the course of my life.

'What exactly do you want?'

'To reach London.'

'Then I can't do anything for you,' says Jacques. 'London is a long way away and I don't have any contacts.'

I'm expecting him to turn his back on me and walk away but Jacques stays in front of me. His eyes are still on me; I try again.

'Can you put me in contact with the Maquis? I would like to go and fight with them.'

'That is also impossible,' Jacques continues, re-lighting his pipe.

'Why?'

'Because you say you want to fight. You don't fight in the Maquis; at best you collect packages, pass on messages, but resistance there is still passive. If you want to fight, it's with us.'

'Us?'

'Are you ready to fight in the streets?'

'What I want is to kill a Nazi before I die. I want a revolver.'

I had said that proudly. Jacques burst out laughing. I didn't understand what was so funny about it; in fact I even thought it was rather dramatic! And that was precisely what had made Jacques laugh.

'You've read too many books; we're going to have to teach you how to use your head.'

His paternalistic question had annoyed me a little, but I wasn't going to let him see my irritation. For months I'd been attempting to establish contact with the

Resistance and now I was in the process of spoiling everything.

I search for the right words that don't come, words that testify that I am someone on whom the partisans can rely. Jacques figures this out and smiles, and in his eyes I suddenly see something that might be a spark of affection.

'We don't fight to die, but for life, do you understand?'

It doesn't sound like much, but that phrase hit me like a massive punch. Those were the first words of hope I had heard since the start of the war, since I had begun living without rights, without status, deprived of all identity in this country that yesterday was still mine. I'm missing my father, my family too. What has happened? Everything around me has melted away; my life has been stolen from me, simply because I'm a Jew and that's enough for many people to want me dead.

My little brother is waiting behind me. He suspects that something important is afoot, so he gives a little cough as a reminder that he's there too. Jacques lays his hand on my shoulder.

'Come on, let's move. One of the first things you must learn is never to stay still, that's how you're spotted. A lad waiting in the street, in times like this, always arouses suspicion.'

And here we are, walking along a pavement in a dark alleyway, with Claude following close on our heels.

'I may have some work for you. This evening, you'll go and sleep at 15, rue du Ruisseau, with old Mme

Dublanc, she'll be your landlady. You will tell her that you're both students. She will certainly ask you what has happened to Jérôme. Answer that you're taking his place, and he's left to find his family in the North.'

I guessed that this was an open sesame that would give us access to a roof and, who could tell, perhaps even a heated room. So, taking my role very seriously, I asked who this Jérôme was, so that I'd be well-informed if old Mme Dublanc tried to find out more about her new tenants. Jacques immediately brought me back to a harsher reality.

'He died the day before yesterday, two streets from here. And if the answer to my question, "Do you want to come into direct contact with the war?" is still yes, then let's say he's the one you're replacing. This evening, someone will knock at your door. He will tell you he's come on behalf of Jacques.'

With an accent like that, I knew very well that this wasn't his real first name, but I knew too that when you entered the Resistance, your former life no longer existed, and your name disappeared with it. Jacques slipped an envelope into my hand.

'As long as you keep paying the rent, old Mme Dublanc won't ask any questions. Go and get yourselves photographed; there's a kiosk at the railway station. Now clear off. We'll have the opportunity to meet up again.'

Jacques continued on his way. At the corner of the alleyway, his lanky silhouette vanished into the mist.

'Shall we get going?' asked Claude.

*   *   *

21

I took my little brother to a café and we had just what we needed to warm ourselves up. Sitting at a table by the window, I watched the tramcar moving up the high street.

'Are you sure?' Claude asked, raising the steaming cup to his lips.

'What about you?'

'Me? I'm sure I'm going to die, but apart from that I don't know.'

'If we join the Resistance, it's to live, not to die. Do you understand?'

'Wherever did you dredge that up from?'

'Jacques said it to me just now.'

'So if Jacques says it . . .'

And then a long silence ensued. Two militiamen entered the café and sat down, paying us no attention. I was afraid that Claude might do something foolish, but all he did was shrug his shoulders. His stomach rumbled.

'I'm hungry,' he said. 'I'm fed up with being hungry.'

I was ashamed of having a seventeen-year-old lad in front of me who didn't have enough to eat, ashamed of my powerlessness; but that evening we might finally join the Resistance and then, I was certain, things would eventually change. Spring will return, Jacques would say one day, so, one day, I will take my little brother to a baker's shop and buy him all the cakes in the world, which he will devour until he can eat no more, and that spring will be the most beautiful of my life.

We left the little café and, after a short stop in the

railway station concourse, we went to the address Jacques had given us.

Old Mme Dublanc didn't ask us any questions. She just said that Jérôme mustn't care much about his things to leave like that. I handed her the money and she gave me the key to a ground-floor room that looked out onto the street.

'It's only for one person!' she added.

I explained that Claude was my little brother, and that he was visiting me here for a few days. I think Mme Dublanc had a slight suspicion that we weren't students, but as long as she was paid her rent, the lives of her tenants were nothing to do with her. The room wasn't much to look at, with some old bedding, a water jug and a basin. Calls of nature were answered in a privy at the bottom of the garden.

We waited for the rest of the afternoon. At nightfall, someone knocked at the door. Not in the way that makes you jump; not the confident rap of the Militia when they're coming to arrest you, just two little knocks. Claude opened the door. Emile entered, and I sensed immediately that we were going to be bound by friendship.

Emile isn't very tall and he hates it when people say he's short. It's a year since he embarked on a clandestine life and everything about his attitude shows he's become accustomed to it. Emile is calm and wears a funny kind of smile, as if nothing were important any more.

At the age of ten, he fled from Poland because his

family were being persecuted. Aged barely fifteen, watching Hitler's armies parading through Paris, Emile realised that the people who had previously wanted to take away his life in his own country had now come here to finish their dirty work. He stared with his child's eyes and could never completely close them again. Perhaps that's what gives him that odd smile; no, Emile's not short, he's stocky.

It was Emile's concierge who saved him. It has to be said that in this sad France, there were some great landladies, the sort who looked at us differently, who wouldn't accept the killing of decent people, just because their religion was different. Women who hadn't forgotten that, immigrant or otherwise, a child is sacred.

Emile's father had received the letter from police headquarters telling him he must go and buy yellow stars to sew onto coats, at chest level and clearly visible, the instructions said. At that time, Emile and his family were living in Paris, on rue Sainte-Marthe, in the tenth arrondissement. Emile's father went to the police station on avenue Vellefaux; there were four children, so he was given four stars, plus one for him and another for his wife. Emile's father paid for the stars and went back home, hanging his head, like an animal who'd been branded with a red-hot iron. Emile wore his star, and then the police raids started. It was no good rebelling, telling his father to tear off that piece of filth, nothing was any use. Emile's father was a man who lived

24

according to the law, and besides, he trusted this country, which had welcomed him in; here, you couldn't do bad things to decent folk.

Emile had found lodgings in a little maid's room in the attics. One day, as he was coming downstairs, his concierge had rushed up behind him.

'Quick, go back up, they're arresting all the Jews in the streets, the police are everywhere. They've gone mad. Quickly Emile, go up and hide.'

She told him to close his door and not answer to anyone; she would bring him something to eat. A few days later, Emile went out without his star. He returned to rue Sainte-Marthe, but there was no one now in his parents' apartment; neither his father, nor his mother, nor his two little sisters, one aged six and the other fifteen, not even his brother, whom he'd begged to stay with him, not to go back to the apartment on rue Sainte-Marthe.

Emile had nobody left; all his friends had been arrested; two of them, who had taken part in a demo at porte Saint-Martin, had managed to escape via rue de Lancry when some German soldiers on motorcycles had machine-gunned the procession; but they had been caught. They ended up being stood up against a wall and shot. As a reprisal, a resistor known by the name of Fabien had killed an enemy officer the following day, on the metro platform at Barbès station, but that hadn't succeeded in bringing back Emile's two friends.

No, Emile had nobody left, apart from André, one

final friend with whom he had taken a few accountancy lessons. So he went to see him, to try and get a little help. It was André's mother who opened the door to him. And when Emile told her that his family had been taken away, that he was all alone, she took her son's birth certificate and gave it to Emile, advising him to leave Paris as quickly as possible. 'Do whatever you can with it; you might even get yourself an identity card.' The name of André's family was Berté, and they weren't Jewish, so the certificate was a golden safe-conduct pass.

At the Gare d'Austerlitz, Emile waited as the train for Toulouse was assembled at the platform. He had an uncle down there. Then he got into a carriage, hid under a seat and didn't move. In the compartment, the passengers had no idea that behind their feet a kid was hiding; a kid who was in fear for his life.

The train set off, but Emile stayed hidden, motionless, for hours. When the train crossed into the free zone, Emile left his hiding place. The passengers' expressions were a sight to see when this kid emerged from nowhere; he admitted that he had no papers; a man told him to go back into his hiding place immediately, as he was accustomed to this journey and the gendarmes would soon be carrying out another check. He would let him know when he could come out.

You see, in this sad France, there were not only some great concierges and landladies, but also generous mothers, splendid travellers, anonymous people who resisted in their own way, anonymous people who refused to do as their neighbours did, anonymous people who broke the rules because they were shameful.

Into this room, which Mme Dublanc has been renting to me for a few hours, comes Emile, with his whole story, his whole past. And even if I don't know Emile's story yet, I can tell from the look in his eyes that we're going to get on well.

'So, you're the new one are you?' he asks.

'We both are,' cuts in my little brother, who hates it when people act as if he isn't there.

'Have you got the photos?' asks Emile.

And he takes from his pocket two identity cards, some ration books and a rubber stamp. Once the papers have been sorted out, he stands up, turns the chair around and sits down again, astride it.

'Let's talk about your first mission, Jeannot. Well, as there are two of you, let's call it the first mission for both of you.'

My brother's eyes are sparkling. I don't know if it's hunger that's gnawing away at his stomach or the new appetite for a promise of action, but I can see clearly that his eyes are sparkling.

'You're going to have to steal some bicycles,' says Emile.

Claude goes back to the bed, looking downcast.

'Is that what resisting means? Pinching bicycles? I've come all this way for someone to ask me to be a thief?'

'So, do you think you're going to carry out your

missions in a car? The bicycle is the partisan's best friend. Think for a moment, if that's not too much to ask of you. Nobody takes any notice of a man on a bike; you're just some guy who's coming back from the factory or leaving for work, depending on the time. A cyclist melts into the crowd, he's mobile, he can sneak around everywhere. You do your job, you clear off on your bike, and while people are still wondering what exactly happened, you're already on the other side of town. So if you want to be entrusted with important missions, start by going and pinching your bicycles!'

So, that was the lesson for the day. We still had to work out where we were going to pinch the bikes from. Emile must have anticipated my question. He had already done some research and told us about the corridor of an apartment building where three bicycles slept, never chained up. We'd have to act fast; if all went well, we were to come and find him early in the evening at the house of a friend. He asked me to learn the friend's address by heart. It was a few kilometres away, in the outskirts of Toulouse; a small, disused railway station in the Loubers district. 'Hurry,' Emile had insisted, 'you must be there before the curfew.' It was spring, darkness would not fall for several hours, and the apartment building with the bikes wasn't far from here. Emile left and my little brother continued to sulk.

I managed to convince Claude that Emile wasn't wrong and also that it was probably a test. My little brother moaned, but agreed to follow me.

We made a remarkable success of our first mission. Claude was hiding in the street; after all, you could get two years in prison for stealing a bicycle. The corridor was deserted and, as Emile had promised, there were indeed three bikes there, resting against each other, and none of them chained up.

Emile told me to nab the first two, but the third one, the one against the wall, was a sports model with a flaming red frame and handlebars with leather grips. I moved the one in front, which fell with a horrifying racket. Already I could see myself having to gag the concierge, but by a stroke of good luck the lodge was empty and nobody disturbed my work. The bike I fancied wasn't easy to capture. When you're afraid, your hands become clumsier. The pedals were caught up and whatever I did, I couldn't separate the two bicycles. After a thousand attempts, all the while trying to calm my pounding heart as best I could, I finally succeeded. My little brother peeped in, finding that time dragged when you were hanging about on the pavement, all alone.

-Good grief, what on earth are you up to?

-Here, take your bike and stop moaning.

-Why can't I have the red one?

-Because it's too big for you!

Claude started moaning again, and I pointed out to him that we were on an official mission and that this was not the time for an argument. He shrugged his shoulders and mounted his bicycle. A quarter of an hour later, pedalling flat out, we were following the route of the disused railway line in the direction of the small former railway station at Loubers.

Emile opened the door to us.

'Look at these bikes, Emile!'

Emile assumed a strange expression, as if he wasn't pleased to see us, and then he let us in. Jan, a tall, thin guy, looked at us and smiled. Jacques was in the room too; he congratulated us both and, seeing the red bike I'd chosen, he burst out laughing again.

'Charles will disguise them so they're unrecognisable,' he added, laughing even louder.

I still didn't see what was funny about it and apparently neither did Emile, in view of the expression he was wearing.

A man in a vest came down the stairs. He was the one who lived here in this little disused station, and for the first time I met the brigade's handyman. The one who took apart and reassembled the bikes, the one who made the bombs to blow up the locomotives, the one who explained how, on railway flat wagons, you could sabotage the cockpits assembled in the region's factories, or how to cut the cables on the wings of bombers, so that once they were assembled in Germany, Hitler's planes wouldn't take off for quite a while. I must tell you about Charles, this friend who had lost all his front teeth in the Spanish Civil War, this friend who had passed through so many countries that he had mixed up the languages and invented his own dialect, to the point where nobody

30

could really understand him. I must tell you about Charles because, without him, we would never have been able to accomplish all that we were going to do in the coming months.

That evening, in that ground-floor room in an old, disused railway station, we're all aged between seventeen and twenty, we're soon going to make war and despite his hearty laugh just now when he saw my red bike, Jacques looks worried. I'm soon going to find out why.

Someone knocks at the door, and this time Catherine comes in. She's beautiful, is Catherine, and what's more, from the look she exchanges with Jan, I'd swear they're a couple, but that's impossible. Rule number one: no love affairs when you're living a secret life in the Resistance, Jan will explain while we're sitting at the table, as he introduces us to the way we must behave. It's too dangerous; if you're arrested, there's a risk that you'll talk to save the one you love. 'A condition of being a partisan is that you don't get yourself attached,' Jan said. And yet he feels an attachment to each one of us and I can work that out already. My little brother isn't listening to anything, he's devouring Charles's omelette; at times, I tell myself that if I don't stop him, he'll end up eating the fork as well. I can see him eyeing up the frying pan. Charles sees him too, and smiles. He gets up and goes to serve him up another portion. It's true that Charles's omelette is delicious, even more so for our bellies, which have been empty for so long. Behind the station, Charles

31

cultivates a kitchen garden. He has three hens and even some rabbits. He's a gardener, is Charles, anyway that's his cover and the people around here like him a lot, even if his accent makes it clear that French isn't his native tongue. He gives them lettuces. And besides, his kitchen garden is a splash of colour in the dreary area, so the people around here like him, this improvised colourist, even if he does have a terrible foreign accent.

Jan speaks in a steady voice. He is hardly any older than I am but he already has the air of a mature man and his calm commands respect. What he tells us thrills us, there is a sort of aura around him. What Jan says is terrible: he talks to us about the missions carried out by Marcel Langer and the first members of the brigade. They've already been operating in the Toulouse area for a year, Marcel, Jan, Charles and José Linarez. Twelve months, in the course of which they've thrown grenades at a dinner party for Nazi officers, blown up a barge filled to bursting with petrol, burned down a garage for German lorries. So many operations that the list alone is too long to tell in a single evening; Jan's words are terrible, and yet he exudes a sort of tenderness that everyone here misses, abandoned children that we are.

Jan's stopped talking. Catherine is back from town with news of Marcel, the leader of the brigade. He's incarcerated in Saint-Michel prison.

His downfall was so stupid. He went to Saint-Agne station to collect a suitcase conveyed by a young woman in the brigade. The suitcase contained explosives, sticks of dynamite, of ablonite EG antifreeze, twenty-four millimetres in diameter. These sixty gramme sticks were put aside by a few Spanish miners who were sympathisers, and who were employed in the factory at the Paulilles quarry.

It was José Linarez who had organised the mission to collect the suitcase. He had refused to let Marcel get on board the little train that shuttled between the Pyrenean towns; the girl and a male Spanish friend had made the return trip alone as far as Luchon and taken possession of the package; the handover was to take place at Saint-Agne. The halt at Saint-Agne was more of a level crossing than a railway station proper. There weren't many people in this undeveloped corner of the countryside; Marcel waited behind the barrier. Two gendarmes were patrolling, looking out for any travellers transporting foodstuffs destined for the region's black market. When the girl got off, her eyes met those of a gendarme. Feeling she was being watched, she took a step back, immediately arousing the man's interest. Marcel instantly realised that she was going to be stopped, so he stepped in front of her. He signalled to her to approach the gate that separated the halt from the track, took the suitcase from her hands and ordered her to get the hell out of it. The gendarme didn't miss any of this and rushed at Marcel. When he asked him what the suitcase contained, Marcel replied that he didn't have the key. The gendarme wanted him to follow him, so Marcel told him that it was a consignment for the Resistance and that he must let him pass.

The gendarme didn't care about his story, and Marcel was taken to the central police station. The typed report stated that a terrorist in possession of sixty sticks of dynamite had been arrested at Saint-Agne station.

The affair was an important one. A police superintendent answering to the name of Caussié took over, and for days Marcel was beaten. He didn't let slip a single name or address. The conscientious superintendent went to Lyon to consult his superiors. At last the French police and the Gestapo had a case that they could use as an example: a foreigner in possession of explosives, and what's more he was a Jew and a Communist too; in other words a perfect terrorist and an eloquent example that they were going to use to stem any desire for resistance in the population.

Once charged, Marcel was handed over to the special section of the public prosecutor's department. Deputy Public Prosecutor Lespinasse, a man of the extreme right who was fiercely anti-Communist and dedicated to the Vichy regime, would be the ideal prosecutor; the Marshal's government could count on his fidelity. With him, the law would be applied without any restraint, without any attenuating circumstances, without any concern for the context. Scarcely had Lespinasse been given the task when, swollen with pride, he swore before the court to obtain Marcel's head.

*   *   *

In the meantime, the young woman who had escaped arrest had gone to warn the brigade. The friends immediately got into contact with Maître Arnal, one of the best lawyers at the court. For him the enemy was German, and the moment had come to take up position in favour of these people who were being persecuted without reason. The brigade had lost Marcel, but it had just won over to its cause a man of influence, who was respected in the town. When Catherine talked to him about his fees, Arnal refused to be paid.

The morning of 11 June 1943 will be terrible, terrible in the memory of partisans. Everyone's leading their own lives and soon destinies will intersect. Marcel is in his cell. He looks out through the skylight at the dawn; today is the day of his trial. He knows he's going to be convicted, he has little hope. In an apartment not far from there, the old lawyer who is in charge of his defence is putting his notes in order. His domestic help comes into his office and asks him if he wants her to make him some breakfast. But Maître Arnal isn't hungry on this morning of 11 June 1943. All night he has heard the voice of the deputy prosecutor demanding his client's head; all night he has tossed and turned in his bed, searching for strong words, the right words that will counter the indictment of his adversary, prosecuting counsel Lespinasse.

And while Maître Arnal revises again and again, the fearsome Lespinasse enters the dining room of his opulent house. He sits down at the table, opens his newspaper and drinks his morning coffee, which is served to him by his wife, in the dining room of his opulent house.

In his cell, Marcel is also drinking the hot brew brought to him by the warder. An usher has just delivered him his citation to appear before the special Session of the Toulouse Court. Marcel looks out through the skylight. He thinks about his little girl, his wife, down there somewhere in Spain, on the other side of the mountains.

Lespinasse's wife stands up and kisses her husband on the cheek. She leaves for a meeting about good works. The deputy prosecutor puts on his overcoat and looks at himself in the mirror, proud of his fine appearance, convinced that he will win. He knows his text by heart, a strange paradox for a man who really doesn't have one – a heart, that is. A black Citroën waits outside his house and is already driving him to the courthouse.

On the other side of town, a gendarme chooses his best shirt from his wardrobe. It is white, and the collar has been starched. He is the one who arrested the accused and today he has been summoned to appear. As he ties his tie, young gendarme Cabannac has moist hands. There is something not right about what is going to happen, something rotten, and Cabannac knows it; what's more, if it happened again he would let him get away, that guy with the black suitcase. The enemies are the Boche, not lads like him. But he thinks of the French State and its administrative mechanism. He is a mere cog and he can't be found wanting. He knows the mechanism well, does Gendarme Cabannac; his father taught him all about it, and the morality that goes with it. At the weekend, he enjoys repairing his motorbike in his father's shed. He knows full well that if one piece happens to be missing, the whole mechanism seizes up. So, with moist hands, Cabannac tightens the knot of his tie on the starched collar of his fine white shirt and heads for the tram stop.

A black Citroën moves away into the distance and overtakes the tram. At the back of the carriage, sitting on the wooden bench, an old man rereads his notes. Maître Arnal looks up and then plunges back into his reading. The game promises to be a hard one but nothing is lost. It is unthinkable that a French court could sentence a patriot to death. Langer is a brave man, one of those who act because they are valiant. He knew that as soon as he met him in his cell. His face was so misshapen; under his cheekbones, you could make out the marks of the punches that had landed there, and the gashed lips were blue and swollen. He wonders what Marcel looked like before he was beaten up like that, before his face was punched out of shape, taking on the imprint of the violence it had suffered. They are fighting for our freedom, mused Arnal; it really isn't complicated to work that out. If the court can't see it yet, he'll do his damnedest to open their eyes. Say they sentence him to prison for example, OK, that will save appearances, but death? No. That would be a judgment unworthy of French magistrates. By the time the tram halts with a screech of metal at the courthouse station, Maître Arnal has recovered

37

the confidence necessary to plead his case well. He's going to win this case, he'll cross swords with his adversary, Deputy Prosecutor Lespinasse and he will save that young man's head. Marcel Langer, he repeats to himself softly as he climbs the steps.

While Maître Arnal walks down the Palais' long corridor, Marcel, handcuffed to a gendarme, waits in a small office.

The trial takes place in camera. Marcel is in the dock, Lespinasse stands up and doesn't even glance at him; he scorns the man he wants to convict, and the last thing he wants is to get to know him. A few scant notes lie in front of him. First, he pays homage to the gendarmerie's perspicacity, which ensured that a dangerous terrorist was prevented from doing harm, and then he reminds the court of its duty, that of observing the law and seeing that it is respected. Pointing at the man on trial without once looking at him, Deputy Prosecutor Lespinasse voices his accusations. He enumerates the long list of murder attempts the Germans have suffered, and he recalls also that France signed the armistice in honour and that the accused, who is not even French, has no right to call the State's authority into question again. To grant him extenuating circumstances would be tantamount to scorning the Marshal's word. 'The reason the Marshal signed the armistice was for the good of the Nation,' Lespinasse continues, with vehemence. 'And a foreign terrorist has no right to judge to the contrary.'

Finally, to add a little humour, he reminds the court that Marcel Langer was not carrying firecrackers for the fourteenth of July, but explosives destined to destroy German installations, and so disturb the citizens' tranquillity. Marcel smiles. The fireworks of the fourteenth of July are a long way away.

Should the defence put forward arguments of a patriotic nature, with the aim of granting Langer extenuating circumstances, Lespinasse again reminds the court that the defendant is a stateless person, that he chose to abandon his wife and little girl in Spain, where he had previously gone to fight, although he was Polish and a stranger to the conflict. That France, in its indulgence, had welcomed him in, but not to come here, to our homeland, bringing disorder and chaos. 'How can a man without a homeland claim to have acted according to a patriotic ideal?' And Lespinasse sniggers at his own witticism, his turn of phrase. Fearing that the court may be afflicted with amnesia, he reminds them of the act of accusation, lists the laws that sentence such acts to capital punishment, and congratulates himself on the severity of the laws in force. Then he pauses for a moment, turns towards the man he is accusing and finally consents to look at him. 'You are a foreigner, a Communist and a partisan, three separate reasons, each of which is sufficient for me to ask the court for your head.' This time, he turns away towards the magistrates and in a calm voice demands that Marcel Langer should be sentenced to death.

*　　*　　*

Maître Arnal is white-faced. He stands up at the same moment as the smug Lespinasse sits down. The old lawyer's eyes are half-closed, his chin tilted forward, his hands clenched in front of his mouth. The court is motionless, silent; the clerk barely dares lay down his pen. Even the gendarmes are holding their breath, waiting for him to speak. But for the moment, Maître Arnal cannot say anything, overcome as he is with nausea.

He is therefore the last person here to realise that the rules have been rigged, that the decision has already been taken. And yet, in his cell, Langer had told him he knew that he was condemned in advance. But the old lawyer still believed in justice and had kept on assuring him that he was wrong, that he would defend him as he should and that the judgment would be in his favour. Behind him, Maître Arnal feels Marcel's presence, thinks he can hear him murmuring: 'You see, I was right, but I don't blame you, in any case, you couldn't do anything.'

So he raises his arms, his sleeves seeming to float in the air, breathes in and launches into a final speech for the defence. How can the gendarmerie's work be praised, when the defendant's face bears the stigmata of the violence he has suffered? How can anyone dare to joke about the fourteenth of July in this France that no longer has the right to celebrate it? And what does the prosecutor really know about these foreigners whom he accuses?

As he got to know Langer in the visiting room, he was able to find out how much these stateless individuals, as Lespinasse calls them, love this country that has welcomed them in even to the point where, like Marcel Langer, they will sacrifice their lives to defend it. The accused is not the man the prosecutor depicts. He is a sincere and honest man, a father who loves his wife and his daughter. He did not leave Spain to join the fighting, but because, more than all, he loves humanity and human freedom. Yesterday, wasn't France still the land of human right? Sentencing Marcel Langer to death means sentencing the hope for a better world.

Arnal's plea lasted more than an hour, using up his last reserves of strength; but his voice rings out without an echo in this court that has already given its verdict. Today, 11 June 1943, is a sad day. The sentence has been pronounced, and Marcel will be sent to the guillotine. When Catherine hears the news in Arnal's office, her lips purse tightly and she takes the blow. The lawyer swears that he has not finished, that he will go to Vichy to plead for clemency.

That evening, in the little disused railway station that serves Charles as lodgings and a workshop, the table has grown. Since Marcel's arrest, Jan has taken command of the brigade. Catherine sat down next to him. From the look they exchanged, I knew this time that they loved each other. And yet the look in Catherine's eyes is sad, and her lips can barely utter the words she has to tell us. She is the one who announces to us that Marcel has been sentenced to death by a French prosecutor. I don't know Marcel, but like all the comrades around the table, I have a heavy heart and as for my little brother, he has completely lost his appetite.

Jan paces up and down. Everyone is silent, waiting for him to speak.

'If they carry it out, we shall have to kill Lespinasse, to scare the hell out of them; otherwise, these scum will sentence to death all the partisans who fall into their hands.'

'While Arnal is lodging his plea for clemency, we can prepare for the operation,' continues Jacques.

'It will take a lot more time,' mutters Charles in his strange language.

'And in the meantime, aren't we going to do anything?' cuts in Catherine, who is the only one who's understood what he was saying.

Jan thinks and continues to pace up and down the room.

'We must act now. Since they have condemned Marcel to death, let's condemn one of their people too. Tomorrow, we'll take down a German officer right in the middle of the street and we'll distribute a tract to explain why we did it.'

I certainly don't have much experience of political operations, but an idea is going around in my head and I venture to speak.

'If we really want to scare the hell out of them, it would be even better to drop the tracts first, and take down the German officer afterwards.'

'And that way they'll all be on their guard. Have you got any more ideas like that?' argues Emile, who seems decidedly mad at me.

'My idea's not bad, not if the operations are a few minutes apart and carried out in good order. Let me explain. If we kill the Boche first and drop the tracts afterwards, we'll look like cowards. In the eyes of the population, Marcel was judged first and only then sentenced.

'I doubt that *La Dépêche* will report on the arbitrary condemnation of a heroic partisan. They'll announce that a terrorist has been sentenced by a court. So let's play by their rules; the town must be with us, not against us.'

Emile wanted to shut me up, but Jan signalled to him to let me speak. My reasoning was logical, I just needed to find the right words to explain to my friends what I had in mind.

'First thing tomorrow morning, we should print a communiqué announcing that as a reprisal for Marcel Langer's death penalty, the Resistance has condemned a German officer to death. We should also announce that the sentence will be applied that very afternoon. I will take care of the officer, and – at the same moment – you will drop the tract everywhere. People will become aware of it immediately, while news of the operation will take a lot of time to spread through the town. The news-papers won't talk about it until tomorrow's edition, and the right chronology of events will appear to have been respected.'

One by one, Jan consults the members seated at the table, and eventually his eyes meet mine. I know that he agrees with my reasoning, except perhaps for one detail: he raised an eyebrow slightly at the moment when I mentioned in passing that I would kill the German myself.

In any event, if he hesitates too much, I have an irrefutable argument; after all, the idea is mine, and besides, I stole my bicycle, so I've complied with the rules of the brigade.

Jan looks at Emile, Alonso, Robert and then Catherine, who agrees with a nod. Charles has missed none of the scene. He stands up, heads for the cupboard under the stairs and comes back with a shoe box. He hands me a barrel revolver.

'Be better if you and brother here sleep tonight.'

Jan approaches me.

'Right, you'll fire the gun; Spaniard,' he said, designating Alonso, 'you will be the lookout; and you, young one, you'll hold the bicycle in the direction of the getaway.'

There. Of course, said like that it's quite anodyne, except that Jan and Catherine went away again into the night, and I now had a pistol in my hand, with six bullets, and my cretin of a little brother who wanted to know how it worked. Alonso leant over towards me and asked me how Jan knew that he was Spanish, when he hadn't said a word all evening. 'And how did he know that the shooter would be me?' I told him with a shrug of my shoulders. I hadn't answered him, but my friend's silence testified that my question must have gained the upper hand over his.

That night, we slept for the first time in Charles's dining room. I lay down completely knackered, but nevertheless with a massive weight on my chest; first my little brother's head – he'd acquired the bloody awful habit of sleeping pressed up against me since we were separated from our parents – and, worse still, the pistol in the left pocket of my jacket. Even though there weren't any bullets in it, I was afraid that in my sleep, it might blow a hole in my little brother's head.

As soon as everyone was properly asleep, I got up on my tiptoes and went out into the garden behind the house. Charles had a dog, which was as gentle as it was stupid.

I'm thinking of it because that night, I had a desperate need for its spaniel muzzle. I sat down on the chair under the washing line, I looked at the sky and I took the gun out of my pocket. The dog came to sniff at the barrel, and I stroked its head, telling it that it would definitely be the only one in my lifetime allowed to sniff the barrel of my weapon. I said that because at that moment I really needed to put on a bold front.

One late afternoon, by stealing two bikes, I had entered the Resistance, and it's only now, hearing my little brother, snoring like a child with a blocked nose, that I really realised it. Jeannot, Marcel Langer brigade; during the months to come, I was going to blow up trains, electricity pylons, sabotage engines and the wings of aircraft.

I belonged to a band of partisans that was the only one to have succeeded in bringing down German bombers . . . on bicycles.

4

It's Boris who wakes us. Dawn has scarcely broken and cramps are gnawing my insides but I mustn't hear its complaint; we won't be having any breakfast. And I have a mission to fulfil. It is perhaps fear, rather than hunger, that ties my stomach into knots. Boris takes his place at the table, Charles is already at work; the red bicycle is transformed before my eyes. It has lost its leather grips; they are now mismatched – one is red, one blue. Too bad for its elegance, I see reason; the important thing is that nobody recognises the stolen bikes. While Charles is checking the derailleur mechanism, Boris beckons me over to join him.

'The plans have changed,' he says. 'Jan doesn't want all three of you to go out. You're novices and, if something bad happens, he wants an old hand to be there as a reinforcement.'

I don't know if that means the brigade doesn't yet trust me sufficiently. So I say nothing and let Boris speak.

'Your brother will stay here. I'm the one who'll accompany you, and ensure you get away. Now listen to me carefully; this is how things must happen. There is a method for bringing down an enemy, and it's very important that you respect it to the letter. Are you listening?'

I nod. Boris must have noticed that for the space of an instant my mind is elsewhere. I'm thinking about my little brother; he's going to sulk when he finds out he's been sidelined. And I can't even admit to him that it relieves me to know that, this morning, his life won't be in danger.

The thing that doubly reassures me is that Boris is a third-year medical student, so if I'm wounded in the operation he may be able to save me, even if that's completely idiotic, because, in an operation, the greatest risk isn't being wounded but quite simply being arrested or killed, which in the end comes to the same thing in most cases.

All that being said, I must admit that Boris wasn't wrong. My mind was perhaps slightly elsewhere while he was speaking; but to be honest, I've always had an annoying penchant for daydreaming; at school, my teachers said I had a 'distracted' nature. That was before the head of the school sent me home on the day I turned up for the baccalaureate examinations. With my name, it really wasn't possible to take the diploma.

Right, I'm focused now on the operation to come; if not, at best I'm going to be ticked off by comrade Boris, who is taking the trouble to explain how things are going to proceed, and at worst, he'll remove me from the mission for not paying attention.

'Are you listening to me?' he says.

'Yes, yes, of course!'

'As soon as we've spotted our target, you will check that the revolver's safety catch is definitely off. We've already seen friends have serious disappointments by thinking that their weapon was jammed, when they'd stupidly forgotten to take off the security catch.'

I did indeed think that this was idiotic, but when you're afraid, really afraid, you're much less skilful; do believe what I say. The important thing was not to interrupt Boris and to concentrate on what he was saying.

'It must be an officer, we don't kill ordinary soldiers. Did you get that? We'll follow him at a distance, neither too close, nor too far. I will deal with the neighbouring perimeter. You approach the guy, you empty your magazine and you count the shots carefully so that you have one bullet left. That's very important for the getaway – you could need it, you never know. I will be covering the getaway. You think only of pedalling. If people try to step in front of you, I'll intervene to protect you. Whatever happens, don't turn back. You pedal and you pedal hard, do you understand me?'

I tried to say yes, but my mouth was so dry that my tongue was stuck to it. Boris concluded that I was in agreement and went on.

'When you're quite a long way away, slow down and mess around like any lad on a bike. Except you're going to ride around for a long time. If anyone has followed you, you must be aware of it and never run the risk of leading him to your address. Go around the docks, and stop frequently, to check if you recognise a face you've encountered more than once. Don't trust coincidences; in our lives there never are any. If you're certain that you're safe, and only then, you can head back.

I had lost all desire to be distracted and I knew my lesson by heart, well almost: the one thing I didn't know at all was how to shoot at a man.

Charles came back from his workshop with my bicycle, which had undergone some serious transformations. The important thing, he said, is that the pedals and chain were reliable. Boris signalled to me that it was time to leave. Claude was still sleeping. I wondered if I ought to wake him. In the event that something happened to me, he might sulk again because I hadn't even said goodbye to him before I died. But I decided to leave him sleeping; when he awoke, he would be famished, with nothing to eat. Each hour of sleep was the same amount of time gained over the gnawing pangs of hunger. I asked why Emile wasn't coming with us. 'Drop it!' Boris muttered to me. Yesterday, Emile had had his bike stolen. That idiot had left it in the corridor of his apartment building without locking it up. It was all the more regrettable that it had been a rather fine model with leather grips, exactly like the one I'd nicked! While we were in action, he'd have to go and pinch another one. Boris added that Emile had hit the roof over the matter!

*   *   *

50

The mission proceeded as Boris had described. Well, almost. The Nazi officer we had spotted was coming down the ten steps of a street staircase, which led to a small square where a *vespasienne* sat imposingly. This was the name given to the green urinals that were found in the town. We called them cups, because of the shape. But as they had been invented by a Roman emperor who answered to the name of Vespasian, that's what they'd been christened. In the end, I might perhaps have got my baccalaureate, if I hadn't made the mistake of being Jewish during the June 1941 exams.

Boris signalled to me that the place was ideal. The little square was below the level of the street and there was no one around. I followed the German, who suspected nothing. To him, I was just someone with whom – although we looked different, with him in his impeccable green uniform and me rather shabbily turned out – he shared the same desire. As the *vespasienne* was equipped with two compartments, there was no reason for him to object to my walking down the same staircase as he was.

So I found myself in a urinal, in the company of a Nazi officer into whom I was going to empty my revolver (less one bullet, as Boris had specified). I had carefully taken off the security catch, when a real problem of conscience passed through my mind. Could one be a decent member of the Resistance, with all the nobility that represented, and kill a guy who had his flies undone and was in such an inglorious posture?

It was impossible to ask comrade Boris for his advice; he was waiting for me with the two bikes at the top of the steps, to ensure a safe getaway. I was alone and I had to make the decision.

I didn't fire, it was inconceivable. I couldn't accept the idea that the first enemy I was going to kill was in the middle of taking a piss as I carried out my heroic action. If I could have talked to Boris about it, he would probably have reminded me that the enemy in question belonged to an army that didn't ask itself any questions when it shot children in the back of the neck, when it machine-gunned kids on the corners of our streets, and even less so when it was exterminating countless people in the death camps. And Boris wouldn't have been wrong. But there you go, I dreamed of being a pilot in a Royal Air Force squadron; well, I might not have a plane, but my honour was safe. I waited until my officer had restored himself to a condition fit to be shot. I didn't allow myself to be distracted by his sidelong smile when he left the urinal and he paid me no further attention when I followed him back to the staircase. The urinal was at the end of a blind alley, and there was only one exit from it.

In the absence of any shots, Boris must have been wondering what I was doing for all that time. But my officer was climbing the steps in front of me and I certainly wasn't going to shoot him in the back. The only way of getting him to turn around was to call him, which wasn't all that easy if one considers that my grasp of German was limited to two words: *ja* and *nein*. Which was unfortunate, since in a few seconds he would reach the street again and the whole thing would be a failure. Having taken all these risks to be found wanting at the last moment would have been too stupid. I filled my lungs and yelled *Ja* with all my strength. The officer must have realised that I was addressing him, because he immediately turned around and I took advantage of this to shoot five bullets into his chest, that is, face-on. What ensued was relatively faithful to the instructions Boris had given. I stuck the revolver in my trouser belt, burning myself in the process on the barrel, which had just fired five bullets at a speed that my level of mathematics didn't enable me to estimate.

Once at the top of the staircase, I mounted my bike and lost my pistol, which slipped out of my belt. I put my feet on the ground to pick up my weapon but Boris's voice shouting at me: 'For God's sake get the hell out of here!' brought me back to the reality of the present moment. I pedalled at breakneck speed, weaving in between the passers-by, who were already running towards the place where the shots had come from.

As I pedalled, I thought constantly about the pistol I had lost. Weapons were rare in the brigade. Unlike the Maquis, we didn't benefit from parachute drops from London; which was really unfair, for the Maquis members didn't do a great deal with the boxes they were sent, apart from storing them in hiding places in preparation for a future Allied landing, which apparently wasn't imminent. For us, the only means of procuring weapons was to get them from the enemy; in rare cases, by undertaking extremely dangerous missions. Not only had I not had the presence of mind to take the Mauser the officer was carrying in his belt, to make things worse, I'd lost my own revolver. I think I thought especially about that to try and forget that in the end, even though everything had happened the way Boris had said, I'd still just killed a man.

Someone knocked at the door. Claude was lying on the bed. His eyes fixed on the ceiling, he behaved as if he hadn't heard anything; anyone would have thought he was listening to music, but since the room was silent I deduced from this that he was sulking.

As a security measure, Boris walked towards the window and gently lifted the curtain to glance outside. The street was quiet. I opened the door and let Robert in. His real name was Lorenzi, but among ourselves we were content to call him Robert; sometimes we also called him 'Death-Cheater' and this nickname was in no way pejorative. It was simply that Lorenzi had accumulated a certain number of qualities. First, his accuracy with a gun; it was unequalled. I wouldn't have liked to find myself in Robert's line of fire, since our comrade's margin for error was in the region of zero. He had obtained permission from Jan to keep his revolver permanently on him, whereas we – because of the brigade's shortage of weapons – had to give them back when the operation was over, so that someone else could have the benefit of them. However strange it may seem, everyone had their own weekly diary, containing, for example, a crane to be blown up on the canal, an army lorry to be set on fire somewhere, a train to be derailed, a garrison post to attack – the list is long. I shall take advantage of this to add that as the months passed, Jan imposed an ever-faster pace upon us. Rest days became rare, to the point where we were exhausted.

It's generally said of trigger-happy types that they're excitable, even to an excessive degree; it was quite the opposite with Robert – he was calm and level-headed. Much admired by the others, with a warm personality, he always had a friendly, comforting word, which was rare in those times. And also, Robert was someone who always brought back his men from a mission, so having him covering you was really reassuring.

One day, I would meet him in a bar on place Jeanne-d'Arc, where we often went to eat vetch, a vegetable that resembles lentils and which is given to livestock; we made do with the resemblance. It's crazy what your imagination can dream up when you're hungry.

Robert dined opposite Sophie and, from the way they were looking at each other I could have sworn that they too were in love. But I must have been wrong since Jan had said that partisans didn't have the right to fall in love, because it was too dangerous for security. When I think back to the number of friends who, the night before their execution, must have hated themselves for respecting this rule, it makes me feel sick to my stomach.

That evening, Robert sat down on the end of the bed and Claude didn't move. One day I shall have to have a word with my little brother about his character. Robert took no notice and stretched out a hand to me, congratulating me on a mission accomplished. I said nothing, torn by contradictory feelings, which, on account of my absent-minded nature, as my teachers said, instantly plunged me into the total silence of deep reflection.

And while Robert stayed there, right in front of me, I mused that I had entered the Resistance with three dreams in my head: to join Général de Gaulle in London, to join the Royal Air Force and to kill an enemy before I died.

Fully comprehending that the first two dreams would remain out of reach, the fact that I had at least been able to fulfil the third ought to have filled me with joy, particularly since I was still not dead, while the operation was now several hours earlier. In reality it was quite the opposite. It gave me no satisfaction to imagine my German officer who, at that time, for the needs of the investigation, was still in the position where I had left him, stretched out on the ground, arms at right angles to his body on the steps of the staircase, with a view downwards to a public urinal.

Boris gave a little cough. Robert wasn't holding out his hand to me in order to shake it – although I am certain he would have had nothing against it, with his natural warmth – but by all accounts he wanted his weapon back. The barrel revolver I had lost was his!

I didn't know that Jan had sent him as a second line of protection, anticipating the risks linked to my inexperience at the moment of the killing and the getaway that was to follow. As I said, Robert always brought his men back. What touched me was that Robert had entrusted his weapon to Charles the previous evening so that he could give it to me, when I had scarcely paid attention to him during dinner, far too absorbed as I was by my share of the omelette. And if Robert, who was responsible for my rear and Boris's, had made such a generous gesture, it was because he wanted me to have the use of a revolver that never jams, unlike automatic weapons.

But Robert mustn't have seen the end of the operation, nor probably the fact that his burning pistol had slipped out of my belt and landed on the road, just before Boris ordered me to get the hell out of there.

As Robert's gaze was becoming persistent, Boris stood up and opened the drawer of the room's sole piece of furniture. From a rustic wardrobe he removed the long-awaited pistol and immediately handed it back to its owner, without a word.

Robert put it back in its proper place and I took advantage of this to learn the correct way to slip the barrel under the belt buckle, to avoid burning the inner thigh and having to deal with the ensuing consequences.

*   *   *

Jan was happy with our operation; we were now accepted into the brigade. A new mission awaited us.

A guy from the Maquis had had a drink with Jan. During the conversation, he had committed an involuntary indiscretion, revealing among other details the existence of a farm where a few weapons parachuted in by the English were stored. It drove us crazy that people were stocking weapons with a view to the Allied landings, when we went short of them every day. So apologies to the Maquis colleagues, but Jan had taken the decision to go and help himself from their stocks. To avoid creating pointless quarrels, and to avert any blunders, we would leave unarmed. I don't say there weren't a few rivalries between the Gaullist movements and our brigade, but there was no question of risking wounding a 'cousin' partisan, even if family relations could sometimes be a bit strained. Instructions were therefore given not to resort to force. If we blundered we'd clear off, and that was that.

The mission was to be conducted with artistry and savoir-faire. What's more, if the plan Jan had devised worked without a hitch, I defied the Gaullists to report what had happened to them to London, at the risk of coming across as real twits and drying up their source of supply.

While Robert was explaining how to proceed, my little brother behaved as if he didn't give a damn, but I could see that he wasn't missing a single word of the conversation. We were to report to this farm, a few kilometres west of the town, explain to the people there that we had come on behalf of a guy called Louis, that the Germans suspected the hiding place and would soon turn up; we had come to help them move the goods and the farmers were supposed to hand us the few cases of grenades and submachine guns they had stored there. Once these were loaded onto the little trailers attached to our bikes, we'd do a bunk and the whole thing was in the bag.

'We'll need six people for it to work,' said Robert.

I knew quite well that I hadn't been wrong about Claude, because he sat up on his bed, as if his siesta had just come to an abrupt end, there and then, just by chance.

'Do you want to take part?' Robert asked my brother.

'With the experience I have now in bicycle theft, I suppose I'm also qualified to nick weapons. I must have the face of a thief for people to think of me automatically for this kind of mission.'

'It's quite the opposite. You have the face of an honest lad and that's why you're particularly well qualified. You don't arouse suspicion.'

I don't know if Claude took that as a compliment or if he was simply pleased that Robert had addressed him directly, offering him the consideration he seemed to lack, but his features instantly relaxed. I think I even saw him smile. It's crazy how the fact of receiving recognition, however tiny it may be, can hearten a person. In the end, feeling anonymous among the people you're with is a much greater pain than people realise; it's as if you're invisible.

It's probably also because of this that we suffered so much from living clandestinely, and for that reason also that in the brigade, we rediscovered a sort of family, a society where every one of us had an existence. And that meant a lot to each of us.

Claude said, 'I'm in.' With Robert, Boris and me, we were still two short. Alonso and Emile would join us.

The six members of the mission must go at the earliest opportunity to Loubers, where little trailers would be attached to their bikes. Charles had asked that we should take turns; not because of the modest size of his work-shop, but to avoid a procession of bikes attracting the neighbours' attention. We were to meet up at around six o'clock on the way out of the village, heading for the countryside and the place called the 'Côte Pavée'.

5

It was Claude who was first to introduce himself to the farmer. He followed to the letter the instructions Jan had obtained from his contact with the Maquis.

'We're here on behalf of Louis. He told me to tell you that tonight, *the tide will be low*.'

'Too bad for the fishing,' the man replied.

Claude didn't contradict him on this point and immediately delivered the second half of his message.

'The Gestapo are on their way, the weapons must be moved!'

'My God, that's terrible,' exclaimed the farmer.

They looked at our bikes and added, 'Where's your lorry?' Claude didn't understand the question, and to be honest nor did I and I think it was the same for our comrades behind. But he'd lost none of his talent for repartee, and immediately replied, 'It's following us,

61

we're here to start organising the transfer.' The farmer took us to his barn. There, behind bales of hay piled several metres high, we discovered what would later give this mission its codename: 'Ali Baba's Cave'. On the ground were rows of stacked-up boxes, stuffed with grenades, mortars, Sten guns, entire sacks of bullets, fuses, dynamite, machine guns and more that I can't remember.

At that precise moment, I became aware of two things of equal importance. First, my political appreciation regarding the point of preparing for the Allied landings had to be revised. My point of view had just changed, even more so when I realised that this cache was probably only one arms-dump among others that were being built up in the country. The second was that we were in the process of looting weapons that the Maquis would probably miss sooner or later.

I was careful not to share these considerations with comrade Robert, the leader of our mission; not through fear of being judged badly by my superior, but rather because, after further thought, I agreed with my conscience: with our six little bicycle trailers, we weren't going to deprive the Maquis of much.

In order to understand what I was feeling as I looked at those weapons, knowing better now how much a single pistol meant within our brigade and at the same time comprehending the meaning of the farmer's well-meaning question, 'But where's your lorry?', all you have to do is imagine my little brother finding himself, by magic, standing in front of a table covered with all kinds of goodies when he was unable to eat.

Robert put an end to our general excitement and ordered that, while we waited for the famous lorry, we should begin loading what we could into the trailers. It was at that moment that the farmer asked a second question that was going to leave us all stunned.

'What do we do with the Russians?'

'What Russians?' asked Robert.

'Didn't Louis tell you?'

'That depends on what it's about,' cut in Claude, who was visibly gaining confidence.

'We're hiding two Russian prisoners who escaped from a prison camp on the Atlantic wall. We have to do something. We can't take the risk of the Gestapo finding them, they'd shoot them on the spot.'

There were two disturbing things about what the farmer had just told us. The first was that, without intending to, we were going to cause a nightmare for these two poor guys who must already have had enough on their plate; but even more disturbing was the fact that not for a single moment had the farmer in question thought about his own life. I shall have to think about adding farmers to my list of magnificent people during that inglorious period.

Robert suggested that the Russians should go and hide in the undergrowth overnight. The peasant asked if one of us was capable of explaining this to them, as his attempts at their language had proved less than brilliant

63

since he took in these two poor devils. After closely observing us, he concluded that he would rather do it himself. 'It's safer', he added. And while he rejoined them, we loaded up the trailers to bursting point. Emile even took two boxes of ammunition that we couldn't use, since we didn't have a revolver of the corresponding calibre, but we didn't know that until Charles told us on our return.

We left our farmer with his two Russian refugees, not without certain feelings of guilt, and we pedalled for all we were worth, dragging our little trailers along the road to the workshop.

As we entered the outskirts of town, Alonso couldn't avoid a pothole, and one of the bags of bullets he was transporting was jolted over the edge. Passers-by stopped, surprised by the nature of the load that had just emptied itself all over the roadway. Two workmen came over to Alonso and helped him to pick up the bullets, replacing them in the little cart without asking any questions.

Charles made an inventory of our booty and found a good place to put it. He returned to us in the dining room, offering us one of his magnificent toothless smiles, and he announced in his own very special language: 'Sa del tris bon trabara. Nous avir à moins de quoi fire sount actions.' Which we instantly translated as: 'Very good work. We have enough there to carry out at least a hundred operations.'

6

June was progressively fading away with every operation we carried out, and the month was almost at its end. Cranes whose foundations had been uprooted by our explosive charges had bowed down into the canals and would never be able to raise their heads again. Trains had been derailed as they travelled along the rails we had moved. The roads that German convoys used were barred by electricity pylons that we had brought down. Around the middle of the month, Jacques and Robert succeeded in placing three bombs in the Feldgendarmerie; the damage there was considerable. The regional Prefect had once again made an appeal to the population; a pitiful message, inviting everyone to denounce any who might belong to a terrorist organisation. In his communiqué, the chief of the French police in the Toulouse region launched a scathing attack on those who claimed to represent a so-called Resistance, those troublemakers who harmed public order and the comfortable lives of French people. Well, the troublemakers in question were us, and we didn't give a damn what the Prefect thought.

Today, with Emile, we collected some grenades from Charles's place; our mission was to hurl them inside a Wehrmacht telephone exchange.

We walked along the street, Emile showed me the windows we must aim at, and on his signal we catapulted our projectiles. I saw them rise up, forming an almost perfect curve. Time seemed to stand still. Next came the sound of breaking glass, and I even thought I could hear the grenades rolling across the wooden floor and the footsteps of the Germans, who were probably rushing towards the first door they could find. It's best if there are two of you when you're doing this kind of thing; alone, success seems improbable.

At this time of day, I doubt that German communications will be re-established for quite some time. But none of this makes me happy, because my little brother has to move out.

Claude has now been integrated into the team. Jan decided that our cohabitation was too dangerous, not in accordance with the rules of security. Each friend must live alone, to avoid compromising a fellow tenant if he happened to be arrested. How I miss the presence of my little brother, and it's now impossible for me to go to bed at night without thinking of him. If he's taking part in an operation, I'm no longer informed. So, stretched out on my bed with my hands behind my head, I search for sleep but can never find it completely. Loneliness and hunger are rotten company. The rumbling of my stomach sometimes disturbs the silence that surrounds me. To think about something else, I gaze at the light bulb on the ceiling of my room and soon, it becomes a flash of light on the canopy of my English fighter plane. I'm piloting a Royal Air Force Spitfire. I fly over the English Channel. All I have to do is tilt the plane and at the ends of the wings I can see the crests of the waves that are running away, like me, to England. A scant few metres away, my brother's plane is purring; I glance at his engine to check that no smoke is going to compromise his return, but already we can see the outline of the coast and its white cliffs. I can feel the wind entering the cockpit, whistling between my legs. Once we've landed, we'll enjoy a delicious meal around a well-laden table in the officers' mess . . . A convoy of German lorries passes by my windows, and the grating of their clutches brings me back to my room and my loneliness.

As I hear the convoy of German lorries fading into the darkness, despite this confounded hunger that gnaws away at me, I finally succeed in finding the courage to switch off the light on my bedroom ceiling. I tell myself that I haven't given up. I'm probably going to die but I won't have given up, in any event I thought I was going to die a lot sooner and I'm still alive, so who knows? Perhaps in the final analysis it's Jacques who's right. Spring will return one day.

*   *   *

In the small hours I receive a visit from Boris; another mission awaits us. While we're pedalling towards the old railway station at Loubers to go and fetch our weapons, Maître Arnal is arriving in Vichy to plead Langer's cause. He's received by the director of criminal affairs and pardons. This man's power is immense and he knows it. He listens to the lawyer distractedly; his thoughts are elsewhere. The end of the week is approaching and he's anxious to know how he'll occupy it, if his mistress will welcome him into the warmth of her thighs after the fine supper he has in store for her at a restaurant in town. The director of criminal affairs swiftly skims the dossier that Arnal begs him to consider. The facts are there in black and white, and they are grave. The sentence is not severe, he says, it is just. The judges cannot be criticised in any way, they did their duty by applying the law. He has already made up his mind, but Arnal continues to persist, so – since the affair is a delicate one – he agrees to call a meeting of the Pardons Committee.

Later, before its members, he will continue to pronounce Marcel's name in such a way as to make it understood that he is a foreigner. And as Arnal, the old lawyer, leaves Vichy, the Committee rejects the pardon. And as Arnal, the old lawyer, steps aboard the train taking him back to Toulouse, an administrative document also follows his little train; it heads for the Keeper of the Seals, who has it sent immediately to the office of Marshal Pétain. The Marshal signs the report, and Marcel's fate is now sealed: he is to be guillotined.

Today, 15 July 1943, with my friend Boris, we attacked the office of the leader of the 'Collaboration' group in the Place des Carmes. The day after tomorrow, Boris will attack a man called Rouget, a zealous collaborator and one of the Gestapo's top informants.

As he leaves the courthouse to go and have lunch, Deputy Prosecutor Lespinasse is in an extremely good mood. The slow train of bureaucracy finally reached its destination this morning. The document rejecting Marcel's request for a pardon is on his desk, and it bears the Marshal's signature. The order of execution accompanies it. Lespinasse has spent the morning contemplating this little piece of paper, only a few square centimetres in size. This rectangular sheet is like a reward to him, a prize for excellence granted to him by the State's highest authorities. It's not the first Lespinasse has hooked. As early as primary school, he brought back a merit point to his father each year, gained thanks to his assiduous work, thanks to the esteem in which his teachers held him . . . Thanks . . . Yes, thanks to him Marcel would never obtain a pardon. Lespinasse sighs and picks up the little china ornament that has pride of place on his desk, in front of his leather desk blotter. He slides over the sheet of paper and replaces the ornament on top of it. It must not distract him; he must finish writing the speech for his next lecture, but his mind wanders to his little notebook. He opens it and turns its pages: one day, two, three, four, there – that's the one. He hesitates to write the words 'Langer execution' beneath 'lunch with Armande', as the sheet is already covered with meetings. So he contents himself with putting a cross. He closes the diary again and resumes writing his speech. A few lines and here he is again, leaning towards that document, which sticks out from underneath the ornament. He opens the diary again and, in front of the cross, writes the number 5. That's the time he has to arrive at the gate of the Saint-Michel prison. Finally Lespinasse puts away the diary in his pocket, pushes away the gold paper knife on the desk, and lines it up, parallel with his fountain pen. It is noon and the deputy prosecutor is now feeling hungry. Lespinasse stands up, adjusts the folds of his trousers and walks out into the corridor of the courthouse.

On the other side of town, Maître Arnal sets down the same sheet of paper on his desk; the sheet he received this morning. His cleaning lady enters the room. Arnal gazes fixedly at her, but no sound emerges from his throat.

'Are you weeping, Maître?' murmurs the cleaning lady.

Arnal bends over the waste paper basket and vomits bile. The spasms shake him. Old Marthe hesitates, not knowing what to do. Then her good sense takes the upper hand. She has three children and two grand-children, does old Marthe, so she's seen quite a bit of vomiting in her time. She approaches and lays her hand on the old lawyer's forehead. Each time he bends towards the basket, she accompanies his movement. She hands him a white cotton handkerchief, and while her employer is wiping his mouth, her gaze lights on the sheet of paper, and this time it is old Marthe's eyes that fill with tears.

This evening, we're at Charles's house. Sitting on the floor are Jan, Catherine, Boris, Emile, Claude, Alonso, Stefan, Jacques and Robert; we all form a circle. A letter passes from hand to hand; everyone searches for words but cannot find them. What can you write to a friend who is going to die? 'We will not forget you,' murmurs Catherine. That's what everyone here is thinking. If our fight leads us to recover freedom, if a single one of us survives, he will not forget Marcel, and one day he will say your name. Jan listens to us, he takes the pen and writes in Yiddish the few phrases we have just said to you. This way, the guards who lead you to the scaffold cannot understand. Jan folds up the letter, Catherine takes it and slides it inside her blouse. Tomorrow, she will go and give it to the rabbi.

Not sure that our letter will reach the condemned man. Marcel doesn't believe in God and he'll probably refuse to have the almoner present, as well as the rabbi. But after all, who knows? A little shred of luck in all of this misery wouldn't be too much. May it ensure that you read these few words written to tell you that, if one day we are free again, your life will have counted for a great deal.

71

7

It is five o'clock on this sad morning of 23 July 1943. In an office within the Saint-Michel prison, Lespinasse is slaking his thirst along with the judges, the director and the two executioners. Coffee for the men in black, a glass of dry white wine to quench the thirst of those who have worked up a sweat putting up the guillotine. Lespinasse keeps looking at his watch. He's waiting for the hand to finish travelling around the face. 'It's time,' he says, 'go and tell Arnal.' The old lawyer didn't want to mix with them; he's waiting alone in the courtyard. Someone goes to fetch him, and he joins the procession, signals to the warder and walks a long way in front.

The morning alarm bell hasn't rung yet but all the prisoners are already up. They know when one of their own is about to be executed. A murmur builds up; the voices of the Spaniards melt into those of the French, and are soon joined by the Italians, then the Hungarians, the Poles, the Czechs and the Romanians. The murmur has become a song that rises, loud and strong. All the accents mingle and are proclaiming the same words. It is the 'Marseillaise' that echoes within the cell walls of the Saint-Michel prison.

Arnal enters the cell; Marcel wakes up, looks at the pink sky through the skylight and instantly realises. Arnal takes him in his arms. Over his shoulder, Marcel looks at the sky again and smiles. He whispers in the old lawyer's ear: 'I loved life so much.'

Then it's the barber's turn to enter; he has to bare the condemned man's neck. The scissors click and the locks of hair slip to the beaten-earth floor. The procession moves forward; in the corridor the 'Song of the Partisans' replaces the 'Marseillaise'. Marcel stops at the top of the stairs, turns around, slowly raises his fist and shouts: 'Farewell, comrades.' The entire prison falls silent for one short moment. 'Farewell, comrade, and long live France,' the prisoners answer in unison. And the 'Marseillaise' fills the space once more, but Marcel's silhouette has already disappeared.

Shoulder to shoulder, Arnal in a cape, Marcel in a white shirt, they walk towards the inevitable. Looking at them from behind, you can't work out which one is supporting the other. The chief warder takes a packet of Gauloises from his pocket. Marcel takes the cigarette he offers, a match crackles and its flame lights up the lower part of his face. A few curls of smoke escape from his mouth, and they continue walking. On the threshold of the door that leads to the courtyard, the prison governor asks him if he wants a glass of rum. Marcel glances at Lespinasse and nods.

'Give it to that man instead,' he says. 'He needs it more than I do.'

The cigarette falls to the ground and rolls away. Marcel signals that he is ready.

The rabbi approaches, but Marcel smiles, indicating to him that he has no need of him.

'Thank you, rabbi, but my only belief is in a better world for men, and perhaps one day men alone will decide to invent that world. For themselves and their children.'

The rabbi knows very well that Marcel does not want his help, but he has a mission to fulfil and time is pressing. So, without further ado, the man of God jostles Lespinasse aside and hands Marcel the book he is holding. He mutters to him in Yiddish: 'There is something for you inside.'

Marcel hesitates, attempts to open it and flicks through it. Between the pages, he finds the note hastily written by Jan. Marcel skims the lines, from right to left; he closes his eyes and hands it back to the rabbi.

'Tell them that I thank them and above all, that I have confidence in their victory.'

It is a quarter past five. The door opens on one of the

74

small, dark courtyards of Saint-Michel prison. The guillotine stands to the right. Out of consideration, the executioners put it up here, so that the condemned man would see it only at the final moment. From the tops of the watchtowers, the German sentries are entertained by the unusual spectacle that is playing out before their eyes. 'Funny people, the French. In principle we're the enemy, aren't we?' one says with irony. His compatriot is content to shrug his shoulders and leans forward to get a better view. Marcel climbs the steps of the scaffold, and turns one last time towards Lespinasse: 'My blood will fall on your head,' he smiles, and adds: 'I am dying for France and for a better humanity.'

Without any help, Marcel lies down on the plank and the blade swishes down. Arnal has held his breath, his gaze is fixed on the sky woven with light clouds, for all the world like silk. At his feet, the paving stones of the courtyard are reddened with blood. And while Marcel's remains are placed in a coffin, the executioners are already setting about cleaning their machine. A little sawdust is thrown on the ground.

Arnal will accompany his friend to his last resting place. He climbs up to ride at the front of the hearse, the prison gates open and the team of horses sets off. At the corner of the street, he passes the silhouette of Catherine but doesn't even recognise her.

Hidden in a doorway, Catherine and Marianne were waiting for the cortège. The echo of the horses' hooves is lost in the distance. On the door of the prison, a warder sticks up the notice confirming the execution. There is nothing more to do. White-faced, they leave their hiding place and walk back up the street. Marianne is holding a handkerchief in front of her mouth, a paltry remedy against nausea and pain. It is scarcely seven o'clock when they join us at Charles's house. Jacques says nothing, just clenches his fists. Boris draws a circle on the wooden table with his fingertip. Claude is sitting with his back to a wall; he's looking at me.

'We must kill an enemy today,' says Jan.

'Without any preparation?' Catherine asks.

'I'm in agreement,' says Boris.

At eight o'clock on a summer evening, it's still full daylight. People are walking about, taking advantage of the opportunity now that the temperature has dropped. The café terraces are bustling with people, a few lovers are kissing on street corners. In the midst of this crowd, Boris seems to be a young man like all the others, inoffensive. But in his pocket he is gripping the butt of his pistol. For the last hour he's been searching for prey. Not any prey though: he wants an officer to avenge Marcel, some gold braid, a uniform jacket with stars on it. But so far he's only encountered two German ship's boys out for a good time, young guys who aren't malicious enough to deserve to die. Boris crosses Lafayette Square, walks up rue d'Alsace, paces up and down the pavements of Place Esquirol. In the distance he can hear the brass section of an orchestra. So Boris allows the music to guide him.

On a bandstand a German orchestra is playing. Boris finds a chair and sits down. He closes his eyes and tries to calm his racing heart. No question of returning empty-handed, no question of letting down the friends. Of course, it isn't this kind of vengeance that Marcel deserves, but the decision has been taken. He opens his eyes again, and Providence smiles at him. A handsome officer has sat down in the front row. Boris looks at the cap the soldier is using to fan himself. On the sleeve of the jacket, he sees the red ribbon of the Russian campaign. This officer must have killed men, to have the right to rest in Toulouse. He must have led soldiers to their deaths, to take such a peaceful advantage of a gentle summer's evening in the south-west of France.

The concert ends, the officer stands up, and Boris follows him. A few steps away from there, right in the middle of the street, five shots ring out, and flames shoot from the barrel of our friend's weapon. The crowd rushes forward. Boris leaves.

In a Toulouse street, the blood of a German officer flows towards the gutter. A few kilometres away, beneath the earth of a Toulouse cemetery, Marcel's blood is already dry.

La Dépêche reports Boris's operation; in the same edition, it announces Marcel's execution. The townsfolk will quickly make the link between the two matters. Those who are compromised will learn that the blood of a partisan does not flow with impunity, while the others will know that, very close to them, some people are fighting.

The regional Prefect made haste to issue a communiqué to reassure the occupiers of the goodwill felt towards them by his departments. 'As soon as I learned of the killing,' he announced, 'I made myself the mouthpiece of the population's indignation to the general chief of staff and the German Head of Security.' The regional police chief also added his hand to the collaborationist prose: 'A very substantial cash reward will be paid by the authorities to any person making it possible to identify the author or authors of the odious murder committed by firearm on the evening of 23 July against a German soldier in rue Bayard, Toulouse.' Unquote! It has to be said that he had only just been appointed to his post, had Police Chief Barthenet. A few years of zeal with the Vichy departments had hewn his reputation as a man who was as efficient as he was formidable and had offered him this promotion that he had dreamed of. The chronicler of *La Dépêche* had greeted his appointment by welcoming him on the front page of the daily. We too, in our own way, had just given him 'our' welcome. And so as to welcome him even better, we distributed a tract all over town. In a few lines, we announced that we had killed a German officer as a reprisal for the death of Marcel.

We won't wait for an order from anyone. The rabbi told Catherine what Marcel said to Lespinasse before dying on the scaffold. 'My blood will fall upon your head.' The message had hit us full in the face, like a will left by our comrade, and we had all decoded his last wish. We would

78

have the deputy prosecutor's hide. The enterprise would demand long preparation. You couldn't kill a prosecutor like that in the middle of the street. The lawyer was certainly protected. He didn't move about unless driven by his chauffeur and our brigade considered it out of the question that an operation should cause the population to run any risk, however small. Unlike those who collaborated openly with the Nazis, those who denounced, arrested, tortured, deported; those who sentenced to death, executed; those who, free from all constraints and with their consciences draped in the togas of pretended duty, assuaged their racist hatred; unlike all of these, we might be ready to soil our hands, but they would remain clean.

Several weeks before, at Jan's request, Catherine had established an information cell. This means that, along with a few of her friends, Damira, Marianne, Sophie, Rosine, Osna, all those we were forbidden to love but whom we loved all the same, she was going to glean the information necessary for preparing our mission.

During the months to come, the girls of the brigade would specialise in tailing people, taking photographs on the sly, noting down itineraries, observing how time was spent, and making neighbourhood enquiries. Thanks to them, we would know everything – or almost – about our targets' actions. No, we wouldn't wait for orders from anyone.

Deputy Prosecutor Lespinasse now headed their list.

8

Jacques had asked me to meet Damira in town; I was to pass on an order regarding the mission. The meeting had been fixed in that café where the friends met up a little too often, until Jan forbade us to set foot in it, as ever for security reasons.

What a shock, the first time I saw her. Now, I had red hair, and white skin dotted with red freckles, so much so that people asked me if I'd been looking at the sun through a sieve, and I was a four-eyes to boot. Damira was Italian and, more important than anything to my short-sighted eyes, she was a redhead too. I figured that this would inevitably create special bonds between us. But well, I'd already been wrong in my appreciation of the importance of the stocks of weapons the Gaullist Maquis were building up, so suffice to say that when it came to Damira, I wasn't sure of anything.

Sitting at a table with our plates of vetch, we must have looked like two young lovers, except that Damira wasn't in love with me, whereas I was already a bit besotted with her. I gazed at her as if, after eighteen years of life spent in the skin of a guy who'd been born with a bunch of carrots on his head, I'd discovered a kindred being, and one of the opposite sex at that; a kind of opposition that for once was bloody good news.

'Why are you looking at me like that?' Damira asked.

'No reason!'

'Is somebody watching us?'

'No, no, absolutely not!'

'Are you certain? Because the way you were staring at me, I thought you were signalling a danger to me.'

'Damira, I promise you we are safe!'

'Then why is there sweat breaking out on your forehead?'

'It's incredibly hot in this café.'

'I don't think so.'

'You're Italian and I'm from Paris, so you must be more used to it than I am.'

'Shall we go for a walk?'

Damira could have suggested I should go for a swim in the canal; I'd still have said yes immediately. Before she'd finished her sentence I was already on my feet, pulling out her chair to help her get up.

'A chivalrous man, that's nice,' she said with a smile.

The temperature inside my body had just climbed even higher and, for the first time since the start of the war, my cheeks must have been so colourful that you might have thought I looked really well.

The two of us walked towards the canal, where I imagined myself frolicking with my splendid Italian redhead in affectionate, loving water games. Which would have been totally ridiculous, since swimming between two cranes and three barges loaded with hydrocarbons has never had anything really romantic about it. That being said, at that moment nothing in the world could have stopped me dreaming. Moreover, as we were crossing Place Esquirol, I landed my Spitfire (whose engine had given out on me while I was looping the loop) in a field beside the delightful little cottage where Damira and I had been living, in England, since she became pregnant with our second child (which would probably be as redheaded as its elder sister). And, just to make my happiness complete, it was tea-time. Damira came out to meet me, hiding a few hot biscuits straight from the oven in the pockets of her green and red checked apron. Unfortunately, I would have to set to work repairing my plane after afternoon tea; Damira's cakes were exquisite; she must have had a terrible job preparing them just for me. For once, I could forget my duty as an officer for a moment and pay her homage. Sitting in front of our house, Damira laid her head on my shoulder and sighed, overjoyed by this moment of simple happiness.

'Jeannot, I think you fell asleep.'

'What!' I said, with a start.

'Your head is on my shoulder!'

I sat up, my face crimson. Spitfire, cottage, tea and cakes had vanished, leaving only the dark reflections of the canal, and the bench where we were sitting.

Searching desperately for some semblance of composure, I gave a little cough and, although I didn't dare look at the girl sitting next to me, I did try to get to know her better.

'How did you come to join the brigade?'

'Weren't you supposed to pass on a mission order to me?' Damira answered rather sharply.

'Yes, yes, but we have time, don't we?'

'You may have, but I don't.'

'Answer me and afterwards, I promise, we'll talk about work.'

Damira hesitated for a moment, then smiled and agreed to answer me. She must certainly have known that I was a bit taken with her, girls always know that, often even before we know it ourselves. There was nothing indelicate in her behaviour, she knew how heavily solitude was weighing on everyone, perhaps on her too, so she just agreed to please me and talk a little. Evening was already upon us, but night would still take a long time to arrive, so we had a few hours ahead of us before curfew. Two kids sitting on a bench, beside a canal, in the middle of the Occupation; there was no harm in taking advantage of the passing time. Who could say how much each of us had left?

'I didn't think the war would reach us,' said Damira. 'It came one evening via the path in front of the house:

83

a gentleman was walking along, dressed like my father, like a workman. Papa went out to meet him and they talked for quite a while. And then the man went away. Papa went back into the kitchen and talked with my mother. I could see perfectly well that she was crying. She said to him, "Haven't we had enough already?" She said that because her brother was tortured in Italy by Mussolini's Blackshirts, like the Militia here.'

I hadn't been able to take my end of school exams, for reasons you know already, but I was well aware of who the Blackshirts were. Nevertheless, I decided not to take the risk of interrupting Damira.

'I realised why that man was talking to my father in the garden; and with his sense of honour, Papa had been expecting it. I knew he had said yes, for himself and for his brothers too. Mother was weeping because we were going to enter the struggle. I was proud and happy, but I was sent to my room. Where I come from, girls don't have the same rights as boys. Back home, there's Papa, my cretinous brothers and then, and only then, there's Mother and me. Suffice to say that when it comes to boys, I know it all by heart – I've got four back home.'

When Damira said that, I thought back over my behaviour since we'd met at a table in the Plate of Vetch, and I told myself that the probability that she hadn't detected how besotted I was with her must lie somewhere between zero and dotted zero. I had no thoughts of interrupting her; I wouldn't have been capable of uttering a single word. So Damira continued.

'I have my father's personality, not my mother's; what's more, I'm well aware that my father likes the fact that I resemble him. I'm like him . . . a rebel. I won't accept injustice. Mother always tried to teach me to keep my mouth shut, but Father's just the opposite: he's always encouraged me to answer back, not to just go along with things, though he did do it mostly when my brothers weren't there, because of the established order in the family.'

A few metres away from us, a barge was casting off its moorings; Damira fell silent, as if the boatmen could hear us. That was idiotic, because of the wind that was blowing through the cranes, but I let her get her breath back. We waited until it headed off towards the lock, and then Damira continued.

'Do you know Rosine?'

Rosine: Italian, slight lilting accent, a voice that could provoke uncontrollable shivers, around 1.70 metres tall, brunette with blue eyes, long hair, beyond fantasy.

As a precaution, I replied timidly:

'Yes, I think we've met once or twice.'

'She's never mentioned you.'

That didn't surprise me too much, and I shrugged my shoulders. That's what you generally do, stupidly, when you're confronted by something inevitable.

'Why are you talking to me about Rosine?'

'Because it's thanks to her that I was able to join the brigade,' Damira went on. 'One evening, there was a meeting at the house, and she was there. When I wanted us to go off to bed, she replied that she wasn't here to sleep, but to be at the meeting. Did I tell you I have a horror of injustice?'

'Yes, yes, less than five minutes ago, I remember it quite clearly!'

'Well, that was just too much to bear. I asked why *I* couldn't take part in the meeting, and Father said I was too young. Now, Rosine and I are the same age. So I decided to take my destiny into my own hands and obeyed my father for the last time. When Rosine came up to join me in my room, I wasn't asleep. I'd been waiting for her. We chattered all night. I confessed to her that I wanted to be like her, like my brothers, and I begged her to introduce me to the commander of the brigade. She burst out laughing and told me that the commander was under my own roof, in fact he was actually sleeping in the sitting room. The commander was the friend of my father who'd come to see him one day in the garden, the day when Mother wept.'

Damira paused for a moment, as if she wanted to be sure that I was following her account closely. Now, this was completely pointless, since at that moment I would have followed her anywhere she asked, and probably even if she didn't ask.

'The next day I went to see the commander while Mother and Father were busy. He listened to me and told me that in the brigade, they needed everyone. He added that to start with I would be given tasks that weren't too difficult, and after that they would see. So there you are, you know everything. Right, so are you going to give me my mission orders now?'

'So what about your father, what did he say?'

'At first he didn't suspect anything, and then he eventually guessed. I think I know that he went to talk to the commander and that the two of them had a real slanging-match. Papa did it just as a matter of paternal authority, because I am still in the brigade. Since then, we behave as if nothing had happened, but I can definitely feel that he and I are even closer. Right, Jeannot, are you going to give me that mission order? I really do have to get back.'

'Damira?'

'Yes?'

'Can I trust you with a secret?'

'I work in clandestine information, Jeannot, so if there's anyone you can trust with a secret, it's me!'

'I've completely forgotten what the mission order was all about . . .'

Damira stared at me and the ghost of a strange smile crossed her lips, as if she was both amused and terribly angry with me.

'You really are a complete idiot, Jeannot.'

But it really wasn't my fault if my hands had been moist for the last hour, if my knees were knocking and there wasn't a drop of saliva left in my mouth. I apologised as best I could.

'I'm sure it's only temporary, but I'm suffering from some kind of terrible mental blank.'

'Right, I'm going back,' said Damira. 'As for you, you're going to spend the night getting your memory back and tomorrow morning at the latest, I want to know what it was about. Good grief, we're at war, Jeannot, this is serious!'

During the month that had passed, I had blown up a number of bombs, destroyed some cranes, a German telephone exchange and several of its occupants; my nights were still haunted by the corpse of an enemy officer sneering as it stared fixedly at a urinal. If there was anyone who knew that what we were doing was serious, it was me; but when it comes to memory problems, in fact problems full stop, they can't be controlled just like that. I suggested to Damira that we should walk a little further; perhaps as we walked it would come back to me.

As we passed Place Esquirol again, our paths had to separate. Damira planted herself in front of me with a resolute look.

'Listen, Jeannot, with us, affairs between boys and girls are forbidden, don't you remember?'

'But you said you were a rebel!'

'I'm not talking about my father, you cretin, I'm talking about the brigade! It's forbidden and it's dangerous, so we'll see each other in the course of our missions and forget the rest, OK?'

And she was outspoken to boot! I stammered that I understood perfectly well and that in any case, I hadn't intended things to be any other way. She said to me that

88

now everything was clear, I might perhaps get my memory back.

'You have to go and walk around the area near rue Pharaon, we're interested in a guy called Mas, head of the Militia,' I said; 'and I swear that it came back to me just like that, all at once!'

'Who'll be in the operation?' Damira asked.

'Since he's a militiaman, there's a strong chance that Boris will take care of it, but nothing official for the moment.'

'When's it planned to take place?'

'Mid-August, I think.'

'That only leaves me a few days, it's very short notice. I'll ask Rosine to give me a hand.'

'Damira?'

'Yes?'

'If we weren't . . . I mean . . . if the security rules didn't exist?'

'Stop, Jeannot, with our identical hair colour, we'd look like brother and sister, and besides . . .'

Damira didn't finish her sentence. She shook her head and left. I was still standing there, arms hanging limply, when she turned around and came back to me.

'You have very beautiful blue eyes, Jeannot, and that short-sighted gaze from behind the lenses of your glasses is lovely for a girl. So try to save those eyes from this war and I have no doubt that you will be a man who's happy in love. Good night, Jeannot.'

'Good night, Damira.'

As I left her that evening, I was unaware that Damira was madly in love with a brigade member called Marc. They were seeing each other secretly, it seems they even went to museums together. Marc was cultivated; he took Damira on visits to churches and talked about painting with her. As I left her that evening, I was also unaware that in a few months Marc and Damira would be arrested together and Damira deported to Ravensbrück concentration camp.

9

Damira went to obtain information on the militiaman called Mas. Simultaneously, Jan had asked Catherine and Marianne to tail Lespinasse. Strange as it may seem, Jan had found the address in the phone book. The deputy prosecutor lived in a middle-class house in a suburb close to Toulouse. There was even a copper plate with his name on, attached to the garden gate. Our two colleagues were stunned by this; the man took no security measures at all. He came and went without any escort, drove alone in his car, as if he feared nothing. And yet, in various different articles the dailies had related that it was thanks to him that an odious terrorist had been permanently prevented from doing harm. Even Radio London had reported that Lespinasse was responsible for Marcel's execution. There was now not a single café customer or factory worker who didn't know his name.

You would have to be amazingly moronic not to suspect even for a moment that the Resistance was after him. Unless, as the two girls thought after two days spent tailing him, his vanity and arrogance were so immense that it seemed inconceivable to him that anyone would dare make an attempt on his life.

The job wasn't easy for our two comrades. The street was most often deserted, which would certainly be an advantage at the moment of the operation, but a woman on her own was more than obvious. Sometimes hidden behind a tree, most of the time spending their days, like all the information-seeking girls, walking, Catherine and Marianne spent a whole week spying.

The affair was all the more complicated by the fact that their prey seemed to have no regularity in the way he spent his time. He never went anywhere except in his black Peugeot 202, which made it impossible to follow him beyond the street. No regular habits except for one, noticed by the two girls: every day he left his home around half-past three in the afternoon. So this would be the time of day when we must act, they had concluded in their report. It was not helpful to continue the investigation still further. It was impossible to follow him because of the car; at the Palais his trail could never be picked up and besides, by persisting for too long, they ran the risk of being spotted.

After Marius had come one Friday morning to carry out a final research operation and decide upon the getaway routes, the operation was timetabled for the following Monday. We had to act quickly. Jan assumed that if Lespinasse lived so quietly, he most probably had the benefit of discreet police protection. Catherine swore that she had not noticed anything of the sort, and Marianne shared her point of view, but Jan was suspicious of everything, and rightly so. Another reason for moving quickly was that during this summer period, our man could go on holiday at any moment.

Tired out by missions carried out in the course of the week, with a belly that was emptier than ever, I imagined my Sunday while stretched out on my bed, dreaming. With a little luck, I might see my little brother. We would go for a walk together along the canal; like two kids out on a stroll, taking advantage of the summer; like two kids who aren't hungry or afraid, two adolescents among all the summer's others. And if the evening wind was in cahoots, perhaps it would do us the favour of lifting the light skirts the girls were wearing, scarcely enough to glimpse a knee, but sufficient to titillate us and make us dream a little more when, in the evening, we regained the mugginess of our sinister rooms.

All of this failed to take account of Jan's fervour. Jacques had just put an end to my hopes by knocking at my door. I'd sworn I was going to sleep in the following morning, but that was all done for, and with reason . . . Jacques unfolded a map of the town and pointed out a crossroads to me. At five o'clock precisely tomorrow afternoon, I was to meet up with Emile and hand him a package that I had previously been to fetch from Charles's house. I didn't need to know any more about it. Tomorrow evening, they would leave on an operation with a new recruit who would safeguard the retreat, someone called Guy, with seventeen years on the clock, but with an incredible turn of speed on a bike. Tomorrow evening, none of us would enjoy any respite until our friends had returned safe and sound.

It's Saturday morning and the sky is clear, with just a few cotton-wool clouds. You see, if life was properly put together, you would smell the scent of an English lawn, I would check the rubber on the tyres of my plane, and the mechanic would signal to me that everything is in order. Then I would climb into the cockpit, close the canopy and fly off on a patrol. But I can hear old Mme Dublanc going into her kitchen, and the sound of her footsteps jolts me out of my reverie. I put on my jacket, look at my watch; it's seven o'clock. I must go to Charles's place and collect that package, which I have to hand over to Emile. Head for the suburbs. Reaching Saint-Jean, I cycle up the route of the railway line as usual. It's a long time since trains ran on the old rails that lead to the Loubers district. A keen breeze blows on the back of my neck, I turn up my collar and whistle the tune from the 'Butte Rouge', a song of the French Revolution. In the distance, I see the little disused railway station. I knock at its door and Charles beckons me inside.

'Want a coffee?' he asks me in his best mumbo-jumbo.

I'm understanding my friend Charles better and better. All I have to do is mix a word of Polish, one of Yiddish, another of Spanish, and a hint of French melody and the thing's in the bag. Charles has learned his strange language while travelling the byways of his exodus.

'Your package is under the stairs, you never know who might knock at the door. Tell Jacques that I mixed the packet. The operation will be heard kilometres away. Tell him to be sure and watch out, after the spark there's two minutes, no more, perhaps a little less.'

Once I'd managed the translation, it was impossible to prevent my head doing the calculation. Two minutes, in other words twenty millimetres of fuse, which would separate life from death for my companions. Two centimetres to set the devices, put them in place and find the getaway route. Charles looks at me and senses my anxiety.

'I always take a small safety margin, for the friends,' he adds with a smile, as if to calm me.

It's a funny smile, is Charles's. He lost almost all his front teeth during an air bombardment, which, I have to say in his defence, doesn't exactly help his diction. Although he is always badly dressed, and incomprehensible for the most part, of all of them he is the one who reassures me the most. Is it that wisdom that seems to dwell within him? His determination? His energy? His love of life? He's so young; how does he manage to be so adult? He's already lived a fair old bit, has Charles. In Poland they arrested him, because his father was a workman, and he was a Communist. He spent several years in the nick. Once freed, like several of our friends, he went off to make war in Spain with Marcel Langer. From Lodz to the Pyrenees, the road wasn't simple, especially without papers or money. I love listening to him when he gives an account of how he crossed Nazi Germany. It wasn't the first time I'd asked him to tell me his story. Charles was well aware of that, but talking a little about his life is for him a way of practising his French and of pleasing me, so Charles sits down on a chair and words of all colours fly free from his lips.

They boarded a train, without tickets, and with his characteristic cheek he pushed his luck as far as sitting in First Class, in a compartment stuffed with uniforms and officers. He spent his journey chatting with them. The soldiers rather liked him and the ticket inspector had been careful not to ask anyone in that compartment any questions. Arriving in Berlin, they even told him how to cross the city and get to the station from which trains left for Aix-la-Chapelle. Paris next, then by coach to Perpignan, and finally he had crossed the mountains on foot. On the other side of the border, other coaches took the fighters to Albacete, on the way to the battle of Madrid, in the Polish brigade.

After the defeat, with thousands of refugees, he crossed back over the Pyrenees in the other direction and reached the frontier again, where he was greeted by gendarmes. Straight off to the internment camp at Vernet.

'I did the cooking for all the prisoners there, and everyone had his daily ration!' he said, not without a certain pride.

Three years' detention in all, until the escape signal. He walked two hundred kilometres to Toulouse.

It's not Charles's voice that reassures me, it's what he tells me. There's a little bit of hope in his story, which gives meaning to my life. I too want to tame the luck in which he wants to believe. How many others must have given up? But even at the foot of a wall, Charles would not admit that he was a prisoner. He would just take the time to think about the best way to get around it.

'You should go now,' said Charles, 'at lunch-time the streets are quieter.'

Charles heads for the cupboard under the stairs, fetches the package and places it on the table. It's funny, he's wrapped up the bombs in sheets of newspaper. On them, you can read the account of an operation led by Boris. The journalist treats him like a terrorist, accuses us all of disturbing public order. The militiaman is the victim, we his executioners; a strange way of regarding the History that is being written each day in the streets of our occupied towns.

Someone scratches at the door. Charles doesn't flinch, but I hold my breath. A little girl enters the room and my friend's face lights up.

'This is my French teacher,' he says, delightedly.

The little girl jumps into his arms and kisses him. Her first name is Camille. Michèle, her mother, is sheltering

97

Charles in this abandoned railway station. Camille's father has been a prisoner in Germany since the start of the war and Camille never asks questions. Michèle pretends not to know that Charles is in the Resistance. To her, as to all the people in the area, he's a gardener who cultivates the finest kitchen garden thereabouts. Sometimes, on a Saturday, Charles sacrifices one of his rabbits to prepare a good meal for them. I would so much have loved a bit of that rabbit, but I must go. Charles signals to me, so I say goodbye to Camille and her mother and I leave, with my package under my arm. There aren't only militiamen and collaborators, there are also people like Michèle, people who know that what we are doing is good, and who take risks to come to our aid, each in their own way. Behind the wooden door, I can still hear Charles articulating the words that a little five-year-old girl makes him repeat conscientiously: 'bread butter cheese,' and my stomach rumbles as I pedal away.

It's five o'clock on the dot. I find Emile, at the place Jacques indicated on the town map, and I hand him the package. Charles has added two grenades to the bombs. Emile doesn't turn a hair. I feel a desire to say, 'See you this evening', but – perhaps out of superstition – I keep quiet.

'Have you got a cigarette?' he asks.

'Do you smoke?'

'It's to light the fuses.'

I rummage in my trouser pocket and hand him a crumpled pack of Gauloises. There are two left. My friend takes his leave and disappears around the corner of the street.

Night has fallen and it's drizzling. The street gleams greasily. Emile is calm; no bomb made by Charles has ever failed. The device is simple: thirty centimetres of cast iron pipe, a section of drainpipe stolen on the sly. A stopper bolted onto each end, a hole and a fuse that goes down into the explosive. They will position the bombs in front of the door of the brasserie, then they'll throw the grenades through the window, and those who succeed in getting out will experience Charles's fireworks.

Three of us are involved in tonight's operation: Jacques, Emile and the little new lad, who is safeguarding the escape route with a loaded revolver in his pocket, ready to fire into the air if any passers-by approach, or horizontally if the Nazis pursue them. Here they are in the street where the operation is to take place. The windows of the restaurant where an enemy officers' banquet is taking place blaze with lights. This is a serious operation: there are at least thirty of them in there.

Thirty officers, that's a hell of a lot of bars on the green Wehrmacht jackets that are hanging in the cloakroom. Emile goes back up the street and passes the glazed door for the first time. He barely turns his head – on no account must he be noticed. It's there that he sees the waitress. He must find a way to protect her, but before that, neutralise the two police officers who are standing

99

guard. Jacques suddenly seizes one of them tightly by the neck; he takes him into a neighbouring alleyway and orders him to get lost. The trembling cop decamps. The one Emile is dealing with won't go along with it. With a jab of the elbow, Emile knocks off his uniform cap and then strikes him with the butt of his revolver. It is the motionless policeman's turn to be dragged towards the blind alley. He will wake up with blood on his forehead and a bad headache. There's still the waitress who's on duty in the restaurant. Jacques is perplexed. Emile suggests signalling to her through the window, but that's not without its risks. She may sound the alarm. Of course, the consequences would be disastrous, but – have I told you this before? – we've never killed an innocent person, not even an imbecile, so we must spare her, even if she is serving Nazi officers the food that we desperately lack.

Jacques approaches the window; from the restaurant, he must look like some poor famished guy who's merely feasting his eyes. A captain sees him, smiles and raises his glass. Jacques smiles back and looks hard at the waitress. The young woman is plump – there's no doubt that the restaurant's food is benefiting her, and maybe her family too. After all, how can you judge? We must survive in these difficult times; everyone has their own way of doing it.

Emile is getting impatient; at the end of the dark street, the young recruit is holding the bicycles in his moist hands. At last, the waitress's eyes meet Jacques'. He signals to her, she nods, hesitates and does an about-turn. She's understood the message, has our plump waitress. To prove it, when the owner enters the room, she takes his arm and holds him back, and drags him firmly towards the kitchens. Now, everything happens very quickly. Jacques gives the signal to Emile; the fuses redden, the pins tumble down into the gutter, the window panes are broken and the grenades are already rolling across the restaurant floor. Emile can't resist the desire to stand up, just to get a glimpse of the chaos.

'Grenades! Get out of here!' roars Jacques.

The blast hurls Emile to the ground. He is a little stunned but this is not the time to yield to a blackout. The acrid smell of smoke makes him cough. He spits; thick blood flows onto his hand. As long as his legs don't fail him, there's still a chance. Jacques takes him by the arm and the two of them run towards the young lad with the three bikes. Emile pedals, Jacques cycles beside him; they have to take care, the roadway is slippery. There's one hell of a racket behind them. Jacques turns around – is the lad still following them? If he's counted accurately, barely ten seconds remain until the big bang. There: the sky lights up; the two bombs have just exploded. The kid on the bike has fallen, brought down by the thunderclap. Jacques does a U-turn, but soldiers are emerging from everywhere and two of them have already caught the struggling kid.

'Jacques, for God's sake, look in front of you!' shouts Emile.

At the end of the street, some police officers are forming

a barricade; the one they allowed to run off a while ago must have gone off to fetch reinforcements. Jacques removes his revolver from its holster. He presses on the trigger, but all he hears is a small click. A brief glance at his weapon, without losing his balance, without losing sight of the target, reveals that the cartridge is hanging down. It's a miracle it hasn't fallen off. Jacques strikes the pistol on the handlebars and manages to push the magazine back into place; he fires three times, the cops clear off and let him through. His bike catches up with Emile's.

'You're pissing blood, old boy.'

'My head's about to explode,' stammers Emile.

'The youngster fell,' confides Jacques.

'Shall we go back?' asks Emile, trying to put his feet on the ground.

'Pedal!' orders Jacques. 'They've already taken him and I only have two bullets left.'

Police cars are arriving from everywhere. Emile lowers his head and pedals as fast as he can. If the night wasn't there to protect him with its darkness, the blood flowing down his face would be an instant betrayal. The pain which is taking him over is terrible, but he tries to ignore his suffering. The fellow-resistor whom they've left back there is going to suffer a lot more than he is; they will torture him. When they beat him black and blue, his temples will be a lot more bruised than his own are.

At the end of his tongue, Emile feels the piece of metal which has gone through his cheek. A fragment of his own grenade, how stupid! He had to be as close as possible, it was the only way to hit the bull's-eye.

The mission has been accomplished, so it's just too bad if he has to die, thinks Emile. His head is spinning, and a red veil is invading his field of vision. Jacques sees the bicycle wobble. He approaches, gets within reach and grabs his friend by the shoulder.

'Keep going, we're almost there!'

They encounter some police officers who are running towards the cloud of smoke. Nobody pays them any attention. An alleyway cuts across; the road to safety isn't very far now. In a few minutes they can slow down.

A few knocks; someone is drumming on my door. I open it. Emile's face is covered in blood, and Jacques is supporting him with his arm.

'Do you have a chair?' he asks. 'Emile is a little tired.'

And when Jacques closes the door behind them, I understand that one friend is missing from the roll-call.

'We have to remove the piece of grenade that's stuck in his face,' Jacques says.

Jacques heats up the blade of his knife in the flame of his lighter and cuts into Emile's cheek. Sometimes, when the pain is too strong, it rises up to his heart to the point of making him vomit, so I hold him up when his head rolls. Emile fights. He refuses to pass out, he thinks of all those days to come, all those nights when the friend who fell in action will be beaten; no, Emile doesn't want to lose consciousness. And while Jacques removes the piece of metal, Emile also thinks back to that German soldier, stretched out in the middle of the street, the body torn apart by his bomb.

10

Sunday has passed. I saw my brother; he has got even thinner but he doesn't talk about his hunger. I can no longer call him my little brother, like before. In a few days, he has aged so much. We do not have the right to tell each other about our operations because of the security rules, but I can read how hard his life is in his eyes. We are sitting beside the canal; to pass the time, we talk about home, about life as it was before, but that doesn't change the look in his eyes. Then we share some long silences. Not far from us, a crane with legs bent sways over the water, looking as if it's in its death throes. It may have been Claude who did the job, but I'm not allowed to ask him the question. He guesses what I'm thinking and laughs.

'Was it you who did the crane?'

'No, I thought it might be you . . .'

'I took care of the lock a bit further upstream, and I can tell you it's nowhere near working. But I swear to you I had nothing to do with the crane.'

All it had taken was a few minutes sitting there, side by side, a few minutes in which we rediscovered each other at last, and he was already becoming my little brother again. From the tone of his voice, it was almost as if he was apologising for doing something stupid by blowing up the machinery of his lock gate. And yet, how many days' delay would accumulate in the movement of heavy marine components, which the German army transported by canal, from the Atlantic to the Mediterranean? Claude laughed; I ran my hand through his tousled hair and I started laughing, too. Sometimes, between two brothers, the complicity is much stronger than all the bans in the world. The weather was nice and hunger was still there. So, a ban for a ban, too bad.

'How do you fancy a stroll around Place Jeanne-d'Arc?'

'To do what?' asked Claude roguishly.

'Eat a plate of lentils, for example.'

'Place Jeanne-d'Arc?' persisted Claude, articulating each of his words very clearly.

'Do you know another place?'

'No, but if Jan nabs us, do you know what we're exposing ourselves to?'

I would have liked to play the innocent but Claude immediately grumbled:

'Well I'll tell you. We run the risk of enduring a very bad Sunday!'

You should know that the whole brigade had been sternly rapped over the knuckles by Jan because of the little café in Place Jeanne-d'Arc. It was Emile, I think, who unearthed the address. The restaurant had two advantages: you could eat there for almost nothing, barely a few coins, but even better, you came out feeling full and that feeling alone was worth all the food in the world. Emile had swiftly passed on the information to the brigade members and, little by little, the café had begun to fill up.

One day, passing by the window, Jan had discovered to his horror that almost every member of the brigade was eating lunch there. One police raid and we were all done for. That same evening, we were summoned *manu militari* to Charles's house, and we were all given a proper dressing down. The place known as the Plate of Vetch was henceforth formally out of bounds to us, under pain of serious punishment.

'I've thought of something,' Claude murmured. 'If nobody is allowed to go there any more, doesn't that mean that nobody from our brigade will be there?'

Up to this point, my little brother's reasoning held water. I allowed him to continue.

'Now, if nobody from our brigade is there, supposing the two of us go there, we won't be putting the brigade in any kind of danger, will we?'

No question, his reasoning still held good.

'And if we go there together, nobody will find out and Jan can't tell us off for it.'

You see, it's crazy what your imagination does when you have an empty belly and that filthy beast hunger gnawing away at it. I took my little brother by the arm and, as soon as we had left the canal behind, we broke into a sprint and headed for Place Jeanne-d'Arc.

As we entered the restaurant we both had a very strange shock. Apparently, all the members of the brigade had reasoned in the same way as we had; and it was more than just apparent, since every one of them was eating lunch there, to the point moreover where there were only two empty chairs left in the dining area. Add to that the fact that the empty seats were right next to those occupied by Jan and Catherine, whose amorous tête-à-tête was frankly compromised, and for a very good reason! Jan pulled a face a hundred paces long and we all tried as best we could to hold back the uncontrollable laughter that was overtaking us. That Sunday, the owner must have wondered why, all of a sudden, his entire restaurant fell about laughing, although it was clear that none of his customers seemed to know each other.

I was the first to regain control of my uncontrollable laughter; not because I found the situation less comical than the others, but because at the back of the café I had just seen Damira and Marc, who were also having an intimate lunch together. And as Jan had been caught unawares in the forbidden café in the company of Catherine, Marc had no reason to deprive himself; I saw him take Damira's hand and she let him do so.

While my amorous hopes were fading away in front of a plate of bogus lentils, the friends dried their tears, their heads lowered over their plates. Catherine hid her face behind her scarf, but it was stronger than she was and in turn she too was overcome by a fit of laughter which revived the joyous humour in the room; even Jan and the owner ended up joining in.

Late in the afternoon, I went back with Claude. Together, we walked back up the little street where he was lodging. Before I went to catch my tram, I turned around, just once, to see his sweet little face before heading back towards loneliness. He didn't turn around, and in the end it was better that way. Because it wasn't my little brother any more who was going back home, but the man he had become. And that Sunday evening, I had a really bad attack of the blues.

11

The weekend buried July. This Monday morning is 2 August 1943. It is today that Marcel will be avenged. This afternoon Lespinasse will be killed when he comes out of his house, at half-past three as usual, since that is his only recurrent habit.

When she got up this morning, Catherine had a strange kind of intuition; she was anxious about those who were going to carry out the operation. One detail might have escaped her. Were there undercover police officers she hadn't noticed, in a car parked alongside the pavement? She constantly goes over her week's surveillance in her head. How many times did she walk up and down the middle-class street where the deputy prosecutor lives – a hundred, maybe more? Marianne didn't see anything either, so why this sudden anguish? To drive away her bad thoughts, she decides to go to the Palais de Justice.

She tells herself it's there that she'll hear the first echoes of the operation.

It's a quarter to three by the big clock that tick-tocks away on the frontispiece of the courthouse. In forty-five minutes, the friends will open fire. So as not to be spotted, she strolls along the main corridor, consults the notices posted up on the walls. But no matter what she does, she keeps on reading the same line, incapable of retaining a single word of it. A man comes forward, his footsteps echoing on the floor. He smiles; a strange smile. Two others come to meet and greet him.

'*Monsieur l'avocat général*,' said the first, 'allow me to introduce one of my friends.'

Intrigued, Catherine turns around and spies on the scene. The man stretches out a hand to the one who is smiling, while the third continues to make the introductions.

'Monsieur Deputy Prosecutor Lespinasse, this is my good friend, Monsieur Dupuis.'

Catherine's expression freezes. The man with the strange smile is in no way the same one she tracked for a whole week. And yet, Jan told her the address, and his name was on the copper plate attached to his garden gate. Catherine's head buzzes; her heart races faster in her chest; and little by little, things become clear. The Lespinasse who lives in the middle-class house in the Toulouse suburbs is someone with the same name! Same name and, still worse, the same Christian name! How could Jan have been so stupid as to imagine that the address of such an important lawyer could be found in a telephone book? And while Catherine is thinking, the clock on the wall in the long corridor continues on its tireless course. It is three o'clock; in twenty minutes, the brigade members are going to kill an innocent man, a poor guy whose only wrong will have been to bear someone else's name. She must stay calm, get a grip on herself. First, she must leave here without anyone noticing the desperation that is overwhelming her. Next, once she has reached the street, she must run, steal a bike if she has to, but at all costs get there in time, to prevent the worst. There are twenty-nine minutes left, unless of course the man she had wanted dead and whom she now wishes to save is not ahead in his timetable . . . for once.

Catherine runs. In front of her is a bicycle that a man has rested against a wall, just long enough to buy his newspaper from the kiosk; time that she does not have, neither to evaluate the risks, nor still less to hesitate. Too bad. She mounts it and pedals with all her strength. Nobody behind her shouts, 'Stop, thief'; the guy can't have noticed yet that his bike has been pinched. She goes through a red light, her scarf comes undone when a car surges forward, a klaxon roars. The front left wing brushes Catherine's thigh, the handle of the door scratches her on the hip; she wobbles but manages to regain her balance. No time to hurt, scarcely time for a grimace, no time to be afraid, she must pedal faster. Her legs speed up, the spokes of the wheels disappear in the light, the speed is infernal. At the pedestrian crossing, the pedestrians shout at her, but there's no time to apologise, not even to brake at the next crossroads. New obstacle: a tram car. Must get past it, pay attention to the rails; if the wheel slips on them she's bound to fall and at this speed there's no chance this time of getting up again. The fronts of buildings fly past; the pavements are no more now than one long grey line. Her lungs are about to explode, her chest hurts fit to burst, but the burning is nothing beside what the poor guy will feel when he takes his five bullets in the chest. What time is it? Quarter past three? Twenty past? She recognises the shape of the hill in the distance. She travelled that way every day that week to come and do her stint.

And to think that she was angry with Jan, but how could she have been stupid enough to imagine that Deputy Prosecutor Lespinasse would take as few precautions as the man she had followed? Each day she mocked him, muttered during her long hours of waiting that the prey was really too easy. The ignorance she had been mocking was her own. It was logical that this poor fellow would have no reason to be wary, that he would not feel he was the target either of the Resistance or of anyone else; logical also that he should have no cares, since he was innocent of everything. Her legs are killing her, but Catherine keeps on going, never slowing down. There, the hill is behind her, just one final crossroads and she might just arrive in time. If the operation had taken place,

113

she would have heard the shots, and for that moment alone a long whistling sound buzzes in her ears. It's the blood, pulsing too hard in her temples, not the sound of death, not yet.

Here's the street; the innocent man is closing the door of his house and crossing his garden. Robert advances across the pavement, his hand in his pocket, his fingers gripping the butt of the revolver, ready to fire. It's now a question of seconds. She brakes, and the bike slides. Catherine lets it run along the roadway and throws herself into the partisan's arms.

'You're crazy! What are you doing?'

She no longer has the breath to speak; her face pale, she holds her comrade's hand. She herself does not know where she is finding so much strength. And as he doesn't understand, Catherine finally succeeds in gasping:

'It's not him!'

The innocent Lespinasse has climbed into his car, the engine gives a little cough and the black Peugeot 202 calmly sets off. As he passes the couple who seem to be intertwined, the driver gives them a little wave. 'Lovers are so beautiful to observe,' he thinks as he glances in his rear-view mirror.

Today is a bad day. The Germans descended on the university. They intercepted ten young men on the concourse, dragged them towards the steps, forcing them forward with blows from rifle butts, and then they took them away. You see, we shall not give up; even if we die of hunger, even if fear haunts our nights, even if our comrades fall, we shall continue to resist.

We had just avoided the worst. As I've already told you, we have never killed an innocent person, not even an imbecile. In the meantime, the deputy prosecutor was still alive, and we must begin the investigation again from zero. Since we did not know where he lived, we would begin tailing him from the courthouse. The enterprise was a difficult one. The real Lespinasse only moved around aboard a large black Hotchkiss, or sometimes in a Renault Primaquatre, but in any event, driven by his chauffeur. So as not to be spotted, Catherine has perfected a method. The first day, a brigade member followed the deputy prosecutor by bike from his exit from the Palais and gave up following after a few minutes. The following day, another brigade member, on a different bicycle, resumed the trail from where it had been abandoned the previous day. By means of successive sections, we thus succeeded in following the route all the way back to the deputy prosecutor's residence. Now, Catherine could begin her long walks again on a different pavement. Another few days of covert work, and we would know all the lawyer's habits.

12

For us, there was an enemy even more hateful than the Nazis. We were at war with the Germans, but the Militia was the worst mob that Fascism and ruthless ambition could produce; walking hatred.

The militiamen violated, tortured and robbed the people they deported, made money from their power over the population. How many women opened their legs, with their eyes closed and teeth desperately clenched, against the false promise that their children would not be arrested? How many of those old men in the long queues outside the empty grocery shops had to pay the militiamen to leave them in peace; and how many of those who couldn't do so were sent to the camps so that the street dogs could calmly empty their homes? Without these scum, the Nazis would never have been able to deport so many people, of whom no more than one in ten would return.

I was twenty years old, I was afraid, I was hungry, hungry all the time, and these black-shirted guys dined in restaurants that were reserved for them. How many of them have I observed behind winter's misted-up windows, licking their fingers, stuffed full after a meal the very thought of which made my stomach rumble? Fear and hunger, a terrible cocktail in the belly.

But we shall have our vengeance, you see, even just saying that word I can feel my heart beating anew. What a horrible idea vengeance is, I shouldn't have said that; the operations we undertook were quite different from vengeance, they were a duty of the heart, to save those who wouldn't have to experience that fate, to take part in the war of liberation.

Hunger and fear, an explosive cocktail in the belly! The small sound of an egg being broken on a counter is a terrible thing, Prévert would one day say, free to write it; I, a prisoner of life, already knew it on that day.

Last August 14th, returning from Charles's place a little late at night and braving the curfew with a few fellow brigade-members, Boris had found himself nose to nose with a group of militiamen.

Boris, who had already dealt personally with several members of their band, knew their organisation better than anyone. All it had taken was the benevolent light from a lamppost for him to recognise instantly the sinister face of a man called Costes. Why him? Because the fellow in question was no other than the general secretary of the *franc-gardes*, an army of savage, bloodthirsty dogs.

As the militiamen walked towards them, arrogant enough to believe that the street belonged to them, Boris drew his weapon. The other brigade members did the same and Costes collapsed in a pool of blood, his own to be precise.

But that evening, Boris had raised the bar a notch; he was going to attack Mas, the head of the Militia.

The operation was almost suicidal. Mas was at his home, along with a good number of his guards. Boris began by beating senseless the guard at the entrance to the detached house, on rue Pharaon. On the first-floor landing, another guard received a fatal blow from a gun-butt. Boris wasn't particular about details; he entered the sitting room, weapon in hand, and he fired. The guys all fell down, the majority of them only wounded, but Mas had taken his bullet in the right place. Curled up under his desk, his head between the legs of the armchair, the position of the body made it clear that Chief Mas would never be able to rape, kill or terrorise anybody ever again.

The press regularly treated us as terrorists, a word brought by the Germans, and which, on their notices, designated the partisans they had executed. But we only terrorised them and the active, Fascist collaborators. To return to Boris, it was after the successful operation that things got complicated. While he was dealing with his business upstairs, the two brigade members who were safeguarding his getaway downstairs had had to face some militiamen who had arrived as reinforcements. Gunfire filled the staircase with smoke. Boris reloaded his revolver and stepped onto the landing. Unfortunately, his undermanned colleagues were forced to fall back. Boris found himself caught in the crossfire. Those who were firing on his friends, and those who were firing on him.

As he was attempting to leave the building, a new squadron of Blackshirts arrived, this time from the upper floors, and got the better of his resistance. Beaten and seized around the waist, Boris fell. After he had copiously perforated their leader's chest and grievously wounded several of their colleagues, it was a fair bet that the guys were going to take it out on him. The two other brigade members had succeeded in getting out. One had taken a bullet in the hip, but Boris could no longer treat it.

It was the end of another of those sad days in August 1943. A friend had been taken, a young student in the third year of his medical studies who, throughout his childhood, had dreamed of saving lives, had been dispatched to a cell at Saint-Michel prison. And none of us doubted that, in order to be seen more favourably by the government and consolidate his authority, Deputy Prosecutor Lespinasse would want to avenge his friend Mas, the deceased head of the Militia, personally.

13

September was flying by, and the russet leaves on the chestnut trees announced the coming of autumn.

We were exhausted, and hungrier than ever, but the operations were growing more numerous and each day the Resistance stretched a little further. During the course of the month, we had destroyed a German garage on Boulevard de Strasbourg, then we attacked the Caffarelli barracks, occupied by a regiment of the Wehrmacht; a little later, we attacked a military train travelling on the route linking Toulouse to Carcassonne. Luck had been with us that day; we placed our charges underneath the wagon that was transporting a gun but the dull-witted types positioned next to it joined in with our gunfire, and the entire train went up. Midway through the month, we celebrated the battle of Valmy a little early by attacking the cartridge factory, making it impossible to manufacture them for a long time; Emile even went to the municipal library to find out other dates of battles that we could celebrate in similar fashion.

But that evening, there was no operation. We were to have brought down General Schmoutz himself, but had thought twice; the reason was a simple one. The chickens that Charles raised in his garden must have had an exciting week as he said: we were invited to his place for an omelette.

At nightfall we met up at the little disused railway station in Loubers.

The table was laid and everyone was already seated around it. Given the number of guests, Charles had judged that there wouldn't be sufficient eggs, so he had decided to make the omelette go further with goose grease. There was always a pot somewhere in the workshop, sometimes serving to improve the air-tightness of his bombs or to lubricate the springs in our revolvers.

We were in celebratory mood. The information-collecting girls were there and we were happy to be together. Of course, this meal broke the most elementary security regulations, but Jan knew how much these rare moments healed us of the isolation that touched every one of us. If the Germans' or the Militia's bullets had not yet killed us, loneliness was doing so, little by little. Not all of us had reached the age of twenty, and even the eldest among us were scarcely more, so although we could not fill our bellies, the presence of our friends filled our hearts.

It was clear from the infatuated glances Damira and Marc were exchanging that they were incontestably taken with each other. As for me, I couldn't take my eyes off Sophie. As Charles was coming back from the workshop with his pot of goose grease under his arm, Sophie gave me one of those smiles she had the knack of giving, one of the most beautiful ones I had ever seen in my life. Carried away by the euphoria of the moment, I promised myself that I would find the courage to invite her to go out with me; perhaps even to have lunch the very next day. After all, why wait? So while Charles was beating his eggs, I was persuading myself to ask her before the end of the evening. I must, of course, look out for a discreet moment, when Jan would not hear; even if, since he had been caught at the Plate of Vetch with Catherine, instructions relating to amorous security had been relaxed slightly in the brigade. If Sophie couldn't manage tomorrow, that wouldn't be serious, I would suggest the following day. Having made my resolution, I was about to move into action when Jan announced that he was appointing Sophie to the team carrying out surveillance on Deputy Prosecutor Lespinasse.

Brave as she was, Sophie accepted immediately. Jan specified that she would take charge of the time slot between 11 a.m. and 3 p.m. That bastard deputy prosecutor really intended to piss me off right to the end.

The evening wasn't a complete failure – there was still the omelette – but all the same, how beautiful Sophie was, with that smile that never left her. In any event, Catherine and Marianne, who watched over the information-gathering girls like two mothers, would never have let us. So in the end, it was better to watch her smile in silence.

Charles emptied the pot of goose grease into the frying pan, stirred a bit and then came and sat down with us, saying, 'Now it has to cook.'

It was while we were trying to translate what he had said that the incident occurred. Shots rang out on every side. We threw ourselves to the ground. Jan raged, weapon in hand. We must have been followed and the Germans were attacking us. Two members who had pistols in their belts found the courage to sneak between the bullets to the windows. I did likewise, which was idiotic since I didn't have a weapon, but if one of them fell I would take his revolver and carry on the chain. One thing seemed rather strange to us – the bullets continued to go off inside the room, bits of wood jumped onto the floor, the walls were dotted with holes and yet in front of us, the countryside was deserted. And then the crackle of bullets ceased. There wasn't a sound any more, nothing but silence. We looked at each other, all very intrigued, and then I saw Charles get up first. He was scarlet-faced and stammering more than ever. Tears in his eyes, he kept repeating, 'Sorry, sorry.'

In fact, there was no enemy outside; Charles had just forgotten that he'd emptied some 7.65mm bullets into his pot of goose grease . . . to prevent them oxidizing! The ammunition had become suddenly hot when it came into contact with the frying pan!

None of us was hurt, apart perhaps from our pride. We collected up what was left of the omelette, sorted through it to make sure it contained nothing more that was abnormal, and sat down at the table again, as if nothing had happened.

It's true that our friend Charles's talents as a pyrotechnist were more reliable than his cooking, but after all, given the times we were living in, it was better that way.

Tomorrow, October began and the war continued. Ours included.

14

The filthy swine have thick hides. When the girls' second period of surveillance reached its end, Jan immediately entrusted Robert with the mission to kill Lespinasse. Boris, who was in prison, was soon to be tried and we must not lose any time if we wanted to prevent him facing the worst. By sending a strong signal to the magistrates, we would eventually make them realise that attacking the life of a partisan was tantamount to signing one's own death warrant. For the last few months, as soon as the Germans posted up a notice of execution on the walls of Toulouse, their officers were instantly killed, and each time, we dropped tracts explaining our actions to the population. Over the last few weeks, they had executed fewer people and their soldiers no longer dared return alone at night. You see, we did not give up and the Resistance was making a little more progress each day.

The mission was to run its course on Monday morning, and we were to meet at the collection point, i.e. the terminus of the number twelve tram line. When Robert arrived, we realised right away that the operation had not been carried out. Something had gone wrong and Jan was furious.

That Monday was the day when the legal profession resumed sitting after the summer vacation, and all the magistrates would be present at the courthouse. The announcement of the deputy prosecutor's death would more than ever have had the effect we were counting on so much. One didn't kill a man like that, not just any time, even if, in the case of Lespinasse, any day would do nicely. Robert waited until Jan calmed down, until he started walking more slowly.

Jan wasn't just furious that we had failed to make the date when the new legal term began. It was more than two months since Marcel had been guillotined, Radio London had announced several times that the person responsible for condemning him to death would pay for his odious crime, and we were going to end up looking like incompetents! But Robert had had a bad feeling just as he was about to carry out the operation, and this was the first time it had happened to him.

His determination to deal with the prosecutor had not changed in any way, but there we were, it was impossible to act today! He promised on his honour that he knew nothing of the importance of this date that Jan had chosen; Robert had never given up; with the calm

126

demeanour that characterised him, he must have had good reasons for doing so.

He had arrived around nine o'clock at the street where Lespinasse lived. According to the information gathered by the brigade's girls, the deputy prosecutor left his house every day at ten o'clock on the dot. Marius, who had taken part in the first operation, and very nearly killed the other Lespinasse, was content this time to take care of protection.

Robert wore a large overcoat, with two grenades in the left pocket, one offensive and one defensive, and his loaded revolver in the right. At ten o'clock, there was nobody. A quarter of an hour later, still no Lespinasse. Fifteen minutes is a long time when you have two grenades knocking against each other in your pocket at every step you take.

A policeman on a bicycle comes up the street and stops near him. A coincidence probably, but with his target still not appearing, questions have to be asked.

Time stretches out slowly, the street is calm; even by going and coming, it's difficult not to be spotted sooner or later.

Further up the street, the two other brigade members also can't pass completely unnoticed any more, with their three bikes ready for the getaway.

A lorry stuffed with Germans turns at the corner of the street; two 'coincidences' in such a short time, that's starting to be a lot! Robert feels ill at ease. In the distance, Marius questions him with a sign and Robert answers him in the same way, that for the moment all is well, they're continuing the operation. Only one problem: still no deputy prosecutor in sight. The German lorry passes without stopping, but it's travelling slowly and this time Robert asks himself more and more questions. The pavements are deserted once more, the door of the house opens at last, a man emerges and crosses the garden. In the pocket of his coat, Robert's hand grips the butt of his revolver. Robert still can't see the face of the man who's closing the gate of the house. Now he's moving towards his car. Robert has a terrible doubt. What if it wasn't him? If it was just a doctor who'd come to visit the prosecutor because he was ill in bed with bad flu? Difficult to introduce himself like this: 'Hello, are you really the guy I'm supposed to empty my gun into?'

Robert goes to meet him and the only thing that comes to his mind is to ask him the time. He wishes this man, who can't be unaware that he's under threat, would show some kind of sign that betrays his fear, that his hand would tremble, that beads of sweat would appear on his brow!

The man merely pushes back his sleeve and replies politely, 'Half past ten.' Robert's fingers let go of the gun butt, incapable of firing. Lespinasse gives him a nod of farewell and gets into his car.

Jan says nothing more; there is nothing more to say. Robert had good reasons and nobody can reproach him for giving up. It's just that the real scumbags have hard skins. As we're going our separate ways, Jan mutters that we're going to have to begin again, very quickly.

*   *   *

128

The bitterness didn't leave him all week. What's more, he didn't want to see anyone. When Sunday came, Robert set his alarm for the early morning. The aroma of the coffee his landlady was preparing rose up to his room. Ordinarily, the smell of toast would titillate his belly, but since last Monday, Robert is heavy of heart. He gets dressed calmly, retrieves his revolver from under the mattress and slips it through his trouser belt. He puts on a jacket and a hat, and leaves his lodgings without telling anyone. It's not the memory of the failure that makes Robert feel sick. Blowing up locomotives, taking the bolts out of rails, destroying pylons, dynamiting cranes, sabotaging enemy equipment, he can do that quite happily, but nobody likes killing. We dreamed of a world where people would be free to exist. We wanted to be doctors, workmen, craftsmen, teachers. It wasn't when they took these rights from us that we took up arms, it was later; when they deported children, shot our comrades. But killing remains a filthy task to us. As I've told you, you never forget the face of someone you're about to shoot, and even if it's a scumbag like Lespinasse, it's a difficult thing.

Catherine confirmed to Robert that every Sunday morning, the deputy prosecutor goes to mass at 10 a.m. precisely, so, his mind made up, Robert battles the sickening feeling inside him and mounts his bike. And besides, Boris must be saved.

It's ten o'clock when Robert enters the street. The prosecutor has just closed his garden gate. Here he is, walking

129

along the pavement flanked by his wife and daughter. Robert cocks his revolver and moves towards him; the group reaches him and goes past. Robert takes out his weapon, spins around and takes aim. Not in the back, so he shouts, 'Lespinasse!' Surprised, the family turns around, sees the weapon pointed at them, but already two shots have rung out and the deputy prosecutor falls to his knees, hands clasping his belly. Wide-eyed, Lespinasse stares at Robert, he gets up, staggers, grabs hold of a tree to support himself. The filthy swine really do have tough hides!

Robert approaches, the deputy prosecutor begs, whispers, 'Mercy.' But Robert thinks of Marcel, head in hands in his coffin, and sees the faces of comrades who have been killed. For all these young kids, there will be neither mercy nor pity; Robert empties his magazine. The two women scream, a passer-by tries to come to their aid, but Robert raises his weapon and the man runs away.

And as Robert pedals into the distance on his bike, cries for help begin to sound behind him.

At noon, he is back in his room. The news has already spread throughout the town. The police have sealed off the area and are questioning the prosecutor's widow. They ask her if she might recognise the man who committed the crime. Mme Lespinasse nods and answers that it's possible, but that she would not wish to. There have already been too many deaths as it is.

15

Emile had succeeded in getting himself a job on the railways. We all tried to get work. We all needed a salary; the rent had to be paid, we had to be fed somehow, and the Resistance struggled to pay us a little each month. A job also had the advantage of allaying suspicions as to our clandestine activities. You attracted less attention from the police or from neighbours when you went off to work every morning. Those who were unemployed had no other choice but to pretend to be students, but they were much more liable to be detected. Obviously, if the work obtained could also serve the cause, then that was ideal! The posts that Emile and Alonso occupied at the marshalling yard in Toulouse were precious to the brigade. Along with a few other railwaymen, they had built up a small team specialising in sabotage of all kinds. One of their specialities, which they executed right under

131

the noses of the German soldiers, was to unstick the labels from the sides of the wagons and immediately re-stick them on others. So when the goods trains were made up, the spare parts anxiously awaited by the Nazis in Calais were sent to Bordeaux, the transformers antici-pated in Nantes arrived in Metz, and the engines destined for Germany were delivered to Lyon.

The Germans accused the French railway of this sham-bles, attacking French inefficiency. Thanks to Emile, François and a few of their fellow railwaymen, the supplies needed by the occupying forces were dispersed in all directions except the right one, and were lost in the middle of nowhere. One or two months would elapse before the goods destined for the enemy were relocated and reached the right place, and that was already a small victory. Often, when night fell, we joined them and sneaked between the stationary goods trains. We strained our ears for every sound around us, taking advantage of the grating noise of a shunting train or the din of a power unit going past to advance towards our target without being caught by the German patrols.

The previous week, we had slid underneath a train, climbing up under its axle-trees until we reached a very special wagon we were wild about: the *Tankwagen*, or 'tank wagon'. Although our sabotage manoeuvre was particularly difficult to put into action without being spotted, it would pass completely unnoticed once it was accomplished.

While one of us kept watch, the others hauled themselves up to the top of the tank, opened the cover and emptied kilos of sand and molasses into the fuel. A few days later, when it reached its destination, the precious liquid we had doctored so carefully was pumped out to fill the fuel tanks of German bombers or fighters. Our knowledge of mechanics was sufficient to know that just after takeoff, the pilot of the plane would have only one choice: try and work out why his engines had just failed, or make an immediate parachute jump before his plane crashed; at worst the planes would be out of action by the end of the runway, which in itself wasn't bad.

With a little sand and a lot of nerve, my friends had succeeded in perfecting a system for destroying enemy aviation from a distance; a system that was extremely simple, yet highly effective. And when I thought about it as I went back with them in the early hours, I told myself that by so doing, they were offering me a little piece of my second dream: to join the Royal Air Force.

Sometimes we also slipped along the railway tracks at Toulouse-Raynal railway station, to lift up the covers of the trains' flatbed wagons and act in accordance with whatever we found there. When we found wings for Messerschmitts, fuselages for Junkers or tail-planes for Stukas manufactured in the region's Latécoère factories, we cut the control cables. When we were dealing with aircraft engines, we tore out the electric cables or fuel pipes. I can't count the number of planes we kept on the ground in this way. As for me, each time I destroyed an enemy plane in this way, it was always best that I did it with someone else, because of my absent-mindedness. As soon as I set about making holes with a bradawl in the aerofoil of a wing, I instantly imagined myself in the cockpit of my Spitfire, pressing the trigger on the joystick, with the wind whistling through the fuselage. Fortunately for me, the benevolent hands of Emile or Alonso always tapped me on the shoulder, and then I saw from their expressions how sorry they were to bring me back to reality when they said, 'Come along, Jeannot, it's time to go back.'

We spent the first fortnight of October operating in this way. But tonight, the job would be much more important than usual. Emile had found out that twelve locomotives were going to be driven into Germany tomorrow.

The mission was a sizeable one, and in order to carry it out there were six of us. It was rare that we acted in such large numbers; if we were taken, the brigade would lose close to a third of its membership. But the stakes justified taking such a risk. Saying twelve locomotives is tantamount to saying twelve bombs. There was no question however of us going in procession to our friend Charles's place. For once, he would be making home deliveries.

In the early hours, our friend placed his precious packages inside a small cart attached to his bike, covered them with freshly-harvested lettuces from his garden and a tarpaulin. He left the little station at Loubers, singing as he pedalled along through the Toulouse countryside.

134

Charles's bicycle, made up of pieces taken from our stolen bikes, was the only one of its kind. With handlebars almost a metre wide, a raised saddle, a frame that was half blue and half orange, mismatched pedals and two women's panniers hanging on either side of the rear wheel, Charles's bicycle really was an odd-looking affair.

Charles was pretty odd-looking, too. He wasn't worried about going into town; the police officers generally paid him no attention, convinced that he was a tramp who had wandered into this part of the world. An inconvenience for the population, it was true, but not a danger in any real sense. Normally, the police, used to his odd look, couldn't have cared less about him – except today, unfortunately.

Charles is crossing the Place du Capitole, towing his extremely special cargo, when two gendarmes stop him for a routine check. Charles holds out his identity card, which states that he was born at Lens. As if the brigadier can't read what's written in black and white, he asks Charles for his place of birth. Charles, who doesn't have the wit for contradictions, answers without hesitation:

'Lountz!'

'Lountz?' asks the brigadier, perplexed.

'Lountz!' insists Charles, folding his arms.

'You say you were born at Lountz but here on your papers, I read that it was in Lens that your mother gave birth to you, so either you are lying, or this is a counterfeit card?'

'But no,' Charles makes an effort to say, with his rather peculiar accent. 'Lountz, that's exactly what I'm saying! Lountz in the Pas-de-Calais!'

The policeman looks at him, wondering if the fellow he's questioning is taking the mickey out of him.

'You also claim to be French, perhaps?' he retorts.

'Si, ti ta fou!' declares Charles . . . this is his version of *tout à fait*, 'completely'.

This time the policeman really does think he's being made a fool of.

'Where do you live?' he demands in an authoritarian tone.

Charles, who has his lesson off pat, immediately replies 'At Brist!'

'Brist? And where exactly is Brist? I don't know anywhere called Brist,' says the police officer, turning to his colleague.

'Brist, in Finistire!' answers Charles with a hint of irritation.

'I think he means Brest in Finistère, chief!' intervenes his impassive colleague.

And Charles delightedly nods his head in a sign of agreement. The annoyed brigadier looks him up and down. It has to be said that what with his multicoloured bicycle, his tramp's pea-coat and his load of lettuces, Charles doesn't entirely look like a sea fisherman from Brest. So the gendarme, who has had enough, orders him to follow him for an identity check.

This time, it's Charles who gives him a fixed stare.

And it seems that little Camille's vocabulary lessons have borne fruit, because our friend Charles leans towards the policeman's ear and whispers:

'I am transporting bombs in my trailer; if you take me to your police station, I will be shot. And tomorrow you will be shot, because the Resistance will know who arrested me.'

Which goes to show that when Charles put his all into it, he spoke excellent French!

The policeman's hand was resting on his service revolver. He hesitated, then let go of the gun butt. There was a brief exchange of looks with his colleague and he said to Charles:

'Clear off, le Brestois, get out of my sight!'

At noon, we took delivery of the twelve bombs, Charles told us about his adventure and the worst thing is that it made him laugh.

Jan, on the other hand, did not find it funny in the least. He lectured Charles, told him that he had taken too many risks, but Charles kept laughing and retorted that soon, twelve locomotives would no longer be able to draw trains filled with deportees, ever again. He wished us good luck for tonight and got back on his bike. Sometimes at night, before I go to sleep, I still hear him pedalling towards Loubers station, perched on his big multicoloured bicycle, with his immense, equally colourful laughter.

Ten o'clock. It's dark enough now for us to act. Emile gives the signal and we jump over the wall that runs along the roadway. We have to be careful when we land, as we're each carrying two bombs in our bags. It's cold, and the damp freezes our bones. François sets off in front, while Alonso, Emile, my brother Claude, Jacques and I form the column that sneaks along the side of a stationary train. The brigade seems almost at full strength.

Ahead of us there's a soldier on guard duty, blocking our progress. Time is moving on, and we must get to the trains, which are parked further away. This afternoon, we rehearsed the mission. Thanks to Emile, we know that the machines are all lined up on marshalling tracks. Each of us will have to take care of two locomotives. First, climb onto it, use the ledge that runs along the side, go up the ladder and haul ourselves up to the top of the boiler. Light a cigarette, then the fuse, and slowly lower the bomb into the smokestack with the aid of the metal wire with which it's held on a hook. Hang the hook on the edge of the funnel, so that the bomb remains suspended several centimetres above the bottom of the boiler. Then go back down, cross the track and begin again on the next locomotive. Once both the bombs are in place, run for a low wall about a hundred metres ahead and, in fact, run full stop, before the whole thing explodes. As far as possible, try to synchronise with the others, to avoid one person still being at work when the other person's locomotives blow up. At the moment when thirty tons of metal go up, it's best to be as far away as possible.

Alonso looks at Emile. We have to get rid of this guy

138

who's barring our way. Emile gets out his pistol. The soldier slips a cigarette between his lips. He strikes a match and the flame lights up his face. Despite his impeccable uniform, the enemy looks more like a poor kid disguised as a soldier than a ferocious Nazi.

Emile puts away his gun and signals to us that we'll make do with knocking him senseless. Everyone is pleased at the news, I a little less than the others because I have to do the job. It's terrible knocking somebody out, terrible striking his skull, with the fear of killing him.

The inanimate soldier is carried into a wagon and Alonso closes its door, as quietly as possible. We carry on walking. And now we've arrived. Emile raises his arm to give the signal, and everyone holds his breath, ready to move into action. As for me, I lift my head and look at the sky, telling myself that doing battle in the air must be more appealing than crawling across gravel and lumps of coal, but one detail attracts my attention. Unless my short sight has suddenly become worse, it seems to me that I can see smoke emerging from the funnels of all the locomotives. Now, if there's smoke in the funnel of a locomotive, you have to presume that its boiler is alight. Thanks to the experience I acquired in Charles's dining room during the omelette party (as the Englishmen of the Royal Air Force would refer to it in their officers' mess) I now know that anything containing gunpowder is extremely sensitive to the proximity of a heat source. Saving a miracle or a peculiarity of our bombs, which might have escaped the field of knowledge I'd acquired in chemistry up to the verge of the diploma, Charles would have thought, just like me, that, 'We have problem.'

Since everything has a reason for being, as my high school maths teacher repeated endlessly, I realise that the railwaymen, whom we forgot to warn about our operation, have left the engines warming up, feeding them with coal, in order to maintain a constant level of steam and ensure that their trains are punctual in the morning.

Although I don't want to upset my comrades' patriotic enthusiasm just before they go into action, I decide that it's a good idea to inform Emile and Alonso of my discovery. I do so by whispering, of course, so as not to attract unnecessarily the attention of any other guards, as I particularly loathed having had to knock out a soldier just before. Whispers or not, Alonso looks worried and, like me, contemplates the smoking funnels. And like me, he analyses perfectly the dilemma we are facing. The plan we have prepared is to lower our explosives via the funnels, to leave them suspended in the locomotives' boilers; now, if the boilers are incandescent, it is difficult, if not almost impossible, to calculate how long it will take before the bombs explode when exposed to the ambient temperature; their fuses having now become somewhat superfluous.

After consulting everyone, he declares that Emile's career as a railwayman has not been sufficiently long to enable us to refine our estimates, and nobody can really reproach him for that.

140

Alonso thinks that the bombs will blow up in our faces halfway up the funnel, whereas Emile is more confident: he thinks that as the dynamite is inside cast-iron cylinders, it should take a certain length of time for the heat to be conducted. To Alonso's question, 'Yes, but how much time?', Emile replies that he hasn't the faintest idea. My little brother concludes that since we're here, we might as well give it a try!

As I've told you, we will not give up. Tomorrow morning the locomotives, smoking or not, will be out of commission. The decision is taken unanimously, without abstentions, to go ahead anyway. Emile raises his arm once again, giving the signal to set off, but this time it's I who dare ask a question, that in the end everyone is asking themselves.

'Should we light the fuses anyway?'

Emile's irritated reply is in the affirmative.

After that, everything happens very quickly. Everyone is now running towards their objectives. We all climb onto our first locomotive, some praying for the best, and the less pious hoping that the worst won't happen. The tinder crackles. I have four minutes, not counting the heat parameter I've already mentioned, to position my first charge, run to the next loco, repeat the process and head for the safety of the low wall. My bomb dangles at the end of its metal wire and descends towards its goal. I guess how important this part is; with the red-hot coals in the firebox, it's vital to avoid any contact.

If my memory is clear, despite the hot and cold that

makes me shiver, a good three minutes had elapsed between the moment when Charles threw his goose grease into the pan and the moment when we threw ourselves to the ground. So, if luck smiled upon me, I might not end my life torn to bits on the boiler of a locomotive, or at least not before I had managed to place my second charge.

What's more, I'm already running between the rails and climbing towards my second objective. A few metres away, Alonso signals to me that all is going well. It reassures me a little to see that he doesn't look any happier than I am. I know people who stand at a distance before striking a match in front of their gas cooker, for fear of a backdraft; I would love to see them in the middle of slipping a three-kilo bomb into the burning chimney of a locomotive. But the only thing that would really reassure me would be to know that my little brother has finished his work and is already about to make good his escape.

Alonso is lagging behind. Climbing back down, he stumbled and caught his foot between the rail and the wheel of his locomotive. The three of us pull him with all our might to free him and I can hear the clock of death tick-tocking in my ear.

Once Alonso's bruised foot is at last freed, we run towards safety and the blast of the first explosion, which produces a terrible din, helps us a little by projecting all three of us as far as the low wall.

My brother comes to help me stand up, and as I see

his sweet, grey little face, even though I am a little groggy, I breathe again and drag him towards the bicycles.

'You saw, we did it!' he says, almost laughing.

'Hey, are you smiling now?'

'On evenings like this, yes!' he replies as he pedals.

In the distance, the explosions come one after another. It's like a rain of iron, falling from the sky. We can feel the warmth even here. Biking through the darkness, we put a foot to the ground and turn around.

My brother is right to smile. This isn't the night of July the 14th, nor New Year's Eve. This is 10 October 1943, but tomorrow the Germans will be short of twelve locomotives, and that's the most beautiful fireworks display we could ever attend.

16

Dawn had broken. I was supposed to be joining my brother, and I was late. The previous evening, when we parted after blowing up the locomotives, we'd promised to have a coffee together. We missed each other, for the opportunities to meet were becoming increasingly rare. Dressing in haste, I hurried off to meet him in a café a stone's throw from Place Esquirol.

'Tell me, exactly what kind of thing are you studying?'

My landlady's voice echoed down the corridor just as I was preparing to leave. From the intonation, I could tell that the question had nothing to do with a sudden interest in my university course on the part of Mme Dublanc. I turned around to face her, forcing myself to be as convincing as possible. If my landlady doubted my identity, I would have to move out with all speed, and probably leave the town today.

'Why do ask, Madame Dublanc?'

'Because if you were in the faculty of medicine, or even better the veterinary school, that would suit me well. My cat is ill, he won't get up.'

'Unfortunately, Mme Dublanc, I would love to help you, I mean your cat, but I'm studying accountancy.'

I thought I'd got out of it, but Mme Dublanc added instantly that this was a great pity; she had a thoughtful air as she said so and her behaviour worried me.

'Can I do anything else for you, Mme Dublanc?'

'It wouldn't bother you to come and take a little look at my Gribouille?'

Mme Dublanc immediately takes me by the arm and drags me into her quarters; as if she wanted to reassure me, she whispers in my ear that it would be better if we talked inside; the walls of her house are not very thick. But in saying that, she does everything but reassure me.

Mme Dublanc's quarters resemble my bedroom, with the addition of furniture and a bathroom, which in the end makes quite a difference. On her armchair sleeps a large grey cat that doesn't look to be in any better state than I am, but I refrain from any comment.

'Listen, young man,' she says, closing the door. 'I don't care if you're studying accountancy or algebra; I've had a few students like you through here, and some of them disappeared without even coming to fetch their things. Now, I rather like you, but I don't want any trouble with the police and still less with the Militia.'

145

My stomach had just twisted. I had the feeling that someone was playing jackstraws in my belly.

'Why do you say that, Madame Dublanc?' I stammered.

'Because unless you're a determined dunce, I don't see you studying much. And besides, your little brother, and those other friends of yours who come here with him sometimes, have the look of terrorists; so I say to you, I don't want any trouble.'

I was desperate to take up Madame Dublanc on the definition of terrorism. Caution should have dictated that I keep my mouth shut, for she had more than mere suspicions about me; and yet I couldn't stop myself.

'I think the real terrorists are the Nazis and the people in the Militia. Because between ourselves, Madame Dublanc, I and my friends are just students who dream of a world at peace.'

'But I want peace too, and to start off I want it in my house! So if it's no problem, my boy, avoid saying such things under my roof. The militiamen have done nothing to me. And when I encounter them in the street, they are always well dressed, very polite and perfectly civilised; which is not the case with all the people one meets in town, far from it, if you see what I mean. I don't want any trouble here, is that understood?'

'Yes, Madame Dublanc,' I replied, in consternation.

'Also, don't make me say what I haven't said. I agree that, in the present times, studying as you and your friends do demands a certain faith in the future, even a certain

146

courage; but all the same, I would prefer that your studies take place outside my walls . . . do you follow me?'

'Do you want me to go away, Madame Dublanc?'

'As long as you pay your rent, I have no reason to throw you out, but be kind enough not to bring your friends back to do their revision in my house. Do your utmost to appear like an ordinary lad with no secrets. It will be better for me and for you too. There, that's all!'

Madame Dublanc winked at me and invited me to use the door of her little apartment to go out again. I said goodbye to her and ran off to meet my little brother, who was probably moaning already, certain that I'd stood him up.

I found him sitting next to the window, drinking coffee with Sophie. It wasn't really coffee, but it really was Sophie opposite him. She didn't see how I blushed as I approached her, at least I don't think so, but I thought it was a good idea to say that I'd just had to sprint because of being late. My little brother looked as if he couldn't give a damn. Sophie got up to leave us together, but Claude invited her to share this moment. Her life as a liaison agent wasn't the easiest one in the world. Like me, she was passing herself off to her landlady as a student. Early in the morning, she left the room she occupied in a house in Côte Pavée and didn't return there until late in the evening, thus avoiding compromising her cover. When she wasn't tailing someone, when she wasn't transporting weapons, she walked the streets, waiting for night to come so that she could finally go back home. In the winter her days were even more difficult. The only moments of respite came when she treated herself to some time off at the counter of a bar, to warm herself up. But she could never stay there very long, as she was at risk of putting herself in danger. A young woman, attractive and alone, was easily noticed.

On Wednesdays, she allowed herself a seat at the cinema, and on Sundays, she told us about the film. Or at least, the first thirty minutes, because more often than not she fell asleep before the interval, lulled by the warmth.

I never knew if there was a limit to Sophie's courage; she was beautiful, she had a smile you'd risk damnation for, and, in all circumstances, an astonishing presence of mind. If with all that I can't be forgiven for blushing in her presence, the world is too unjust.

'Something incredible happened to me last week,' she said, running her hand through her long hair.

No need to mention that neither I nor my brother felt like interrupting her.

'What's wrong with you boys? Have you lost your tongues?'

'No, no, go on,' my brother replied with a beatific smile.

Perplexed, Sophie looked at as both in turn and then continued her tale.

'I was going to Carmaux, to carry three submachine guns which Emile was waiting for. Charles had hidden them in a suitcase, but it was quite heavy. There I am, taking my train at Toulouse station; I open the door of my compartment and happen upon eight gendarmes! I sneak off on tiptoe, praying that they haven't noticed me, but then one of them stands up and offers to squeeze up to make a little bit of room for me. Another even offers to help me with my case. What would you have done in my place?'

'Well, I'd have prayed that they'd shoot me there and then!' replies my little brother.

And he adds:

'Why wait? When the game's up the game's up, isn't it?'

'Well, since the game was up as you say, I just let things happen. They took the case and put it at my feet, under the seat. The train set off and we chatted until we got to Carmaux. But wait, that's not all!'

I think that at that moment, if Sophie had said to me: 'Jeannot, I'll gladly kiss you if you change that hair colour,' not only would I have done so, but I'd have had it dyed that very second. But anyway, the question's not asked, I'm still a redhead and Sophie continues her narrative with increased vigour.

'So the train arrives at Carmaux station and bang! There's a check. Through the window, I can see the Germans opening everyone's luggage on the platform; this time, I tell myself I'm really done for!'

'But you're here!' ventures Claude, in the absence of a sugar lump, he's dipping his finger in what's left of the coffee at the bottom of his cup.

149

'The gendarmes laugh when they see my face. They tap me on the shoulder and say they'll accompany me until we're past the check. And to my astonishment, their brigadier adds that he'd rather it was a girl like me who benefited from the hams and sausages I'd hidden in my suitcase, rather than a few Wehrmacht soldiers. It's a great story, isn't it?' Sophie concludes, bursting out laughing.

Actually, her story sends cold shivers down our backs, but our friend is laughing, so we're happy, happy to be simply here with her. As if in the end all of this were nothing but a children's game, a children's game in which she could have been shot ten times . . . for real.

Sophie had her seventeenth birthday this year. At the start, her father, who's a miner at Carmaux, wasn't very keen on her joining the brigade. When Jan took her into our ranks, he even gave him a real dressing down about it. But Sophie's father has been in the Resistance since the beginning, so it's hard for him to find a valid argument to forbid his daughter from doing the same thing he does. His row with Jan was for form's sake.

'Wait, the best is to come,' adds Sophie, even more cheerfully.

Claude and I listen to the rest of her tale with good grace.

'At the station, Emile is waiting for me at the end of the platform. He sees me coming towards him, surrounded by eight gendarmes, one of them carrying the suitcase containing the submachine guns. You should have seen Emile's face!

'How did he react?' asked Claude.

'I signalled wildly to him, called him "darling" from a distance, and literally threw myself at him, kissing him so that he didn't run away. The gendarmes handed him my suitcase and left, wishing us a good day. Even now, I think Emile's still trembling about it.'

'I may stop eating kosher if ham brings as much happiness as this,' observes my little brother.

'They were submachine guns, imbecile,' retorts Sophie, 'and besides, the gendarmes were just in a good mood, that's all.'

Claude wasn't thinking of the luck Sophie had had with the gendarmes, but about Emile's . . .

Our friend glanced at her watch and leapt to her feet, saying, 'I have to go,' then she kissed both of us and left. My brother and I remained sitting side by side, saying nothing, for a good hour. We parted in the early afternoon, and we each knew what the other was thinking.

I suggested postponing our tête-à-tête to tomorrow evening, so that we can talk a little.

'Tomorrow evening? I can't', Claude said.

I didn't ask him any questions, but I could tell from his silence that he was going out on an operation and as for him, he could see from my face that anxiety had begun to gnaw away at me as soon as he fell silent.

'I'll come to your place afterwards,' he adds. 'But not before ten o'clock.'

It was very generous on his part, because once his mission was accomplished, he would still have to pedal

151

for quite some time in order to find me. But Claude knew that if he didn't, I wouldn't get a wink of sleep all night.

'OK, see you tomorrow, bro'.'

'See you tomorrow.'

My little conversation with Mme Dublanc was still on my mind. If I told Jan about it, he would make me leave town. For me there was no question of being parted from my brother . . . nor from Sophie. On the other hand, if I didn't tell anyone and I was taken, I would have committed an unforgivable error. I straddled my bike and headed for the little railway station at Loubers. Charles always gave good advice.

He greeted me with his usual good humour and invited me to come and give him a hand in the garden. I had spent a few months working on the vegetable garden at the Manor before joining the Resistance, and I had acquired some knowledge when it came to hoeing and weeding. Charles appreciated my help. Very quickly, we engaged in conversation. I repeated what Mme Dublanc had said to me and Charles reassured me immediately.

According to him, if my landlady didn't want any problems, she wouldn't denounce me, for fear of being harassed in one way or another; and besides, her little phrase on the merit she accorded to 'students' let it be known that she wasn't so bad after all. Charles even added that we mustn't misjudge people too quickly. Many do nothing, simply because they are afraid; that didn't necessarily make them stool-pigeons. Mme Dublanc is like that. The

Occupation hasn't changed her life to the point where she would run the risk of losing it, that's all.

It takes a true awareness to understand that we're alive, he explained as he pulled up a clump of radishes.

Charles is right. The majority of men are content with a job, a roof over their heads, a few hours' rest on a Sunday and they consider themselves happy like that; happy to be alive, not happy to have a life! Their neighbours may suffer, but as long as the pain doesn't affect them, they choose to see nothing; to act as if the bad things didn't exist. It's not always cowardice. For some, living itself demands a lot of courage.

'Avoid bringing friends back to your house for a few days. You never know,' added Charles.

We carried on hoeing the earth in silence. He busied himself with the radishes, and I, the lettuces.

'It's not just your landlady who's bothering you, is it?' Charles asked, handing me a rake.

I waited a little before replying, and he began instead.

'Once, a woman came here. Robert asked me to give her shelter. She was ten years older than me, she was ill and was coming to rest. I said I wasn't a doctor, but I agreed. There's only one bedroom upstairs, so what was I supposed to do? We shared the bed: her on one side, me on the other, the pillow down the middle. She spent two weeks in my house, we laughed all the time, we told each other all kinds of things and I got used to having her around. One day, she got better, so she left. I didn't ask for anything, but I had to get used to living with silence again. At night, when the wind whistled around the house we heard it. Alone, it doesn't make the same music.'

'You've never seen her again?'

'She knocked at my door two weeks later and told me she wanted to stay with me.'

'And?'

'I told her it was better for us that she went back to her husband.'

'Why are you telling me this, Charles?'

'Which girl in the brigade have you fallen in love with?'

I didn't reply.

'Jeannot, I know how heavily loneliness weighs upon us, but that's the price you pay when you live in secrecy.'

And as I remained silent, Charles stopped weeding.

We went back towards the house. Charles handed me a bunch of radishes in thanks for my help.

'You know, Jeannot, that lady friend I told you about just now, she gave me an amazing bit of luck; she let me love her. It was only for a few days, but with the face I've got, that was a fine gift in itself. Now, all I have to do is think of her to find a moment of happiness. You should go back. Night falls early at this time of year.'

And Charles accompanied me back to the doorstep.

As I mounted my bike, I turned around and asked him if he thought I had a chance with Sophie anyway, if I should see her again one day, after the war, when we didn't live secretly any more. Charles looked saddened. I saw him hesitate and he answered me with a sad smile:

'If Sophie and Robert aren't together any more at the

end of the war, who knows? Have a good journey, old chap, and watch out for patrols on the way out of the village.'

That evening, as I dropped off to sleep, I thought back to my conversation with Charles. I went back to his reasoning. Sophie would be a wonderful friend and it would be better. In any case, I would have hated dyeing my hair.

We had decided to continue Boris's action against the Militia. From now on, the street-dogs in their black uniforms, those who spied on us in order to arrest us, who tortured, and sold human misery to the highest bidder, would be fought without mercy. Tonight, we would go to rue Alexandre, to blow up their lair.

In the meantime, lying on his bed with his hands behind his head, Claude looks at the ceiling of his room, thinking of what awaits him.

'Tonight, I won't come back,' he says.

Jacques enters. He sits down beside him, but Claude says nothing; with his finger, he is measuring the fuse that enters the bomb – only fifteen millimetres – and my little brother murmurs:

'Too bad, but I'm going anyway.'

Then Jacques smiles sadly. He didn't order this, it was Claude who suggested it.

'Are you sure?' he asks.

Claude is sure of nothing, but he can still hear my

father's question in the Café des Tourneurs . . . Why did I tell him about that? So he says, 'Yes.'

'Tonight, I won't come back,' murmurs my little brother, who is scarcely seventeen years old.

Fifteen millimetres of tinder is short; a minute and a half of life when he hears the fuse crackle; ninety seconds in which to flee.

'Tonight, I won't come back,' he repeats ceaselessly, 'but tonight, the militiamen won't be going home either. So lots of people we don't know will have gained a few months of life, a few months of hope, the time it takes for other dogs to come along and repopulate the lairs of hatred.'

One minute and a half for us and a few months for them, it's worth the trouble, isn't it?

Boris had begun our war against the Militia on the very same day when Marcel Langer had been sentenced to death. So if for nothing else but the man who was rotting in a cell at Saint-Michel prison, it must go ahead. It was also to save him that we had brought down Deputy Prosecutor Lespinasse. Our tactics had worked: at Boris's trial, the judges had declined to give a verdict one after the other, the lawyers were so afraid that they had made do with twenty years in prison. Tonight, Claude is thinking about Boris, and about Ernest too. It is he who will give him courage. Ernest was sixteen when he died, do you realise? It seems that when the militiamen arrested him, he started pissing himself in the middle of the street; the scum gave him permission to undo his fly, long enough

156

to relieve his fear, there in front of them, to humiliate him; in reality, long enough to take the pin out of the grenade he was hiding in his trousers and take that filth to hell. And Claude again sees the grey eyes of a kid who died in the middle of the street; a kid who was only sixteen years old.

It's November the 5th today; almost a month has passed since we killed Lespinasse. 'I won't come back,' says my little brother, 'but it doesn't matter; others will live in my place.'

Night has fallen, and it is raining continuously. 'It's time,' whispers Jacques, and Claude raises his head and unfolds his arms. Count the minutes, little brother, memorise each moment and let courage engulf you; let this strength fill your belly, which is so empty of everything. You will never forget Mother's eyes, her tenderness when she came to say good night to you, just a few months ago. See how long time has taken to pass since then; so, even if you don't come back tonight, you still have a little left to live. Fill your chest with the scent of the rain, let your body carry out the movements you have rehearsed so many times. I would like to be at your side, but I'm elsewhere, and you are there, Jacques is with you.

Claude grips his package under his arm. A few pieces of bravura, whose tinder fuses stick out. He tries to forget the moisture on his skin, like the mist on the darkness. He is not alone; even if I'm elsewhere, I'm here.

On Place Saint-Paul he feels his heart beating in his

157

temples and tries to match its rhythm to that of his steps, which are leading him to courage. He continues walking. If luck smiles upon him, he will soon flee along rue des Créneaux. But he mustn't think now about the way out . . . only if luck smiles on him.

My little brother enters rue Alexandre; courage is with him. The militiaman who is guarding the lair tells himself that if they're walking so determinedly, Jacques and you must be part of his mob. The large carriage entrance door closes behind you. You strike the match, the incandescent ends crackle, and the tick-tock of prowling death clicks in your heads. At the far end of the courtyard, a bicycle is propped up against a window; a bicycle with a basket to take the first of the bombs Charles has made. A door. You set off along the corridor, the tick-tock continues, how many seconds are left? Two steps for each of them, thirty paces in all, don't calculate, little brother, keep to your track, salvation is behind you, but you have to go further on.

In the corridor, two militiamen are talking without paying him any attention. Claude enters the room, puts down his package beside a radiator, pretends to rummage in his pocket, as if he's forgotten something. He shrugs his shoulders, how can someone be so scatterbrained? The militiaman flattens himself against the wall to allow him to go out again.

Tick-tock, must keep walking to a regular rhythm,

don't show any sign of the moistness hidden under your clothes. Tick-tock, here he is in the courtyard. Jacques shows him the bike and Claude sees the incandescent fuse disappear under the newspaper. Tick-tock, how much more time left? Jacques guesses the question and his lips whisper, 'Thirty seconds, maybe less?' Tick-tock, the guards on duty let you pass; they've been told to watch those who come in, not those who are leaving.

Here's the street and Claude shivers when his sweat mingles with the cold. He isn't yet smiling at his boldness, as he was the other day after the locomotives. If his calculations are right, they should get past the police supplies office before the explosion blasts a hole into the night. At that moment, it will be as bright as day for the children of freedom and he will be visible to the enemy.

'Now!' says Jacques, gripping his arms. Jacques' embrace tightens like a vice at the moment of the first explosion. The bombs' burning breath scorches the walls of the houses, the windows blow out in shards, a woman cries out her fear, and the police officers whistle theirs, running in all directions. At the crossroads, Jacques and Claude separate; head pulled down into the collar of his jacket, my brother once more becomes someone going home from the factory, one among the thousands coming back from work.

Jacques is already far away, on Boulevard Carnot. His silhouette has melted into invisibility; and Claude, without understanding why, imagines him dead, and fear

159

overtakes him again. He thinks of the day when one of the two will say, 'Tonight, I had a friend,' and he hates himself for thinking that he would be the survivor.

Join me at Mme Dublanc's house, little brother. Jacques will be at the terminus of the number twelve tram tomorrow and when you see him, you'll finally be re-assured. Tonight, huddled under your bedclothes, your head buried in your pillow, your memory will offer you the gift of Mother's perfume, a little bit of childhood that it still keeps, deep inside you. Sleep, my little brother. Jacques is home from work. And neither you nor I know that one night in August 1944, in a train that will deport us to Germany, we shall see him stretched out with a bullet in his back.

I invited my landlady to the opera, not to thank her for her relative benevolence, not even in order to have an alibi, but because, according to Charles's advice, it was preferable for her not to encounter my brother when he arrived at my place on his way back from the mission. God knows what state he would be in.

The curtain rose and in the darkness, seated in the balcony of the large theatre I thought constantly of him. I had hidden the key under the doormat; he knew where to find it. However, although anxiety was gnawing away at me, and I followed nothing of the show, it felt strangely good to me simply to be somewhere.

It may not seem like anything, but when you're a fugitive, being safe is a form of healing. Knowing that for

160

two hours I wouldn't have to hide or run away, plunged me into unexpected bliss. Of course, I sensed that once the interval was over, the fear of the return would nibble away at this patch of freedom I'd been granted; the show had been playing for barely an hour, and all it took was a silence to bring me back to this reality, to the loneliness that was mine in the middle of this audience borne away into the wondrous world of the stage. What I could not imagine was that the sudden entrance of a handful of German gendarmes and militiamen would suddenly tip my landlady over to the side of the Resistance. The door had opened with a din and the barking of the Feldgendarmes had put an end to the opera. And opera, for Madame Dublanc, was something sacred. Three years of harrying, deprivation of freedom, summary assassinations, and all the cruelty and violence of the Occupation had not succeeded in provoking my landlady's indignation. But interrupting the premiere of *Pelleas and Melisande*: that was too much! So Mme Dublanc whispered, 'What savages!'

Thinking back to my conversation the previous day with Charles, I realised that evening that the moment when a person becomes really aware of his or her own life would forever remain a mystery to me.

From the balcony, we watched the bulldogs evacuating the hall with a haste that was exceeded only by their violence. It is true that they had the look of bulldogs, those barking soldiers with their silver badges that hung on a heavy chain around their necks. And the black-clad militiamen who accompanied them resembled those miserable dogs belonging to people you meet on the streets of abandoned towns, the saliva trickling down their chops, a menacing look in their eyes and eager to bite, more through hatred than hunger. If Debussy had been swept aside and the militiamen were furious, it meant that Claude had succeeded in his mission.

'Let's go,' said old Mme Dublanc, draped in her scarlet coat, which lent her dignity.

To get up, I still had to calm my heart down, which was beating furiously in my chest, so hard that it took away my legs from under me. And what if Claude had been caught? If he were shut up in a damp cellar, facing his torturers?

'Are we going or not?' repeated Mme Dublanc. 'We're certainly not going to wait for these animals to dislodge us.'

'So, at last?' I said, a smile at the corner of my lips.

'At last what?' my landlady asked, more angrily than ever.

'Are you going to start "studying" too?' I replied, finally managing to get to my feet.

17

The queue stretches out in front of the food store. Everyone waits, ration tickets in their pockets: violet for margarine, red for sugar, brown for meat – but since the start of the year meat has deserted the shelves, you only find it there once a week – green for tea or coffee, and for a long time now coffee has been replaced by chicory or grilled barley. A three-hour wait before you get to the counter, in order to obtain just enough to live, but people no longer count the time passing, they watch the carriage entrance opposite the grocer's shop. One regular isn't in the queue. 'Such a good lady,' some say. 'A courageous woman,' lament others. On this pale morning, two black cars are parked outside the building where the Lormond family lives.

'They took her husband away earlier, I was already here,' whispers a housewife.

'They're keeping Mme Lormond upstairs. They want to catch the little one, she wasn't in when they arrived,' explains the building's concierge, who is also in the queue.

The little one they are talking about is called Gisèle. Gisèle isn't her real first name and her real surname isn't Lormond. Here in the district, everyone knows they're Jews, but the only important thing was that the police and the Gestapo didn't. Now they've finally found out.

'It's terrible what they do to the Jews,' says one lady, weeping.

'Mme Lormond was so kind,' replies another, lending her her handkerchief.

Upstairs in the building, there are two militiamen, and the same number of Gestapo accompanying them. In all, four men with black shirts, uniforms, revolvers and more force than a hundred others, motionless in the queue that stretches out in front of the grocer's shop. But people are terrified, they barely dare speak, so actually doing anything . . .

It was Mme Pilguez, the fifth-floor tenant, who saved the little girl. She was at her window when she saw the cars arrive at the end of the street. She rushed up to warn the Lormonds of their impending arrest. Gisèle's mother begged her to take her child and hide her. The little one is only ten years old! Mme Pilguez said yes straight away.

Gisèle didn't have time to kiss her mother, or her father for that matter. Mme Pilguez had already taken her hand and was leading her away. 'I've seen a lot of Jews leave,

164

and not a single one has returned up to now!' says an old gentleman as the queue moves forward a little.

'Do you think there will be sardines today?' asks a woman.

'I haven't a clue; on Monday there were still a few tins left,' replied the old gentleman.

'They still haven't found the little one, and so much the better!' sighs a lady behind them.

'Yes, that is preferable,' replies the old gentleman with dignity.

'Apparently they send them to camps and kill a lot of them there; a Polish worker colleague told my husband at the factory.'

'I don't know anything at all, but you'd do better not to talk about such things, and your husband too.'

'We're going to miss Monsieur Lormond,' sighs the lady again. 'Whenever there was a witty remark in the crowd, he was always the one who made it.'

In the early hours of the morning, neck enveloped in his red scarf, he had come to queue outside the grocer's shop. It was he who comforted them during the long wait on frozen early mornings. He offered nothing more than human warmth, but during this winter, that was what was missing the most. There, it's over, now Monsieur Lormond won't ever say anything again. His humorous words, which always provoked a laugh, a feeling of relief, his funny or affectionate little phrases, which turned the humiliation of rationing into derision, had gone in a Gestapo car, two hours ago already.

The crowd falls silent, barely uttering a murmur. The procession has just emerged from the building. Mme Lormond's hair is dishevelled; the militiamen are on either side of her. She walks, head high; she's not afraid. Her husband has been stolen from her, her daughter has been taken away, but they won't take either her dignity as a mother or her dignity as a woman. Everyone is looking at her, so she smiles; the people in the queue don't matter, it's just her way of saying goodbye to them.

The men from the Militia push her towards the car. Suddenly, behind her, she senses the presence of her child. Little Gisèle is up there, her face pressed to the fifth-floor window; Mme Lormond can feel it, she knows. She would like to turn around, to give her daughter one last smile, a gesture of affection that would tell her how much she loves her; a glance, just for a fraction of a second, but long enough for her to know that neither the war, nor the madness of men will dispossess her of her mother's love.

But no; if she turned around she would attract attention to her child. A friendly hand has saved her little girl, she cannot take the risk of putting her in danger. Her heart in a vice, she shuts her eyes and walks towards the car, without turning around.

On the fifth floor of an apartment building in Toulouse, a little ten-year-old girl watches her mother who is going away for ever. She knows very well that she won't come back, her father told her; the Jews who are taken away never come back, that's why she must never make a mistake when she gave her new name.

Mme Pilguez has laid a hand on her shoulder, and with the other she holds the net curtain over the window, so that they can't be seen from below. And yet Gisèle sees her mummy getting into the black car. She would like to tell her that she loves her and that she always will, that of all mummies she was the best in the world, that she will never have any other. Talking is forbidden, so she thinks with all her strength that so much love must inevitably be able to pass through a window. She tells herself that, in the street, her mummy can hear the words she is whispering through her lips, even if she holds them so tightly closed.

Mme Pilguez placed her cheek on her head, and a kiss too. She feels Mme Pilguez's tears trickling down the back of her neck. But she won't cry. She just wants to watch until the end, and she swears to herself that she will never forget this December morning in 1943, the morning when her mummy left for ever.

The car door has just closed and the cortège sets off. The little girl stretches out her arms, in a final gesture of love.

Mme Pilguez has knelt down to be closer to her.

'My little Gisèle, I'm so sorry.'

Mme Pilguez weeps her heart out. The little girl looks at her; she wears a fragile smile. She wipes Mme Pilguez's cheeks and tells her:

'My name is Sarah.'

*   *   *

In his dining room, the fourth-floor tenant leaves his window in a foul mood. On the way, he stops and blows on the frame he has placed on the chest of drawers. Some dust had unfortunately gathered on the photo of Marshal Pétain. From now on, the neighbours from downstairs won't make any more noise; he won't have to listen to piano scales any more. And, while he's at it, he thinks he'd also better continue his surveillance and find out who's managed to hide the dirty little Yid.

18

I'd soon have been in the brigade for eight months and we were in action almost every day. In the course of the previous week alone, I'd carried out four operations. I'd lost ten kilos since the start of the year, and my spirits were suffering just as much as my body from hunger and exhaustion. At the end of the day, I went around to find my little brother at his lodgings and, without prior notice, I took him to share a real meal at a restaurant in town. Claude's eyes were out on stalks as he read the menu. Meat casserole, vegetables and apple tart; the prices charged at the Reine Pédauque were out of reach and I sacrificed all the money I had left for it, but I had got it into my head that I was going to die before the end of the year and it was already the start of December!

On entering the establishment, which was only accessible to the wallets of militiamen and Germans, Claude thought I'd brought him there for some kind of action. When he realised that we were there to feed our faces, I saw the expressions of his childhood come to life again on his face. I saw the rebirth of the smile he wore when Mother was playing hide and seek in the apartment where we lived, the joy in his eyes when she walked past the wardrobe, pretending not to have seen that he was inside.

'What are we celebrating?' he whispered.

'Whatever you like! The winter, us, being alive, I don't know.'

'And how are you planning to pay the bill?'

'Don't worry about that. Just enjoy the food.'

Claude's eyes devoured the pieces of crusty bread in the basket, with the appetite of a pirate who'd found gold pieces in a chest. At the end of the meal, my spirits restored after seeing my brother so happy, I asked for the bill while he went to the lavatory.

I saw him return with a mocking look. He didn't want to sit down again; we must leave immediately, he told me. I hadn't emptied my coffee cup, but my brother insisted that we hurry. I must have sensed a danger of which I was as yet unaware. I paid, put on my coat and we both left. In the street, he clung to my arm and dragged me forward, forcing me to speed up.

'Hurry up, I tell you!'

I threw a brief glance over my shoulder, assuming that someone was following us, but the street was deserted and I could see quite well that my brother was having difficulty battling an attack of the giggles.

'What on earth is going on? You're starting to frighten me!'

'Come on!' he insisted. 'Over there, in that little alleyway, I'll explain.'

He led me to the end of a blind alley and, making the most of the moment, he unbuttoned his overcoat. In the cloakroom of the Reine Pédauque, he'd pinched a German officer's uniform belt and the Mauser pistol suspended in its holster.

The two of us walked through the town, closer than ever. The evening was fine, the food had given us back some strength and almost as much hope. As we parted, I suggested we see each other again the next day.

'I can't, I'm off on an operation,' Claude whispered. 'Oh, and to hell with the regulations, you're my brother. If I can't tell you what I'm doing, what's the point of it all?'

I said nothing. I didn't want to force him to speak, nor to prevent him confiding in me.

'Tomorrow, I have to go and pinch the takings from the post office. Jan must think I'm really made for thievery of all kinds! If you knew how much that annoys me!'

I understood his turmoil, but we were cruelly short of money. Those among us who were 'students' had to feed ourselves somehow if they wanted us to continue the fight.

'Is it very risky?'

'Not at all! That's possibly the most annoying aspect of all!' complained Claude.

And he explained the plan for his mission.

Each morning, an official arrived alone at the post office on rue Balzac. She was transporting a satchel containing sufficient cash to keep us going for a few months more. Claude was to knock her out and take the bag. Emile would be supplying cover.

'I've refused to use violence!' said Claude, almost angry.

'And what are you planning to do?'

'I will never strike a woman! I'll frighten her, at worst push her around a bit; then I grab her bag and that's that.'

I didn't know quite what to say. Jan ought to have understood that Claude would never hit a woman. But I was afraid that things might not go as Claude hoped.

'I'm to take the money to Albi. I won't be back for two days.'

I took him in my arms, and before leaving I made him promise to be careful. We waved a last goodbye to each other. I too had a mission to carry out two days later, and I was to go to Charles's place to fetch ammunition.

As planned, at seven o'clock in the morning Claude was crouching behind a bush in the little garden bordering the post office. As planned, at ten past eight, he heard the van drop off the official and the gravel on the path crunch under her footsteps. As planned, Claude leapt to his feet, clenching his fist menacingly. As was not at all planned, the official weighed a hundred kilos, and she was wearing spectacles!

The rest happened very quickly. Claude attempted to unbalance her by charging at her; if he had charged at a wall, the effect would have been the same! He found himself on the ground, slightly stunned. He had no other solution but to return to Jan's plan and knock out the official. But as he looked at her spectacles, Claude thought of my terrible short-sightedness; the idea of knocking slivers of glass into his victim's eyes made him give up once and for all.

'Stop, thief!' roars the official. Claude summons up all his strength and tries to seize the satchel, which she's clutching to her gigantic chest. Is it the fault of fleeting emotion? A matter of unequal strength? The hand-to-hand combat is engaged and Claude finds himself on the ground again with a hundred kilos of femininity on his thorax. He fights as best he can, frees himself, seizes hold of the satchel, and, watched in dismay by Emile, mounts his bike. He flees without anyone following him. Emile makes sure that this is so and heads off in the opposite direction. A few passers-by gather, the post-woman is hauled to her feet, and is calmed.

A policeman on a motorbike comes out of a side road and understands the situation straightaway; he spots Claude in the distance, accelerates and gives chase. A few seconds later, my little brother feels the sudden bite of a truncheon, which throws him to the ground. The policeman gets off his machine and rushes at him. He's kicked with unexpected violence. Revolver to his temple, Claude is already handcuffed. He doesn't care though; he's out cold.

*　　　*　　　*

When he regains consciousness, he's attached to a chair, with his hands tied behind him. He doesn't remain awake for long; the first beating from the commissaire who's interrogating him sends him sprawling. His head hits the ground and everything goes dark again. How much time has elapsed between then and when he opens his eyes again? His sight is clouded with red. His swollen eyelids are stuck together with blood, and his mouth is cracked and misshapen under the blows. Claude says nothing, not a groan, not even a murmur. Only a few episodes of fainting save him from the brutality, and as soon as he raises his head again, the inspectors' batons begin again.

'You're a little Jew-boy, aren't you?' demands Commissaire Fourna. 'And the dough, who was that for?'

Claude makes up a story, a story in which there are no children fighting for freedom, a story without friends, without anyone to finger. This story doesn't stand up; Fourna roars:

'Where's your room?'

He must hold out for two days before answering this question. That's the regulation, the time necessary for the others to go and do the 'cleaning'. Fourna hits him again. The light bulb hanging from the ceiling sways and leads my little brother into its waltz. He vomits and his head falls again.

'What day is it today?' asks Claude

'You've been here two days,' replies the warder.

174

'They've done a real job on you, if you could see your face.'

Claude moves a hand to his face, but scarcely has he brushed it when pain overwhelms him. The warder mutters, 'I don't like this.' He leaves him his mess tin and closes the door on him.

So, two days have passed. Claude can finally let slip his address.

Emile had checked that he'd seen Claude escaping. Everyone thought he must have delayed in Albi. After a second night of waiting, it's too late to go and clean his room. Fourna and his men have already cordoned it off.

The thirsty policemen smell the odour of the Resistance. But in the miserable room there's not much to find, almost nothing to destroy. The mattress is torn open: nothing! The pillow is torn open: again, nothing! The drawer in the dressing table is broken: still nothing! There's nothing left but the stove in the corner of the room. Fourna pushes open the metal grille.

'Come and see what I've found!' he roars, mad with joy.

He's holding a grenade. It was hidden under old ashes.

He bends forward, almost sticks his head inside; one after the other, he removes the pieces of a letter my brother had written to me. I never received it. As a security measure, he'd chosen to tear it up. All he'd lacked was the wherewithal to buy a little coal to burn it.

*　　*　　*

When I left Charles, he was in a good mood as always. At that time, I don't yet know that my little brother has been arrested; I hope he's hiding in Albi. Charles and I had a chat in the vegetable garden, but we went back inside because of the icy cold. Before I left, he handed me the weapons for the mission I must carry out tomorrow.

I have two grenades in my pockets, a revolver in my trouser belt. Not easy to pedal down the Loubers road with all that paraphernalia.

Night has fallen, and my street is deserted. I put my bike in the corridor and look for my room key. I'm exhausted after the journey I've just made. There it is, I can feel the key at the bottom of my pocket. In ten minutes I'll be under the covers. The light in the corridor goes out. It's not serious, I can locate the lock in the dark.

A sound behind me. I don't have time to turn around; I'm flattened to the ground. In a few seconds my arms are twisted, my hands cuffed and my face covered in blood. Six police officers were waiting for me inside my room. There was the same number in the garden, not counting the ones who cordoned off the street. I can hear Mme Dublanc howling. The car tyres crunch. The police are everywhere.

It's really idiotic. On the letter my little brother wrote to me, he put my address. He must just have lacked a few bits of coal to burn it with. Life hangs on as little as that.

In the small hours, Jacques doesn't see me at the rendez-vous point for the mission. Something must have happened to me on the way, a checkpoint that went wrong. He gets on his bike and hurries to my place to 'clean' my room, that's the rule.

The two policemen who were hiding there arrested him.

I underwent the same treatment as my brother. Commissaire Fourna had the reputation for being ferocious, and it wasn't an exaggeration. Eighteen days of interrogations, punches, beatings; eighteen nights that were a succession of cigarette burns and sessions of varying tortures. When he's in a good humour, Commissaire Fourna forces me to get on my knees, arms stretched out, with a telephone book in either hand. As soon as I flinch, his foot flies at me, sometimes between my shoulder blades, sometimes in the belly, sometimes in my face. When he's in a bad mood, he aims for between the legs. I haven't talked. There are two of us in the cells at the police station on rue du Rempart-Saint-Etienne. Sometimes, at night, I can hear Jacques moaning. He hasn't said anything either.

December 23, twenty days now, and we still haven't talked. Mad with rage, Commissaire Fourna finally signs our committal orders. At the end of one final day of regulation beatings, Jacques and I are transferred.

*　　　*　　　*

177

In the van taking us to Saint-Michel prison, I don't yet know that in a few days, martial courts will be put in place. I don't know that the judgments pronounced will be executed in the courtyard immediately, since that is the fate promised to all Resistance members who are arrested.

The English sky is a long way away, beneath my bruised skull I no longer hear the purring of my Spitfire's engine.

In the van that is taking us towards the end of the journey, I think back to my childhood dreams. That was scarcely eight months ago.

And on 23 December, in 1943, the warder of Saint-Michel prison closed the door of our cell behind me again. Difficult to see anything in this half-light. The light barely filtered beneath our puffy eyelids. They were so swollen that we could barely open them a fraction.

But in the shadow of my cell in Saint-Michel prison, I still remember, I recognised a fragile voice, a voice that was familiar to me.

'Merry Christmas.'
  'Merry Christmas, little brother.'

PART TWO

19

It's impossible to become accustomed to prison bars, impossible not to jump at the sound of the cell doors closing, impossible to endure the screws' rounds. All of this is impossible, when you are in love with freedom. How can we find a meaning to our presence within these walls? We were arrested by French policemen, we will soon appear before a court martial, and those who will shoot us in the courtyard, just afterwards, will be French too. If there is a meaning to all of this, then I cannot find it from the bottom of my cell.

Those who have been here for several weeks tell me that you get used to it, that a new way of life organises itself as time goes by. But I think of the time lost, I count it. I shall never know my twentieth birthday; my eighteenth has gone, without my ever experiencing it. Of course, there's the evening mess tin, says Claude. The food is vile, a kind of cabbage soup, sometimes a few beans already eaten away by weevils, not enough to give us back an ounce of strength; we are dying of hunger. There aren't just a few companions of the MOI (*Main-d'oeuvre immigrée*) or FTP (*Francs-tireurs et partisans*) sharing this cell. We also have to cohabit with the fleas, the bugs and the scabies, all of which gnaw away at us.

At night, Claude stays close to me. The prison walls are shiny with ice. In this cold, we huddle against each other to gain a little warmth.

Jacques is already not the same person. As soon as he wakes he starts pacing silently. He too is counting the lost hours, forever done for. Perhaps he's also thinking of a woman, outside. Missing someone is an abyss; sometimes, at night, his hand lifts and attempts to hold the impossible, the caress that no longer exists, the memory of a skin whose touch has gone, a look where intimacy lived in peace.

Occasionally a benevolent warder slips us a clandestine leaflet printed by our friends the *francs-tireurs partisans*. Jacques reads it to us. This is compensation for the feeling of frustration that never leaves him. His powerlessness to act eats away at him a little more each day. I assume that the absence of Osna does, too.

It is in watching him, walled-in by his despair, here in this very place, at the middle of this sordid universe, that I have, however, seen one of the most unexpected kinds of beauty in our world: a man can resolve himself to the idea of losing his life, but not to the absence of those he loves.

Jacques is silent for a moment, then he carries on reading and gives us news of our friends. When we learn that a pair of aeroplane wings has been sabotaged, that a pylon lies on its side, torn up by a friend's bomb, that a militiaman has been killed in the street, when ten wagons have been put out of service, wagons used to deport innocent people, we are sharing a little of their victory.

Here, we are at the bottom of the world, in an obscure, cramped place; a territory where the only ruler is sickness. But in the middle of this vile lair, at the very darkest part of the abyss, a minuscule particle of light still dwells, like a whisper. The Spaniards who occupy the neighbouring cells sometimes call to it at night as they sing; they have baptised it Esperanza.

20

New Year's Day, there had been no celebration, for we had nothing to celebrate. It's here, in the middle of nowhere, that I met Chahine. January was advancing and already a few of us had been brought before their judges and, while the semblance of a trial was in progress, a van came and placed their coffins in the courtyard. Then there was the sound of rifles, the din of the prisoners, and silence fell again on their death and ours to come.

I never knew Chahine's real first name; he no longer had the strength to speak it. I gave him this nickname because the fevered deliriums which troubled his nights sometimes made him talk. He then called out to a white bird that would come and free him. In Arabic, Chahine is the name given to the peregrine falcon with a pale plumage. I searched for it after the war, in memory of these moments.

Locked up for months, Chahine was dying a little more each day. His body suffered from malnutrition and his stomach had become so small that it could not even tolerate the soup any more.

One morning, as I was delousing myself, his eyes met mine; his gaze called to me silently. I came towards him, and it took him all his strength to smile at me; barely, but it was a smile all the same. His gaze turned towards his legs. Scabies was ravaging them. I understood his torment. Death would soon carry him away from here, but Chahine wanted to join it with dignity, as clean as was still possible. I moved my mattress towards his, and when night came again, I removed his fleas, and the lice that were lodged in the folds of his shirt.

From time to time, Chahine gave me one of his fragile smiles, which demanded so much effort, but which said thank you in his own way. It was I who really wanted to thank him.

When the evening mess-tin was distributed, he signalled to me to give his to Claude.

'What's the use of feeding this body, since it's already dead,' he whispered. 'Save your brother, he is young, he still has life to live.'

Chahine waited until the day faded away to exchange a few words. Probably he needed the silences of night to surround him in order to regain a little strength. Together in these silences, we shared a little humanity.

Father Joseph, the prison chaplain, sacrificed his ration tickets to come to his aid. Each week, he brought him a little packet of biscuits. To feed Chahine, I crushed them into crumbs and forced him to eat. It took him more than an hour to nibble one biscuit, sometimes twice that. Worn out, he begged me to give the remainder to our friends, so that Father Joseph's sacrifice should have some purpose.

You see, it's the story of a priest who deprives himself of food to save an Arab, of an Arab who saves a Jew by giving him reason to believe again, of a Jew who holds the Arab in his arms as he is dying, while awaiting his own turn; you see, it's the story of the world of men with its moments of unsuspected marvels.

The night of January 20th was icy; the cold went bone-deep. Chahine was shivering, and I held him tightly to me; the trembling exhausted him. That night, he refused the food I brought to his lips.

'Help me, I just want to find my freedom again,' he said to me suddenly.

I asked him how I could give what I didn't have. Chahine smiled and replied:

'By imagining it.'

Those were his last words. I kept my promise and washed his body until dawn; then I wrapped him in his clothes, just before sunrise. Those among us who had faith prayed for him; and the words of their prayers mattered because they came from the heart. I had never believed in God, but for an instant I prayed too, that Chahine's wish could be granted, and he could be free somewhere else.

21

Last days of January, the pace of executions in the court-yard lessens, allowing some of us to hope that the country will be liberated before their turn comes. When the warders take them away, they hope that their sentencing will be put back, so that they can be allowed a little more time, but that never happens and they are shot.

We may be cloistered inside these dark walls, power-less to act, but we learn that outside, our friends' activities are increasing. The Resistance is spinning its web and deploying it. The brigade now had organised detachments throughout the region; moreover the battle for freedom is taking shape all over France. Charles said one day that we had invented the war in the streets; it was an exaggeration, we weren't the only ones, but in the region we had shown the example. The others followed us and each day the enemy's task was being thwarted, paralysed by the number of our operations. Not a single German convoy moved around without the risk that a wagon or a load might be sabotaged; not a single French factory produced items for the enemy army without the transformers that supplied them with electricity being blown up, without its installations being destroyed. And the more the friends did, the more the population regained its courage, and the ranks of the Resistance grew.

During the exercise period, the Spanish told us that the brigade had a big success yesterday. Jacques is trying to find out more from a Spanish political detainee. He's called Boldados, and the screws are a little afraid of him. He's a Castilian who, like all his people, feels great pride for his land. He defended that land in the battles of the Spanish civil war; he loved it throughout his exodus, crossing the Pyrenees on foot. And in the camps of the West where he was locked up, he has never stopped singing its praises. Boldados signals to Jacques to approach the wire fencing that separates the Spaniards' exercise yard from the French one. When Jacques is close to him, he tells him what he heard from the mouth of a warder who's a sympathiser.

'It was one of your people who carried out the operation. Last week, he got on the last tram a bit late, not even realising that it was reserved for Germans. Your friend must have had his mind on something else, to have done something like that. An officer made him get off immediately with a kick in the backside. Your friend didn't like that at all. I can understand that; a kick in the backside is humiliating and it's not good. So he carried out a sort of investigation and quickly realised that every evening, this tram brought back the officers who'd just come out of the Variétés cinema. A little as if the last service was reserved for those *hijos de putas*. With three of your guys, they came back a few days later, in other words last night, to the same place where your mate got his arse booted, and they waited.'

Jacques didn't say anything; he drank in Boldados's words. Closing his eyes, it was as if he were taking part in the action, as if he could hear Emile's voice, imagine the wicked smile on his lips when he smells a real success. Told this way, the story may seem simple. A few grenades hurriedly thrown on a tram, Nazi officers who'll no longer be officiating and street kids with the faces of heroes. But that's not the whole picture; the story shouldn't be told that way.

They're hiding, barely concealed in the shadow of a few murky porches, fear in their bellies, their bodies shivering because the night is icy cold, so cold that the frosty surface of the deserted street gleams in the moonlight. The drops of some old rain running out of a broken gutter fall in the silence. Not a soul in sight. Clouds of steam form in front of their mouths the moment they breathe out. From time to time, they have to rub their hands, to keep their fingers mobile. But what can they

189

do to fight the trembling when fear is mixed with the cold? All it takes is one detail to betray them, and it will all end here. Emile remembers his friend Ernest, stretched out on his back, his chest cut open and reddened with the blood that flows from his throat, his mouth, his legs the wrong way around, his arms dangling limply and his neck hanging down. God, but a body is flexible when it's just been shot dead.

No, believe me; nothing in this story happens as you'd imagine it. When fear inhabits all your days, all your nights, it takes a lot of guts to go on living, to go on fighting, to believe that spring will come again. To die for the freedom of others is difficult when you're only sixteen years old.

In the distance, the din of the tram betrays its approach. Its headlight draws a line in the darkness. André is taking part in the operation, alongside Emile and François. It is because they are together that they can act. If one was without the others, everything would be different. Their hands slide into their coat pockets; they've removed the pins from the grenades, keeping a tight grip on the safety catches. One moment of clumsiness and everything would end here. The police would pick up the pieces of Emile, scattered across the roadway. Death is disgusting, that's not a secret to anybody.

The tram gets nearer; the silhouettes of the soldiers are reflected in the windows, lit up by the vehicle's lights.

They must keep resisting, remain patient, control the heartbeats that make the blood rise to the temples. 'Now,' whispers Emile. The pins slip to the ground. The grenades shatter the window-panes, and roll onto the floor of the tram.

The Nazis have lost all their arrogance; they're attempting to flee from the hell. Emile signals to François on the other side of the street. The submachine guns are armed and fire; the grenades explode.

The words Boldados utters are so precise that Jacques feels he's almost touching the carnage. He says nothing; his silence mingles with the silence that returned last night to the desolate street. And in that silence, he hears the moans of pain.

Boldados looks at him. Jacques thanks him with a nod; the two men part, each one returning to his own yard.

'One day spring will come again,' he whispers as he rejoins us.

22

January has faded away. Sometimes, in my cell, I think of Chahine. Claude has lost a lot of his strength. From time to time, a friend brings back a sulphur lozenge from the infirmary. He doesn't use it to calm the burning in his throat, but to strike a match. Then the friends gather around a cigarette given by a warder; we smoke it together. But today, our hearts aren't in it.

François and André went to give a hand to the Maquis, who have just set themselves up in Lot-et-Garonne. On their return from the mission, a detachment of gendarmes was waiting to nab them. Twenty-five cops against two street urchins: the fight was an unequal one. They proclaimed that they belonged to the Resistance; because since the rumours of a probable German defeat have been circulating, the forces of order are sometimes less assured; some are already thinking about the future and asking themselves questions. But those who were waiting for our friends haven't yet changed their minds, nor changed sides; and they took them away roughly.

Entering the police station, André wasn't afraid. He removed the pin from his grenade and threw it on the ground. Without even attempting to run away, while everyone else was running for cover, he remained alone, standing, motionless, watching it roll along the floor. It ended up lodged between two floorboards, but it didn't explode. The gendarmes charged at him and punished his taste for bravery.

He was incarcerated that morning, with his face covered with blood and his body swollen. He's in the infirmary. They broke his ribs and his jaw, and split open his forehead: nothing out of the ordinary.

The head of the screws at Saint-Michel prison is called Touchin. He's the one who unlocks our cells for the afternoon exercise period. Around five o'clock, he jangles his bunch of keys and begins the cacophony of locks rattling open. We have to wait for his signal before we can come out. But when chief warder Touchin's whistle sounds, we all count a few seconds before we cross the thresholds of our cells, just to get on his nerves. All together, the doors open onto the footbridge where the prisoners line up against the wall. The chief warder, escorted by two colleagues, stands very upright in his uniform. When he deems that everything is in order, truncheon in hand, he walks back up the line of prisoners.

*   *   *

We all have to acknowledge him in our own way; a movement of the head, the raising of an eyebrow, a sigh, it doesn't matter, the chief warder wants his authority to be recognised. When the review is over, the line moves forward in close formation.

After we return from our walk, our Spanish friends undergo the same ceremonial. There are fifty-seven of them occupying the part of the area that is set aside for them.

Everyone walks past Touchin and greets him once again. But our Spanish friends also have to undress on the footbridge and leave their clothes on the guardrail. They all have to go back into the dormitory cell as naked as the day they were born. Touchin says it is for security reasons that the regulations force prisoners to undress for the night. Underpants have to come off, too. 'One seldom sees a naked man attempting to escape with his bollocks on display,' says Touchin by way of justification. 'One thing's for sure: he'd swiftly be spotted in town.'

Here, we are well aware that this isn't the reason for this cruel regulation; the people who instituted it are gauging the humiliation they force prisoners to undergo.

Touchin also knows all this, but he doesn't care; the highpoint of his day is still to come, when the Spaniards walk past him and acknowledge him; that's fifty-seven acknowledgements, since there are fifty-seven of them; fifty-seven frissons of pleasure for Touchin the chief screw.

So the Spaniards walk past him and acknowledge him, since the regulations oblige them to do so. With them, Touchin is always a little disappointed. There's something about those lads that he will never subdue.

The line moves forward; it's friend Rubio who's leading it. Normally Boldados should be at the front, but as I've told you, Boldados is Castilian and with his proud nature, he might well drive his fist into a screw's face, or even throw the screw over the balustrade while calling him a *hijo de puta*; so it's Rubio who leads the way. It's safer that way, especially this evening.

I know Rubio better than the others. We share something in common, a peculiarity that makes us almost indistinguishable from each other. Rubio is a redhead, with freckles and pale-coloured eyes, but nature has been more generous with him than with me. He has perfect eyesight, whereas I am short-sighted to the point where, without my spectacles, I'm blind. Rubio has a matchless sense of humour. All he has to do is open his mouth and everyone's laughing. Here, within these dark walls, that's a precious gift, because the desire to laugh is rather rare beneath the glass roof, grey with filth, which hangs over the footbridges.

Rubio must have been a success with the girls, when he was outside. I must ask him to give me a few tips, just in case I see Sophie again one day.

The line of Spaniards moves forward, Touchin counting them one by one. Rubio walks, his face imperturbable. He stops, genuflects a few times in front of the chief screw who, delighted, sees this as a kind of bow, whereas Rubio's face quite openly says the opposite. Behind Rubio is the old teacher who wanted to teach in Catalan, the

195

peasant who learned to read in his cell and now recites verses from Garcia Lorca, the former mayor of a village in the Asturias, an engineer who knew how to find water even when it was hidden at the bottom of the mountain, and a miner in love with the French Revolution, who sometimes sings the words of 'Rouget de Lisle', although no one knows if he really understands them.

The prisoners halt in front of the dormitory cell and, one by one, begin to undress.

The clothes they take off are those in which they fought during the Spanish civil war. Their linen trousers are held together by worn-out cords, the espadrilles they sewed in the camps of the West have practically no soles left, the shirts are torn, but even dressed in their old rags, our Spanish comrades have a proud look to them. Castile is beautiful and so are her children.

Touchin rubs his belly, belches, wipes a hand under his nose, and wipes the snot off on the lapel of his jacket.

This evening, he notices that the Spaniards are taking their time; they're more pernickety than usual. Here they are folding up their trousers, taking off their shirts and hanging them on the guardrail; all together, they bend down and line up their espadrilles on the tiled floor. Touchin shakes his truncheon, as if this gesture could emphasize time.

Fifty-seven thin, opaline bodies now turn towards him. Touchin looks, scrutinises; a detail isn't right, but what is it? The screw scratches his head, lifts his cap, leans back as if the posture were going to give him a bit of perspective. He's certain of it, something isn't right, but what? A quick glance to the left at his colleague, who shrugs his shoulders, then one to the colleague on the right, who does the same, and Touchin discovers the inadmissible: 'What's going on with these underpants? They're still wearing them, when they ought to have their nuts on show!' Touchin is sure he's not chief for nothing – his two acolytes hadn't noticed the ploy at all. Touchin leans to one side to check if there isn't at least one man who's obeyed, but no, they're all without exception still wearing their underpants.

Rubio is careful not to laugh, even though the desire takes him as he sees Touchin's expression of pique. A battle is being played out. It may seem very trivial, but the stakes are substantial. It's the first one, and if it is won, there will be others.

Rubio, who has no equal when it comes to messing Touchin about, gazes at him with the innocent look of a man who is wondering why they're waiting to go back into the cells.

And as the stunned Touchin doesn't say anything, Rubio takes a step forward and so does the line of prisoners. Then Touchin rushes helplessly to the doorway of the dormitory and flings his arms out sideways, blocking the way.

'Come on, come on, you know the regulations,' warns Touchin, who doesn't want any trouble. 'The prisoner and his underpants can't enter the cell at the same time. The underpants stay on the guardrail and the prisoner

197

in the dormitory; it's always been that way, why change tonight? Come on, come on, Rubio, don't act like an imbecile.'

Rubio won't change his mind. He looks Touchin up and down and tells him calmly in his own language that he won't take them off.

Touchin threatens, attempts to push Rubio around, grabs him by the arm and shakes him. But beneath the chief warder's feet, the tiled floor worn out by the prisoners' footsteps is very slippery in this damp cold. Touchin loses his footing and falls backwards. The warders rush forward to pick him up. Furious, Touchin raises his arm to Rubio; Boldados takes a step forward and places himself in front of Rubio. He clenches his fists, but he has sworn to the others that he won't use them, that he won't undermine their stratagem with a fit of anger, however legitimate.

'I won't take my underpants off either, chief!'

Scarlet-faced, Touchin shakes his truncheon and shouts to anyone who wants to hear:

'So this is a rebellion, is it? You'll see what you'll see! A month's solitary for both of you, I'll teach you!'

Hardly has he finished speaking when the fifty-five other Spaniards take a step forward and also head for solitary. With two people in it, the solitary confinement cell is a bit of a squeeze. Touchin isn't very hot on geometry, but all the same he can see the size of the problem he's faced with.

He continues brandishing his truncheon, giving himself

time to think; if he stopped shaking it around, it would be like recognising that he's lost face. Rubio looks at his friends, he smiles, and in turn begins shaking his arms, without ever touching a warder, so that there is no pretext for sending for reinforcements. Rubio gesticulates, forming large circles in the air, and his friends do likewise. Fifty-seven pairs of arms whirl around and the noise of the other prisoners rises up from the lower floors. In one place they're singing the 'Marseillaise', in another the 'Internationale', and on the ground floor it's the 'Chant des partisans'.

The chief warder no longer has a choice. If he lets this go on, the entire prison will mutiny. Touchin's truncheon falls back, motionless; he signals to the prisoners to go back into their dormitory cell.

You see, that night, the Spaniards won the war of the underpants. It was only a first battle, but when Rubio told me every detail the next day in the exercise yard, we shook hands through the wire. And when he asked me what I thought of it all, I answered:

'There are still bastilles to capture.'

The peasant who was singing the 'Marseillaise' died one day in his cell, the old teacher who wanted to teach Catalan never returned from Mauthausen, Rubio was deported but came back anyway, Boldados was shot in Madrid, the mayor of the village in the Asturias returned home, and the day they dismantle the statues of Franco, his grandson will take over at the town hall.

As for Touchin, when the Liberation came he was appointed chief warder at the prison in Agen.

23

In the small hours of 17 February, the warders come and fetch André. As he leaves the cell, he shrugs his shoulders and gives us a little sidelong glance. The door closes again, and he leaves between two screws for the court martial, which sits within the prison walls. There will be no debate; he has no lawyer.

In one minute he is sentenced to death. The execution squad is already waiting for him in the yard.

The gendarmes have come specially from Grenade-sur-Garonne, the same place where André was on a mission when they arrested him. The job must be finished properly.

André would like to say farewell, but it's against regulations. Before dying, André writes a little note to his mother, which he hands to chief warder Theil, who is standing in for Touchin today.

Now André is tied to the stake. He asks for a stay of a few seconds, just long enough to remove the ring he wears on his finger. Chief warder Theil grumbles a bit but accepts it when André entrusts it to him, begging him to give it back to his mother. 'It was her wedding ring,' he explains; she gave it to him the day he left to join the brigade. Theil promises, and this time the ropes are tied around André's wrists.

Gripping the bars of our cells, we imagined the twelve helmeted men forming the execution squad. André stands up straight. The rifles are raised, we clench our fists and twelve bullets tear apart the thin body of our friend, which folds in two and remains there, dangling from its stake, the head to one side, the face dripping blood.

The execution is over, and the gendarmes leave. Chief warder Theil tears up André's letter and puts the ring in his pocket. Tomorrow, he will take care of another of our friends.

Sabatier, who was arrested in Montauban, was shot at the same stake. André's blood had barely dried behind him.

At night, I still sometimes see little pieces of torn paper fluttering in the yard of Saint-Michel prison. In my nightmare, they pirouette as far as the wall behind the execution post and stick together to re-form the words André wrote just before he died. He had just passed his eighteenth birthday.

At the end of the war, chief warder Theil was promoted to chief supervisor at the prison in Lens.

In a few days it was the turn of Boris's case and we feared the worst. But we had brothers in Lyon.

Their group is called Carmagnole-Liberté. Today they settled his account with a counsel for the prosecution who, like Lespinasse, had succeeded in cutting off the head of a Resistance member. Friend Simon Frid was dead, but Prosecutor Fauré-Pingelli had a hole in his skin. After this success, no more magistrates would dare to demand the life of one of our members. Boris, who got a twenty-year prison sentence, doesn't give a damn about his punishment, his fight continues outside. The proof is that the Spaniards told us that the house of a militiaman was blown up yesterday evening. I managed to pass a note to Boris so that he could know about it.

Boris doesn't know that on the first day of spring 1945, he will die at Gusen, in a concentration camp.

'Don't pull that face, Jeannot!'

Jacques's voice jolts me out of my torpor. I raise my head, take the cigarette he's holding out to me and beckon to Claude to come over and have a few puffs. But my little brother is exhausted, and prefers to remain stretched out against the wall of the cell. What's exhausting Claude is not the lack of food, or the thirst, or the fleas that devour us at night, nor the screws' harassment; no, what's making my little brother so sullen is remaining here, far

202

from the action, and I understand him, because I feel the same sadness.

'We won't give up,' Jacques goes on. 'Outside, they're continuing to fight and the Allies will eventually land, you'll see.'

While he's saying these words to comfort me, Jacques doesn't suspect that our friends are preparing for an operation against the Variétés cinema: only Nazi propaganda films are shown there.

Rosine, Marius and Enzo are involved, but for once it's not Charles who has prepared the bomb. The explosion must occur once the film is over, when the cinema is empty, to avoid there being any victims among the civilian population. The device that Rosine must place under a seat in the orchestra stalls is equipped with a delayed-action mechanism, and our gardener from Loubers didn't have the equipment necessary to manufacture it. The strike was supposed to happen yesterday evening; programme listing: *The Jew Süss*. But the police were everywhere, entry was controlled, bags and briefcases searched, so the friends were unable to enter with their cargo.

Jan decided to postpone until the next day. This time there's no police cordon at the ticket window. Rosine enters the auditorium and sits down next to Marius, who slides the bag containing the bomb under his seat. Enzo takes his place behind them, to check that they haven't been spotted. If I had caught wind of the story, I would have envied Marius, spending an entire evening at the cinema next to Rosine. She's so pretty, with her slight, sing-song accent and her voice that arouses uncontrollable shivers.

The lights go out and the news parades across the screen at the Variétés cinema. Rosine huddles low in her seat, her long brown hair slipping onto her shoulder. Enzo hasn't missed any of the smooth, elegant movement of her neck. It's difficult to concentrate on the film that is starting, when you have two kilos of explosives between your legs. It's no good Marius trying to persuade himself to the contrary; he's a little nervous. He doesn't like working with equipment he doesn't know. When Charles prepares the charges, he's confident; his friend's work has never failed; but here, the mechanism is different, the bomb too sophisticated for his taste.

At the end of the show, he has to slip his hand into Rosine's bag and break a glass tube, which contains sulphuric acid. In thirty minutes, the acid will have eaten through the side of a little iron box stuffed with potassium chlorate. As they mix together, the two substances will set off the detonators implanted in the charge. But all these chemists' tricks are much too complicated in Marius's eyes. He likes simple systems, the ones Charles manufactures with dynamite and a fuse. When it crackles, you just have to count the seconds; if there's a problem, with a little courage and agility you can always take off the tinder cord. In addition, the bomb-maker has added another system under the belly of his bomb; four little batteries and a ball of mercury are linked together to unleash the explosion immediately if a night watchman happened to find it and attempt to pick it up once the mechanism was armed.

So Marius sweats and tries in vain to interest himself in the film. Failing that, he casts discreet glances at Rosine, who pretends not to have seen anything; up to the moment when she gives him a tap on the leg to remind him that the show is happening in front of them, and not on her neck.

Even sitting next to Rosine, the minutes seem to pass very slowly at the Variétés cinema. Of course, Rosine, Enzo and Marius could have set off the mechanism in the interval and legged it immediately. The die would be cast and they would already be back, instead of suffering and sweating as they were. But as I've already told you, we have never killed an innocent, not even an imbecile. So they wait for the end of the show and when the auditorium empties, they will then set off the delayed-action mechanism, and only then.

At last the lights go up again. The spectators stand up and head for the exit. Sitting in the middle of the row, Marius and Rosine stay in their seats, waiting for the people to leave. Behind them, Enzo sits tight too. At the end of the row, an old lady takes her time putting on her coat. Her neighbour can't wait any longer.

Exasperated, he makes an about-turn and heads for the opposite aisle.

'Get a move on, push off, the film's over!' he grouses.

'My fiancée is a little tired,' answers Marius. 'We're waiting until she gets her strength back before we get up.'

Rosine seethes and thinks very quietly that Marius has got a cheek, and she'll tell him so as soon as they're outside! In the meantime, all she wants is for this guy to go back the way he came.

The man glances at the row; the old lady has left but he'd have to go all the way back. Too bad; he flattens himself to the back of the seat, and forces his way past this imbecile of a boy who's still sitting down when the credits have completely rolled, strides over his neighbour, who he thinks is a bit young to be feeling tired, jostles her about a bit and leaves without an apology.

Marius turns his head slowly towards Rosine. Her smile is strange, something isn't right, he knows it, he can sense it. Rosine's face is haggard.

'That bastard crushed my bag!'

Those were the last words Marius will ever hear; the mechanism has been set into motion; in the jostling, the bomb turned over, the bead of mercury came into contact with the batteries and instantly triggered the explosion. Marius is cut in two, killed instantly. Enzo, thrown backwards, sees Rosine's body rise slowly and fall three rows in front. He tries to help her but collapses instantly, his leg opened up, almost torn off.

Stretched out on the ground, his eardrums burst, he can no longer hear the police officers as they rush in. In the auditorium, ten rows of stalls have been blown out of place.

He's picked up and carried off. He's losing blood and his consciousness is vague. Before him, on the ground, Rosine is bathed in an ever-expanding red lake, her face frozen.

This happened yesterday, at the Variétés cinema, at the end of the film, Enzo remembers. Rosine had the beauty of springtime. They were taken to the Hôtel-Dieu hospital.

Rosine died in the small hours, without ever regaining consciousness.

They sewed Enzo's leg back on. The surgeons did what they could.

Outside his door, three militiamen are standing guard.

Marius's remains were thrown into a trench at the cemetery in Toulouse. Often at night, in my cell in Saint-Michel prison, I think of them. So that their faces are never wiped away, so that their courage can never be forgotten either.

The following day, Stefan, who is coming back from a mission he's carried out in Agen, meets up with Marianne; she's waiting for him at the train station, her face haggard. Stefan puts an arm around her and leads her outside the station.

'Have you heard?' she asks, a lump in her throat.

From his expression, she realises that Stefan knows nothing of the drama that was played out yesterday in the auditorium of the Variétés cinema. On the pavement they're walking along, she tells him of the deaths of Rosine and Marius.

'Where is Enzo?' asks Stefan.

'At the Hôtel-Dieu,' answers Marianne.

'I know a doctor who works in the surgical team. He's pretty liberal. I'll see what I can do.'

Marianne accompanies Stefan to the hospital. They don't exchange a word throughout the journey; both are thinking of Rosine and Marius. Arriving outside the front of the Hôtel-Dieu, Stefan breaks the silence.

'What about Rosine? Where is she?'

'In the mortuary. This morning, Jan went to see her father.'

'I understand. You know, the deaths of our friends would not have any purpose if we didn't follow through to the end.'

'Stefan, I don't know if the "end" you're talking about really exists, if we will wake up one day from this nightmare we've been living through for months. But if you want to know, yes, I am afraid since Rosine and Marius died, yes, Stefan, I'm afraid; getting up in the morning, I'm afraid; all through the day, when I walk the streets to glean information or tail an enemy, I'm afraid; at each crossroads, I'm afraid I'm being followed, afraid I'm going to be shot at, afraid I'll be arrested, afraid that other

Mariuses and Rosines won't come back from operations, afraid that Jeannot, Jacques and Claude will be shot, afraid that something will happen to Damira, to Osna, to Jan, to all of you who are my family. I'm afraid all the time, Stefan, even when I'm asleep. But not more than yesterday or the day before yesterday, not more than since the first day I joined the brigade, not more than ever since that day when they took away our right to be free. So yes, Stefan, I shall continue to live with this fear, until this "end" you speak of, even if I don't know where it is.'

Stefan comes up to Marianne and wraps his awkward arms around her. With just as much modesty, she lays her head on his shoulder; and too bad if Jan considers this liberty dangerous. Solitude is their daily fare, so if Stefan wishes, she will let him, she will allow herself to be loved, even for a moment, provided it is with tenderness. To experience a moment's comfort, to feel within her the presence of a man who could tell her, through the gentleness of his gestures, that life goes on, that she, quite simply, exists.

Marianne's lips slide towards Stefan's and they kiss, there, in front of the steps of the Hôtel-Dieu, where Rosine lies in a dark basement.

On the pavement, passers-by slow down, amused to see this entwined couple whose kiss seems never to want to end. In the middle of this horrible war, some people still find the strength to love. Spring will come again, Jacques said one day, and this kiss stolen by the front steps of a sinister hospital allows one to believe that he was perhaps right.

'I have to go,' mutters Stefan.

Marianne loosens her embrace and watches her friend climb the steps. When he reaches the door, she waves to him. A way of telling him, 'see you this evening,' perhaps.

Professor Rieuneau officiated in surgery at the Hôtel-Dieu. He had been one of Stefan and Boris's teachers, when they still had the right to follow their medical studies at the faculty. Rieuneau did not like Vichy's unworthy laws; of a liberal sensibility, his heart inclined towards the Resistance. He greeted his former pupil benevolently and drew him to one side.

'What can I do for you?' asked the professor.

'I have a friend,' replied Stefan hesitantly, 'a very good friend, who is somewhere here.'

'In which department?'

'The one that takes care of people who've had their legs torn off by a bomb.'

'Then I assume he's in surgery,' replied the professor. 'Has he been operated on?'

'Last night, I think.'

'He's not in my department, I would have seen him when I did my morning round. I shall find out.'

'Professor, we need to find a way of . . .'

'I understood you very well, Stefan,' the professor interrupted him. 'I shall see what it is possible to do. Wait for me in the lobby. I shall go and find out about his state of health.'

Stefan complied and headed down the staircase.

Arriving at the ground floor, he recognised the door with the flaking panelling; behind, other steps led to the basements. Stefan hesitated. If he was caught, he was bound to be asked questions that he would find very hard to answer. But duty was more pressing than the risk he ran, and without further ado he pushed open the double doors.

At the bottom of the staircase, the corridor seemed a long intestine penetrating the hospital's entrails. On the ceiling, interlaced cables ran around sweating pipework. Every ten metres, an electric lamp diffused its halo of pale light; in places, the bulb was broken and the corridor plunged into half-light.

Stefan didn't care about the darkness; he knew his way. He had had to come here before. The place he was looking for was on his right. He entered.

Rosine lay on a table, alone in the room. Stefan approached the sheet, stained with dark blood. The slight angle at which the head lay betrayed the fracture at the base of the neck. Was it this wound that had killed her or the many others he could see? He meditated before the remains.

He had come on behalf of the friends to say goodbye to her, to say that her face would never be wiped from our memories and that we would never give up.

'If wherever you are, you happen to meet André, say hello from me.'

Stefan kissed Rosine on the forehead and left the mortuary, heavy of heart.

When he got back to the lobby, Professor Rieuneau was waiting for him.

'I've been looking for you, where were you, for God's sake? Your friend is out of the woods, the surgeons have sewn his leg back on. Understand that I'm not saying he will walk again, but he will survive his wounds.'

And as the silent Stefan kept staring at him, the old professor concluded:

'I can do nothing for him. He is guarded permanently by three militiamen; those savages didn't even let me into the room where he is. Tell your friends to attempt nothing here, it's much too dangerous.'

Stefan thanked his professor and left immediately. Tonight, he would meet up with Marianne and tell her the news.

They only allowed Enzo a few days' rest before removing him from his hospital bed to transfer him to the prison infirmary. The militiamen did so without gentleness and Enzo lost consciousness three times during the course of his transfer.

His fate was sealed even before he was incarcerated. As soon as he was recovered, he would be shot in the courtyard. As he had to be capable of walking to the execution stake, we were counting on him not being able to stand upright for a while. We were at the start of March 1944, and the rumours of an imminent landing by the Allies were becoming increasingly numerous. Nobody here doubted that on that day, the executions would cease and we would be freed. To save our friend Enzo, we must play against the clock.

Charles has been furious since yesterday. Jan came to visit him in the little disused railway station at Loubers. A new brigade of French Resistance fighters is forming in the hinterland. They need experienced men, and Jan is to join them. He's not the one who's decided this, those are the orders, that's all. He's just obeying them.

'But who gives these orders?' demands Charles, his anger not abating.

French resistors, in Toulouse, outside the brigade, that didn't even exist last month! Now a new network is being set up and his team is being stripped! There aren't enough guys like Jan; many friends have fallen or been arrested, so he finds it unjust that he should be allowed to leave like this.

'I know,' says Jan, 'but the directives come from on high.'

Charles says that he doesn't know anything about 'on high' either. Through all these long months, it's here below that the fighting's been going on. The war on the streets, it's they who invented it. Easy for others to copy their work.

Charles doesn't really believe what he's saying, it's just that saying farewell to his friend Jan hurts him almost more than the day he told a woman that it was better if she returned to her husband.

Of course, Jan is a lot less pretty than she was and he would never have shared his bed with him, even if he'd been at death's door. But before being his leader, Jan is first of all his friend, so seeing him leave like this . . .

'Have you time for an omelette? I'm got some eggs,' grumbles Charles.

'Keep them for the others, I really have to go,' replies Jan.

'What others? At this rate, I shall end up being the only one in the brigade!'

'Others will come, Charles, don't worry. The battle is only just beginning, the Resistance is being organised and it's normal that we should give a hand where we can be useful. Come on, say goodbye to me and don't pull that face.'

Charles accompanied Jan onto the road.

They embraced, swore to meet again one day, when the country was free. Jan got on his bike and Charles called to him one last time.

'Is Catherine coming with you?'

'Yes,' replied Jan.

'Then kiss her for me.'

Jan promises with a nod and Charles's face lights up as he asks him one final question.

'So technically, since we've said goodbye, you're not my leader any more?'

'Technically, no!' replied Jan.

'So, you big cretin, if we win this war, you and Catherine try to be happy. And it is I, the bomb-maker of Loubers, who's giving you that order!'

Jan saluted Charles as you might salute a soldier you respect, and pedalled off on his bike.

Charles returned his salute and stood there, at the end of the lane leading to the disused railway station, until Jan's bicycle disappeared over the horizon.

While we are dying of hunger in our cells, while Enzo is writhing in pain in the infirmary at Saint-Michel prison, the fight is continuing in the streets. And not a day passes without the enemy experiencing its share of sabotaged trains, uprooted pylons, cranes plunging into the canal, or a few grenades suddenly landing on some German lorries.

But, in Limoges, an informer has told the authorities that some young people, surely Jews, are meeting furtively in an apartment in his block. The police carry out arrests immediately. The Vichy government then decides to send one of its best sleuths to the area.

Commissaire Gillard, charged with anti-terrorist repression, is sent with his team to investigate how to gain the means to follow the thread back to the Resistance network in the South West, which must be wiped out at all costs.

At Lyon, Gillard proved his worth. He's used to inter-rogations, and he won't lower his guard in Limoges. He returns to the police station to take personal care of the questions being asked. From harassment to torture, he ends up finding out that 'packages' are sent, poste restante, to Toulouse. This time, he knows where to cast his net. All he needs to do now is watch for the fish coming to bite.

The time has come to get rid once and for all of these wops who disturb public order and call into question the State's authority.

In the early hours of the morning, Gillard abandons his victims at the police headquarters in Limoges and takes the train for Toulouse with his team.

24

As soon as he arrives, Gillard gets rid of the Toulouse
police officers and shuts himself away in an office on the
first floor of the police headquarters. If the cops in
Toulouse had been competent, there would have been no
need to call him in, and the young terrorists would already
be under lock and key. And besides, Gillard is not unaware
that even in the ranks of the police, as at the prefecture,
here and there you can find a few people who sympa-
thise with the Resistance cause, sometimes even organising escapes. Isn't it the case that from time to time,
certain Jews are warned that they are about to be arrested?
If that were not so, the militiamen would not find apart-
ments emptied of their occupants, when they arrive to
take them in for questioning. Gillard reminds the members
of his team to be suspicious: Jews and Communists are
everywhere. Within the framework of his investigation,

he doesn't want to take any risks. At the end of the meeting, surveillance of the post office is organised straight away.

This morning, Sophie is ill. A bad case of flu keeps her in bed. And yet someone must go and collect the package that has arrived, as it does every Thursday, and without which the friends won't get their money; they must pay their rent, buy something to eat, at the very least. Simone, a new recruit who has recently come from Belgium, will go in her place. When she enters the post office, Simone doesn't spot the two men who are pretending to fill in documents. They, however, instantly identify the young kid who's opening letterbox number 27, to collect the packet it contains. Simone leaves; they follow her. Two experienced cops against a young girl of seventeen, the game of hide-and-seek is played out before it begins. One hour later, Simone comes back to Sophie's place to bring back her 'shopping'. She doesn't know that she has just enabled Gillard's men to locate where she lives.

The girl who knew so well how to hide in order to follow others, the girl who tirelessly walked the streets so as not to be spotted, the girl who knew, better than we did, how to find out the timetable, the movements, contacts and smallest details of the lives of those she followed, doesn't suspect that outside her windows two men are watching her and that she is now the one who is being tracked. Cats and mice come to swap their roles.

218

That very afternoon, Marianne pays Sophie a visit. When evening comes and she leaves, it's her turn to be followed by Gillard's men.

They have arranged to meet on the banks of the Midi canal. Stefan is waiting for her on a bench. Marianne hesitates and smiles at him from a distance. He stands up and says good evening. Another few steps and she'll be in his arms. Since yesterday, life isn't quite the same any more. Rosine and Marius are dead and there's nothing to do to stop thinking about it, but Marianne is not alone. You can love so strongly at seventeen, you can love to the point of forgetting that you're hungry, you can love so much that you forget that yesterday you were still afraid. But since yesterday life isn't the same any more, since now she is thinking about someone.

Sitting side by side, on this bench close to the Demoiselles bridge, Marianne and Stefan kiss and nothing and no one can come and steal away these moments of happiness. Time passes and it's time for curfew. Behind them, the gas-lights are already lit; they must part. Tomorrow, they will meet again, and every evening after that. And every evening after that, beside the Midi canal, Commissaire Gillard's men will spy at their ease upon two adolescents who love each other in the middle of the war.

The next day, Marianne meets up with Damira. When they part, Damira is followed. The day after, or is it later? Damira meets Osna; in the evening, Osna has a meeting with Antoine. In a few days, almost all the brigade has been logged by Gillard's men. The net tightens around them.

We weren't yet twenty, scarcely more for a few of us, and we still had a lot to learn in order to make war without being spotted, things that the bloodhounds of the Vichy police knew like the back of their hands.

The police are preparing to haul in their nets. Commissaire Gillard has gathered all his men in the office they have set up at the Toulouse police headquarters. Nevertheless, in order to make arrests, they will have to request reinforcements from the police officers of the 8th brigade. Upstairs, an inspector has missed nothing of what is being planned. He leaves his post discreetly and goes to the main post office. He goes to the window and asks the operator for a Lyon number. He is connected to the number in a phone booth.

A glance through the glazed door, and the official discusses with his colleague. The line is secure.

The other man does not speak; he is content to hear the terrible news. In two days, the entire 35th Marcel Langer brigade will be arrested. The information is rock-solid; they must be warned with all urgency. The inspector hangs up and prays that the information will be relayed.

In an apartment in Lyon, a lieutenant in the French Resistance replaces the phone on its hook.

'Who was it?' asks his commander.

'A contact in Toulouse.'

'What did he want?'

'To inform us that the lads of the 35th brigade are going to fall in two days' time.'

'The Militia?'

'No, cops sent by Vichy.'

'Then they have no chance.'

'Not if we alert them; we still have time to get them out.'

'Perhaps, but we are not going to,' answers the commander.

'But why?' asks the man, stunned.

'Because the war isn't going to last. The Germans lost two hundred thousand men at Stalingrad, and they say that another hundred thousand are in the hands of the Russians, among them thousands of officers and a good twenty generals. Their armies are being routed on the Eastern fronts and whether they come from the west or the south, the Allied landings will come soon. We know that London is preparing for them.'

'I know all this, but what's it got to do with the guys in the Langer brigade?'

'It's now a matter of good political sense. These men and women we're talking about are all Hungarian, Spanish, Italian, Polish and goodness knows what else; all or almost all foreigners. When France is liberated, it's preferable that History tells that it was Frenchmen who fought for her.'

'So we're going to let them be caught, just like that?'

rages the man who thinks of these adolescents, fighters from the very beginning.

'They won't necessarily be killed . . .'

And seeing his lieutenant's sickened expression, this commander of the French Resistance sighs and concludes:

'Listen to me. In a little while, the country will have to get back on its feet after this war, and it must have its head high, the people must be reconciled around a single leader, and that will be de Gaulle. The victory has to be ours. It's regrettable, I agree, but France will need its heroes to be Frenchmen, not foreigners!'

In his little railway station in Loubers, Charles was disgusted. At the start of the week, he had been informed that the brigade would no longer be receiving any money. There would be no more deliveries of weapons, either. The links woven with the Resistance networks that were organising in the area had been cut. The reason given was the attack on the Variétés cinema. The press had refrained from saying that the victims were Resistance fighters. In the eyes of public opinion, Rosine and Marius passed for two civilians, two kids who fell victim to a cowardly attack, and nobody cared that the third child-hero who accompanied them was writhing in pain on a bed in the infirmary at Saint-Michel prison. Charles had been told that such actions cast opprobrium upon the entire Resistance, and that the Resistance preferred to cut off its links.

To him, this abandonment had the taste of treason.

That evening, with Robert, who had taken command of the brigade since the departure of Jan, he expressed all his disgust. How could people abandon them, turn their backs on them, they who had been there at the beginning? Robert wasn't sure what to say, he loved Charles like a brother, and he reassured him on the point that probably preoccupied him the most, the one that made him suffer the most.

'Listen, Charles, nobody is duped by what they write in the press. Everyone knows what really happened at the Variétés cinema, who lost their lives there.'

'At what price!' growled Charles.

'The price of their freedom,' answered Robert, 'and the whole town knows it.'

Marc joined them a little later. Charles shrugged his shoulders as he saw him and he went out to walk for a while in the garden behind the house. As he tapped on a mound of earth, Charles told himself that Jacques must have been mistaken. This was the end of March 1944 and spring still wasn't here.

Commissaire Gillard and his second-in-command Sirinelli gathered all their men together. On the first floor of the police headquarters, it is time for preparations to be made. Today the arrests will be carried out. The order is given for absolute silence. They must avoid anyone alerting those who, in a few hours, will fall into their net. However, from the neighbouring office, a young police officer hears what is being said on the other side of the partition wall. His job is common law crime; the war hasn't made offenders disappear and somebody has to deal with them. But Commissaire Esparbié has never locked up partisans, on the contrary. When something is brewing, he's the one who warns them; it's his way of belonging to the Resistance.

Informing them of the danger they're in will involve danger and risk, and time is very short; Esparbié isn't alone, one of his colleagues is also his accomplice. The young police officer abandons his armchair and goes to find him immediately.

'Go straight to the public revenue office. In the pensions department, ask to see someone called Madeleine, and tell her that her friend Stefan must leave immediately on a journey.'

Esparbié has entrusted this mission to his colleague as he is going to another meeting. By taking his car, he can be in Loubers in half an hour. There, he must talk with a friend; he has seen his identification sheet in a file, one in which it would have been better that he didn't feature.

At noon, Madeleine leaves the public revenue office and goes to look for Stefan, but although she visits all the places he frequents, she can't find him. When she goes back to her parents, the police are waiting for her. They don't know anything about her, except that Stefan comes to see her almost every day. While the police officers are searching the place, Madeleine, taking advantage of a moment's inattention, hastily scrawls a note and hides it in a box of matches. She claims to be feeling ill and asks if she can take the air at the window . . .

Under her windows lives one of her friends, an Italian grocer who knows her better than anyone. A box of matches falls at his feet. Giovanni picks it up, looks up and smiles at Madeleine. It's time to close the shop! Giovanni tells the astonished customer that in any case, he hasn't had anything to sell on his shelves for ages. Pulling down the blind, he gets on his bike and goes to warn anyone who it concerns.

At the same moment, Charles is going back with Esparbié. As soon as he has left, he packs his suitcase and, with a heavy heart, closes the door of his disused railway station for the last time. Before turning the key in the lock, he casts a final glance around the room. On the hotplate sits an old frying pan, which recalls a dinner when one of his omelettes almost caused a catastrophe. That evening, the whole group were gathered together. It was one of those terrible days, but the times were better than today.

On his strange bicycle, Charles pedals as fast as he can. He has so many of us to find. The hours are passing and his friends are in danger.

Warned by the Italian grocer, Stefan is already on his way. He won't have time to say goodbye to Marianne, nor even to go and kiss his girlfriend Madeleine, whose insolence has saved his life, by endangering her own.

Charles has joined Marc in a café. He informs him of

225

what is afoot and gives him the order to leave immediately and join the maquisards near Montauban.

'Go there with Damira, they'll welcome you into their ranks.'

Before leaving him, he entrusts an envelope to him.

'Pay close attention. I've noted down the majority of our operations in this log book,' says Charles. 'Give it on my behalf to the people you find there.'

'Isn't it dangerous to keep these documents?'

'Yes, but if we all die, someone must know one day what we have done. I can accept being killed, but not being made to disappear.'

The two friends part. Marc must find Damira as quickly as possible. Their train leaves early in the evening.

Charles had hidden a few weapons on rue Dalmatie, and others in a church not far from there. He must try to save what can still be saved. When he reaches the vicinity of the first cache, Charles notices two men at the crossroads, one of them reading a newspaper.

'Shit, it's blown,' he thinks.

There's still the church, but as he's approaching, a black Citroën emerges onto the forecourt, four men spring out and fall upon him. Charles struggles the best he can, but the fight is an unequal one and blows rain down. Charles is pissing blood, he staggers; Gillard's men finish the job by knocking him unconscious; they take him away.

*　　*　　*

226

Dusk is falling as Sophie returns home. Two men are watching her from the end of the street. She spots them, does a U-turn, but two others are already advancing towards her. One opens his jacket, takes out his revolver and aims at her. Sophie has no means of escape. She smiles and refuses to put her hands up.

Tonight, Marianne is having dinner at her mother's house; an approximation of artichoke soup is on the menu. Nothing very tasty, but enough to allow one to forget one's hunger until the next day. Someone knocks violently at the door. The young woman starts; she has recognised this way of knocking and has no illusions about the nature of her visitors. Her mother looks at her, anxious.

'Don't move, it's for me,' says Marianne, laying down her napkin.

She walks around the table, takes her mother in her arms and embraces her tightly.

'Whatever anyone says to you, I don't regret any of what I've done, Mother. I have fought for a just cause.'

Marianne's mother gazes fixedly at her daughter, she strokes her cheek, as if this gesture of ultimate tenderness might enable her to hold back her tears.

'Whatever anyone says to me, my love, you are my daughter and I am proud of you.'

The door trembles at the blows. Marianne kisses her mother one last time and goes to open it.

*   *   *

It's a warm evening; Osna is at the window, propped up on her elbows, smoking a cigarette. A car comes up the street and parks opposite her house. Four men in rain-coats get out. Osna has realised. In the time it takes them to climb upstairs, she might perhaps still hide, but the tiredness is so strong, at the end of all these months of secrecy. And besides, where would she hide? So Osna closes the window. She goes towards the washbasin, turns on the tap and dabs her face with water.

'The time has come,' she whispers to her reflection in the mirror.

And already she hears the footsteps coming up the stairs.

On the platform at the railway station, the clock reads seven thirty-two. Damira is edgy. She leans forward, hoping to see the train appear that will carry them far from here.

'It's late, isn't it?'

'No,' replies Marc calmly, 'it will be here in five minutes.'

'Do you think the others have managed to get away?'

'I don't know anything, but I'm not too worried about Charles.'

'Well I'm worried about Osna, Sophie and Marianne.'

Marc knows that no words can reassure the young woman he loves. He takes her in his arms and kisses her.

'Don't worry, I'm certain they've all been warned in time. Just like us.'

'And what if we were arrested?'

'Well, at least we'd be together, but we won't be arrested.'

'I'm not thinking about that, I'm thinking about Charles's log book – after all, I'm the one who's carrying it.'

'Ah!'

Damira looks at Marc and smiles at him tenderly.

'I'm sorry, that's not what I wanted to say, I'm so afraid that I end up talking rubbish.'

In the distance, the locomotive's nose stands out against the curving railway track.

'You see, all will be well,' says Marc.

'Until when?'

'One day spring will come again, you'll see, Damira.'

The train moves past them, the wheels of the engine stop, striking clusters of sparks behind them, and the train comes to a halt with a screech of brakes.

'Do you think you will always love me, when the war is over?' asks Marc.

'Who told you that I loved you?' replies Damira with a mischievous smile.

And as she pulls him towards the carriage steps, a hand falls heavily on her shoulder.

Marc is flattened to the ground; two men handcuff him. Damira struggles, but a masterful slap sends her sprawling against the side of the carriage. Her face is crushed against the train's name-plate. Just before she loses consciousness, she reads, written in large letters, 'Montauban'.

*   *   *

At police headquarters, the officers search her and find the envelope which Charles entrusted to Marc.

On that day, 4 April 1944, the brigade fell almost entirely into the hands of the police. A few managed to get away. Catherine and Jan escaped the net. The police officers failed to track down Alonso. As for Emile, he left just in time.

That evening, 4 April 1944, Gillard and his terrible second-in-command Sirinelli toast each other in champagne. As they raise their glasses, they congratulate themselves with their colleagues on putting an end to the activities of a band of young 'terrorists'.

Thanks to the work they have done, these foreigners who were harming France will spend the rest of their lives behind bars. 'Although . . .!' he added, going through Charles's log book, 'with the evidence here to convict them, we can be certain that the lives of these scumbags won't be long before they're shot.'

While the police were beginning to torture Marianne, Sophie, Osna and all those arrested that day, the man who had betrayed them by his silence, the one who had decided for political reasons not to relay the information communicated by Resistance members working at the prefecture, that very same man was already preparing for his entrance into the Liberation's staff headquarters.

When he learned, the next day, that the 35th Marcel Langer brigade, which belonged to the MOI, had almost entirely fallen, he shrugged his shoulders and dusted off his jacket; in the very same place where, a few months later, a Légion d'honneur medal would be pinned. Today a commanding officer in the French Forces of the Interior, he will soon be a colonel.

As for Commissaire Gillard, congratulated by the authorities, at the end of the war he was entrusted with running the drugs squad. He ended his career peacefully there.

25

As I've told you, we never gave up. The few surviving members were organising themselves already. A few friends from Grenoble joined them. Their leader, Urman, who had been sent to take over command and rebuild the brigade, was determined to allow the enemy no respite, and the following week operations recommenced.

It had been dark for a long time. Claude was asleep, like the majority of us; I on the other hand, was trying to spot the stars in the sky, through the bars.

Amid the silence, I heard a friend sobbing. I approached him.

'Why are you crying?'

'My brother, you know, he couldn't kill, he couldn't ever raise his weapon against a man, even some shit of a militiaman.'

Samuel was a strange mixture of wisdom and anger. I thought the two things were irreconcilable, until I met him.

Samuel runs his hand across his face. As he spreads out his tears, he reveals the pallor of his emaciated cheeks. His eyes have sunk deep into their sockets, and you'd think they were only held there by a miracle. There's almost no muscle left on his face, and his bones show through his translucent skin.

'It was so long ago,' he continues, his voice barely audible. 'There were only five of us back then. Five Resistance fighters in the whole town and all together, we were less than a hundred years old. I only fired once, at point blank range, but he was a bastard, one of those who denounced, raped and tortured. But my brother was incapable of doing anything bad, even to people like that.'

Samuel began to laugh nervously and his chest, ravaged by tuberculosis, kept rattling. He had a strange voice, sometimes with the timbre of a man, sometimes stamped with a kind of childlike clarity. Samuel was twenty years old.

'I shouldn't tell you, you know, it's not good, it reawakens the pain, but when I talk about him, I make him live again a little, don't you think?'

I really didn't know, but I gave a nod of agreement. It didn't matter what he had to say; the guy needed someone to listen to him. There were no stars in the sky and I was too hungry to sleep.

'It was at the beginning. My brother had the heart of

an angel, the cheerful face of a kid. He believed in good and evil. You know, I realised right from the start that he was done for. With such a pure soul, you can't wage war. And his soul was so beautiful that it shone above the filth of factories, below that of prisons; it lit up the paths of dawn, when you leave for work with the warmth of the bed still there at your back.

'You couldn't ask him to kill. I told you that, didn't I? He believed in forgiveness. But listen; my brother had courage, he never refused to come on an operation, but always without a weapon. "What good would it do me, I don't know how to shoot?" he would say, mocking me. It was his heart that prevented him from taking aim, a heart as big as this, I tell you,' insisted Samuel, spreading his arms wide. 'He went empty-handed and tranquil into battle, certain of his victory.

'We were asked to sabotage a production line in a local factory. Cartridges were manufactured there. My brother said he must go, for him it was logical, the more cartridges that couldn't be made any more, the more lives would be saved.

'Together, we conducted the investigation. We never split up. He was fourteen, I had to keep watch on him, take care of him. If you want the truth, I think that all that time, it was he who was protecting me.

'His hands were filled with talent, if you'd only seen him with a pencil in his fingers, capable of drawing anything and everything. In two lines of charcoal, he could have drawn your portrait and your mother would

234

have hung it on her sitting-room wall. Well, perched on the low surrounding wall, in the deep of night, he drew the factory's surroundings, coloured in each of the buildings that grew on his sheet of paper in the same way that wheat emerges from the earth. I kept watch and waited for him down below. And then, all of a sudden, he started laughing, like that, in the middle of the night; a full, clear laugh, a laugh I shall carry forever with me, right to the tomb when my tuberculosis has won its war. My brother laughed because he had drawn a man in the middle of the factory, a guy with bow legs like the headmaster of his school.

'When he'd finished his drawing, he jumped into the street and said to me: "Come on, we can go now." You see, my brother was like that; gendarmes could have passed that way, and we'd certainly have ended up in prison, but he didn't give a damn; he looked at his factory plan, with his little bow-legged man and he gave a full-throated laugh; that laugh, believe me, I swear to you, filled up the night.

'Another day, while he was at school, I went on my own to visit the factory. I was hanging about in the yard, trying not to draw too much attention to myself, when a workman came over to me. He said that if I'd come for the job interviews, I had to take the path that ran past the transformers, the ones he pointed out to me; and as he added "comrade", I understood his message.

'When I got back, I told everything to my little brother, who had completed his plan. And this time, as he looked

235

at the finished drawing, he no longer laughed, even when I showed him the little fellow with the bandy legs.'

Samuel stopped talking, long enough to get a bit of breath back. I had kept a dog-end in my pocket. I lit it but didn't suggest that he should share it, because of his cough. He gave me time to savour a first puff and then continued his tale, with his voice changing in intonation according to whether he was talking about himself or his brother.

'A week later, my friend Louise arrived at the railway station with a cardboard box under her arm. In the box there were twelve grenades. God knows how she'd found them.

'You know we had no help from the parachute drops, we were alone, so alone. Louise was one hell of a girl, I had a thing for her and she for me. Sometimes we went to make love around by the marshalling yard and you really had to love each other not to pay any attention to the surroundings, but in any event, we never had the time. The day after the one when Louise had arrived with her package, we left for an operation; it was a cold, dark night, like this one, only different, because my brother was still alive. Louise accompanied us to the factory. We had two revolvers, taken from some policemen I had knocked around a bit, in an alleyway. My brother didn't want a weapon, so I had the two pistols in my bicycle bag.

'I must tell you what happens to me, because you

aren't going to believe it, even if I swear it to you, here in front of you. We're cycling along, the bicycle juddering over the cobbles, and behind me I hear a man's voice saying "Monsieur, you've dropped something." I didn't want to listen to this guy, but a bloke who continues on his way when he's lost something is suspicious. I put my foot on the ground and turned around. On the pavement that runs alongside the railway station, workmen are going home from the factory, their satchels slung across their bodies. They're walking in groups of three, because the pavement isn't wide enough for four. You must understand that this is the whole factory, walking up the street. And in front of me, thirty metres away, is my revolver, which has fallen out of my saddlebag; my revolver, lying shining on the cobbles. I lean my bike against the wall and walk towards the man who bends down, picks up my weapon and hands it back to me as if it were a handkerchief. The guy takes his leave and rejoins his friends who are waiting for him, wishing me good evening. That night, he goes home to his wife and the food she's prepared for him. As for me, I get back on my bike, the weapon under my jacket, and I pedal to catch up with my brother. Can you imagine? What do you think the expression on your face would be if you lost your weapon in action and somebody brought it back to you?'

I didn't say anything to Samuel; I didn't want to interrupt him. But images instantly resurfaced from my memory: the look on the face of a German officer, his

arms at right angles to his body as he lay beside a urinal;
the looks on the faces of Robert and my friend Boris,
too.

'The cartridge factory lay before us like a line drawing
in Indian ink in the darkness. We walked along the
surrounding wall. My brother scaled it, his feet finding
holds on the mill-stones as though he were climbing a
staircase. Before jumping down on the other side, he
smiled at me and said that nothing could happen to him,
and that he loved us, Louise and me. I climbed the wall
too and joined him as we'd agreed, in the yard, behind
a pylon he had marked on his map. We could hear the
grenades rattle against each other in our bags.

'We must be careful of the watchman. He sleeps a
long way from the building we're going to burn and the
explosion will get him out in time so that he doesn't run
any risk, but what about us? What risk do we run if he
sees us?

'Already my brother is sneaking ahead in the drizzle.
I follow him to the point where our paths separate; he's
dealing with the warehouse, and I'm taking care of the
workshop and the offices. I have his map in my head
and the darkness doesn't frighten me. I enter the building,
walk along the assembly line and up the steps to the
footbridge that leads to the offices. The door is closed
with a steel crossbar, firmly padlocked in place; too bad,
the windowpanes are fragile. I take two grenades, pull
out the pins and throw them, one in each hand. The

windows break; just enough time for me to crouch down, the blast reaches me. I'm flung backwards and land with my arms stretched out sideways. Dazed, with buzzing eardrums, gravel in my mouth and smoke in my lungs, I spit out as much as I can. I try to get up, but my shirt's on fire, I'm going to be burned alive. I hear other explosions thundering in the distance, from the direction of the warehouses. I must finish my work too.

'I roll down the iron steps and fetch up in front of a window. The sky is reddened by my brother's work. Other buildings light up in their turn, following the explosions, which make them burst into flames in the darkness. I reach into my satchel, remove the pins from my grenades and throw them, one by one, running in the smoke towards the way out.

'Behind me, explosions come one after another; at each of them, my entire body shakes. There are so many flames that it's like broad daylight, and at moments, the brightness is masked, giving way to the most profound black. My eyes are giving up on me, the tears trickling from them are burning hot.

'I want to live, I want to escape from this hell, get out of here. I want to see my brother, hold him in my arms, tell him that everything was just an absurd nightmare; that when I awoke I rediscovered our lives, just like that, by chance in the chest where Mother kept my things. These two lives, his, mine, the ones where we went off to pinch sweets from the grocer on the corner, the ones where Mother waited for us on our return from school, the ones where she made us recite our homework; just before they come to take us away and steal our lives.

'In front of me, a wooden beam has just collapsed. It's in flames and it's barring my way. The heat is terrible but outside, my brother is waiting and I know he won't leave without me. So I take the flames in my hands and I push away the beam.

'You can't imagine the fire's bite until you've felt it. You know, I howled, like a beaten dog, I howled for death, but I want to live, I told you; so I continue on my way through the inferno, praying that someone will cut off my hands so that the pain will stop. And in front of me, at last the little courtyard appears, just as my brother had drawn it. A little further, the ladder that he has already placed against the wall. "I was wondering what you were doing, you know?" he says when he sees my face, as black as a miner's. And he adds, "You've got yourself into quite a state." He orders me to go first, because of my injuries. I climb as best I can, leaning on my elbows, my hands hurt too much. At the top, I turn around and call him, to tell him that it's his turn, he mustn't hang about.'

Once again, Samuel has fallen silent. As if to gain the strength to tell me the end of his story. Then he opens his hands and shows me his palms; they are those of a man who has spent all his life working the land, a man a hundred years old; Samuel is only twenty.

'My brother is there, in the yard, but when I call it's the voice of another man that answers. The factory watchman takes aim with his rifle and shouts "Halt, halt." I take my revolver out of my satchel, I forget the pain in my hands, and I aim; but now my brother shouts, "Don't do that!" I look at him and the weapon slides between my fingers. When it falls at his feet he smiles, as if reassured that I can't do any harm. You see, I've told you, he has the heart of an angel. Empty-handed, he turns and smiles at the watchman. "Don't shoot," he says. "Don't shoot, it's the Resistance." He spoke as if to reassure him, this podgy little man with his rifle at the ready, as if to tell him that we didn't wish him any harm.

'My brother adds, "After the war, they will build you a brand new factory, it will be even more beautiful to guard." And then he turns around and places his foot on the first rung of the ladder. The podgy man shouts again, "Halt, halt," but my brother continues his walk towards the heavens. The watchman pulls the trigger.

'I saw his chest explode, his expression freeze. He smiled at me and his blood-drenched lips murmured, "Run away, I love you." His body fell backwards.

'I was there on the top of the wall, he down below, bathing in that red lake that spread out beneath him, red with all the love that was spreading away.'

Samuel said nothing more that night. When he had finished telling me his story, I went to lie down next to

241

Claude, who moaned a little because I woke him up.

From my straw mattress, I looked through the bars and at last saw a few stars shining in the sky. I don't believe in God, but that night I imagined that on one of them sparkled the soul of Samuel's brother.

26

The May sunshine warms our cell. In the middle of the day, the bars on the skylights trace three black lines on the ground. When the wind is just right, the first scents of the lime trees reach us.

'Apparently the comrades have got a car.'

It's Etienne's voice that breaks the silence. I got to know Etienne here, he joined the brigade a few days after Claude and I were arrested; like the others, he fell into Commissaire Gillard's nets. And while he is speaking, I try to imagine myself outside, in another life than my own. I can hear the passers-by walking in the street, their footsteps light with their liberty, not knowing that a few metres away from them, behind a double wall, we are prisoners awaiting death. Etienne sings to himself, as if to kill the boredom. And then there's the confinement, it's like a snake that winds around us, gripping us without

243

respite. Its bite is painless, its poison spreads. Then the words our friend is singing call us back to the moment; no, we are not alone, but all together here.

Etienne is sitting on the ground, back to the wall, his fragile voice is soft, it's almost that of a child telling a story, that of a brave kid, quivering with hope:

Sur c'te butte-là, y avait pas d'gigolette,
Pas de marlous, ni de beaux muscadins.
Ah, c'etait loin de moulin d'la Galette,
Et de Paname, qu'est le roi des pat'lins

C'qu'elle en a bu, du beau sang, cette terre,
Sang d'ouvrir et sang de paysan,
Car les bandits, qui sont cause des guerres,
N'en meurant jamais, on n'tue qu'les innocents.

Etienne's voice is joined by Jacques'; and the friends' hands that were beating their straw mattresses continue their task, but now to the rhythm of the refrain:

La Butte Rouge, c'est son nom, l'baptême s'fit un
  matin
Où tous ceux qui grimpèrent, roulèrent dans le ravin
Aujord'hui y a des vignes, il y pousse du raisin
Qui boira d'ce vin-là, boira l'sang des copains

In the next cell, I hear the accents of Charles and Boris joining in the song. Claude, who was scribbling words

244

on a piece of paper, abandons his pencil to hum about others. And now he is on his feet and he's singing too:

> Sur c'te butte-là, on n'y f'sait pas la noce
> Comme à Montmartre, où l'champagne coule à flots.
> Mais le pauv' gars qu'avaient laissé des gosses,
> I f'saient entendre de pénibles sanglots.

> C'qu'elle en a bu, des larmes, cette terre,
> Larmes d'ouvriers et larmes de paysans,
> Car les bandits, qui sont cause des guerres
> Ne pleurent jamais, car ce sont des tyrans.

> La Butte Rouge, c'est son nom, l'baptême s'fit un
>   matin
> Où tous ceux qui grimpèrent , roulèrent dans le ravin
> Aujourd'hui y a des vignes, il y pousse du raisin
> Qui boit de ce vin-là, boira les larmes des copains

Behind me, the Spaniards are singing too. They don't know the words but hum along with us. Soon, the whole floor resounds to a unison rendition of 'La Butte Rouge'. Now there are a hundred people singing:

> Sur c'te butte-là, on y r'fait des vendanges,
> On y entend des cris et des chansons.
> Filles et gars, doucement y échangent
> Des mots d'amour, qui donnent le frisson.

245

Peuvent-ils songer dans leurs folles étreintes,
Qu'à cet endroit où s'échangent leurs baisers,
J'ai entendu, la nuit, monter des plaintes,
Et j'y ai vu des gars au crâne brisé?

La Butte Rouge, c'est son nom, l'baptême s'fit un matin
Où tous ceux qui grimpèrent, roulèrent dans le ravin
Aujourd'hui y a des vignes, il y pousse du raisin
Mais moi j'y vois des croix, portant l'nom des copains

You see, Etienne was right, we are not alone, but all here
together. Silence falls again and with it darkness at the
window. We all turn back to our boredom, our fear. Soon,
we'll have to go out onto the footbridge, take off our
clothes, except for our underpants since now, thanks to a
few Spanish friends, we have the right to keep them on.

The first glimmers of daylight have returned. Everyone
is dressed again and all waiting for the meal. On the
footbridge, two prisoners on duty drag along the cooking
pot, serving the mess tins that are held out to them. The
detainees go back into their cells, the doors close again
and the concert of keys in locks comes to an end. Everyone
sits on their own, left to their own solitude, warming
their hands on the sides of their metal bowls. Lips move
forward towards the broth and blow on the unpleasant
liquid. It is the coming day that they drink down in little
sips.

*   *   *

Yesterday when we were singing, one voice was missing from the roll call. Enzo is in the infirmary.

'They're calmly waiting there for him to be executed, but I think we must act,' says Jacques.

'From here?'

'You see, Jeannot, from here we indeed can't do much, which is why we ought to pay him a visit,' he replied.

'And . . .?'

'As long as he can't stay on his feet, they can't shoot him. We must prevent him from getting better too quickly, do you understand?

From my expression Jacques saw that I hadn't yet grasped the role he had in mind for me; we'll draw straws for which of us two must writhe in pain.

I've never been lucky in gambling, and the old saying that claims I should be lucky in love is idiotic: I know what I'm talking about!

So here I am, rolling on the ground, feigning illnesses that my imagination doesn't have to travel very far to find.

The warders take an hour before they come to see who's in so much pain that they're howling like I am; and while I carry on doing so, conversation goes on energetically in the cell.

'Is it true that the friends have got old cars?' asks Claude, who pays no attention to my acting talents.

'Yes, apparently,' replies Jacques.

'Just think, there they are outside, going off to an

247

operation in a car, and here we are, like idiots with nothing that we can do.'

'Yes, I realise all right,' growls Jacques.

'Do you think we'll go back?'

'I don't know, perhaps.'

'Who knows if we'll have help?' asks my little brother.

'You mean from outside?' replies Jacques.

'Yes,' continues Claude, almost cheerfully. 'Perhaps they'll give it a try.'

'They won't be able to. Between the Germans on the watchtowers and the French warders in the yard, it would take an army to free us.'

My little brother considers this. His hopes crushed, he sits down again with his back to the wall, adding a sad expression to his pale complexion.

'Good grief Jeannot, couldn't you moan a bit more quietly? We can hardly hear ourselves speak!' he grumbles before shutting up for good.

Jacques stares fixedly at the cell door. We heard the sounds of clodhopping boots on the gangway.

The little hatch in the door slides up and the warder's red face appears. His eyes seem to be searching for the source of the groaning. The lock clicks open, and two warders lift me up off the ground and drag me outside.

'You'd better have something serious, disturbing us out of hours; if you haven't, we'll take away your taste for walking,' says one of them.

'You can count on that!' adds the other.

But I don't care about a bit of additional harassment, since it's taking me to see Enzo.

He's lying on his bed, in a restless sleep. The male nurse receives me and makes me lie down on a stretcher, next to Enzo. He waits for the warders to leave and then turns towards me.

'Are you pretending, so you can have a few hours' rest, or are you really hurting somewhere?'

I point to my belly and grimace. He palpates it hesitantly.

'Have you already had your appendix removed?'

'I don't think so,' I stammer, not really thinking about the consequences of my reply.

'Let me explain something to you,' the man goes on curtly. 'If the answer to my question is still no, it is possible that we're going to open up your belly to take this inflamed appendix out. Of course, there are advantages to that. You exchange two weeks in your cell against the same length of time in a nice bed, and you'll get better food. If you were about to stand trial, it will be delayed for that length of time and if your pal is still here when you wake up, the two of you can even have a little chat.'

The nurse takes a packet of cigarettes out of his white coat, offers me one, sticks the other one between his lips, and carries on in an even more solemn tone.

'Of course, there are also disadvantages. First, I am not a surgeon, just an external student; otherwise, as you

249

suspect, I wouldn't be working as a nurse in Saint-Michel prison. Now listen, I don't say that I have no chance of performing your operation successfully, for I know my manuals off by heart; but you'll understand that it's still not the same as being in expert hands. Next, I won't hide from you that the conditions of hygiene here are not ideal. You're never safe from infection, and if you get one, I also can't hide from you the fact that a nasty fever could carry you off well before the execution squad does. Right; I'm going for a walk outside, just long enough to smoke this cigarette. During this time, you are going to try and remember if the scar I can see low down on your belly, on the right-hand side, mightn't actually be from an appendix operation!'

The nurse left the room, leaving me alone with Enzo. I shook my friend, probably jolting him out of a dream, since he was smiling at me.

'What the hell are you doing here, Jeannot? Did you get yourself beaten up?'

'No, there's nothing wrong with me; I've just come to visit you.'

Enzo sat up on his bed and this time the smile didn't come from any dream.

'That's really nice! You put yourself to all this trouble just to come and see me?'

I nodded in lieu of an answer, because to tell the truth, I felt deeply emotional at seeing my friend Enzo. And the more I looked at him, the more the emotion intensified; also because being close to him, I saw Marius at the Variétés cinema and Rosine smiling at his side.

'You shouldn't have gone to such lengths, Jeannot, I'll soon be walking again, I'm almost better.'

I looked down. I didn't know how to tell him.

'Well, old chap, you don't look very pleased that I'm better!'

'The thing is, Enzo, it's just that it would be better if you weren't doing quite so well, do you understand?'

'Not really, no!'

'Listen to me. As soon as you can walk again, they will take you into the yard to sort out your fate. But as long as you're unable to walk to the stake, you'll be safe. Now do you understand?'

Enzo said nothing. I felt ashamed, because my words were harsh and because if I had been in his place, I wouldn't have liked what he was saying to me. But it was to help him and save his skin, so I swallowed my awkwardness.

'You mustn't get better, Enzo. The Allied landings will eventually come; we have to play for time.'

Enzo suddenly lifted up his sheets to reveal his leg. The scars were immense, but had almost closed.

'And what can I do about it?'

'Jacques hasn't told me anything about that yet; but don't worry, we'll find a way. In the meantime, try to pretend that the pain has suddenly got worse again. If you want I can show you, I've acquired a certain expertise.'

251

Enzo said that he didn't need me to show him that; when it came to pain, his memories were very fresh. I heard the nurse's footsteps returning. Enzo pretended he was still having a nap, and I turned over on my stretcher.

After mature reflection, I decided to reassure the man in the nurse's uniform; my memory had come back to me during that short spell of rest; I was almost certain that, at the age of five, I had been operated on for appendicitis. In any case, the pain seemed to have gone away, and I could even go back to my cell. The nurse slipped a few sulphur tablets into my pocket, to light our cigarettes. He told the warders who were taking me back that they had done the right thing in bringing me here. I had the beginnings of an intestinal blockage, which could have turned nasty, and without their intervention, I could even have died.

On the footbridge, the more cretinous of the two dared to remark that he had saved my life, and I had to thank him. That thank you sometimes still burns in my mouth; but when I think that it was to save Enzo, then the fire goes out.

Back in the cell, I give news of Enzo and it's the first time I've ever seen people sad because their friend is getting better. That tells you that this era is a crazy one, that life has lost all logical meaning and to what extent our world is turning upside down.

So we all pace up and down, arms behind our backs, seeking a solution to save a friend's life.

'In fact,' I ventured, 'we just have to find a way of making sure that the scars don't close up.'

'Thank you, Jeannot,' growls Jacques, 'so far, we're all in agreement with you!'

My little brother, who dreams of studying medicine one day, which in his situation points to a certain optimism, instantly jumps in.

'All you'd need for that is for the wounds to get infected.'

Jacques looks him up and down, wondering if the two brothers might possess a congenital defect predisposing them to say such clichés.

'The problem,' adds Claude, 'is finding the way for the wounds to get infected; from here, it's not easy!'

'Then we need to gain the cooperation of the nurse.'

I reach into my pocket and take out the cigarette and sulphur pills he gave me just now, and tell Jacques that I sensed a certain degree of compassion towards us in the man.

'Enough to take risks in order to save one of us?'

'You know, Jacques, there are heaps of people who are still ready to take risks to spare the life of a kid.'

'Jeannot, I don't care what these people do or don't do; what interests me is this nurse you met. How do you rate our chances with him?'

'I have no idea, or at least, I think he's not a bad guy.'

Jacques walks towards the window, thinking; his hand moves constantly across his emaciated face.

'We have to go back and see him,' he said. 'We have

to ask him to help us so that Enzo falls ill again. He'll know how to do it.'

'And what if he won't?' cuts in Claude.

'Talk to him about Stalingrad, tell him that the Russians are at the borders of Germany, that the Nazis are losing the war, that the Allies will soon invade and that the Resistance will find a way of thanking him when it's all over.'

'And what if he still isn't convinced?' insists my little brother.

'Then we'll threaten him with settling his account when Liberation comes,' replies Jacques.

And Jacques detests his own words, but what do the means matter? Enzo's wound must become gangrenous.

'And how are we going to say all this to the nurse?' asks Claude.

'I haven't a clue yet. If we play the sickness trick again, the screws will smell a rat.'

'I think I know a way,' I say without much thought.

'What are you planning?'

'During the exercise period, the warders are all in the yard. I'll do the one thing they're not expecting: I'll escape to the inside of the prison!'

'Don't act the fool, Jeannot. If you get caught, they'll give you a beating.'

'I thought we had to save Enzo at any cost!'

Darkness returns and the following morning rises, as grey as the others. It's exercise time. At the sound of the warders' boots on the footbridge, I remember Jacques' warning. 'If they catch you, they'll give you a beating', but I think of Enzo. Keys clunk in locks, the doors open, and the prisoners line up in front of Touchin, who counts them.

We acknowledge the chief warder and the cohort sets off down the spiral staircase that leads to the ground floor. We pass beneath the glass roof, which casts a sad light over the gallery; our footsteps echo on the worn stone and we enter the corridor that stretches out towards the yard.

My whole body is tense. It's at the turn that I have to escape, slip, invisible in the midst of the procession, towards the little half-open door. I know that in daytime it is never closed, so that the warder can cast an eye over the occupants of the condemned cell from his chair. I know the way; yesterday I walked it under guard. In front of me is a dual-entrance passage scarcely a metre long and at the end, a few steps leading to the infirmary. The screws are in the yard; luck is with me.

When he sees me, the nurse jumps. From my manner, he knows he has nothing to fear. I talk to him, and he listens without interrupting; and suddenly he sits down on a chair, looking depressed.

'I've had enough of this prison,' he says, 'I've had enough of knowing you're all above my head, I've had enough of my own powerlessness, having to say hello, goodbye, each time I encounter those scum who guard you and beat you up the first chance they get. I've had enough of people being shot in the yard; but I have to live, don't I? I have to feed my wife, and the child we're expecting, you understand?'

And now here I am comforting the nurse! It's me, the Jew, red-haired and bespectacled, dressed in rags, emaciated and covered in the blisters the fleas leave me each morning as a souvenir of their night; it's me, the prisoner watching for death like someone waiting for his turn at the doctor's, me, with the rumbling stomach, me reassuring him about his future!

Hear me telling him everything I still believe: the Russians at Stalingrad, the Eastern fronts collapsing, the landings that are being prepared for and the Germans who will soon fall from the tops of the watchtowers, like apples in the autumn.

And the nurse listens to me: he listens to me like a child who has almost lost his fear. At the end of the story, here we are, the two of us, partners to some extent, our fates linked. When I sense that his bitterness has passed, I tell him again that the life of a lad aged only seventeen lies in his hands.

'Listen to me,' says the nurse. 'Tomorrow, they are going to take him down to the condemned prisoners' cell; between now and then, if he agrees, I will put a bandage around his wound. With a little luck, the infection will come back and they'll bring him back up here. But in the days to come, you will have to find a way of keeping the stratagem going.'

In his cupboards you'll find disinfectant, but the product called an 'infectant' just doesn't exist. So, this luck the nurse is talking about consists of urinating on the bandages.

'Now get out,' he says, looking out of the window. 'The exercise period is finishing.'

I'm back with the prisoners, the screws didn't see anything and little by little, Jacques gets closer to me.

'Well?' he asks me.

'Well, I have a plan!'

And the next day, the day after next and all the days that follow, during exercise period I organised my own, away from the others. As I passed the dual-entrance passage, I made a swift exit from the line of prisoners. All I had to do was turn my head and see Enzo, in the condemned prisoners' cell, sleeping on his bed.

'Gosh, is that you again, Jeannot?' he would always say, stretching.

And each time he would sit up, anxious.

'But what are you doing here again, it's crazy, if they catch you you'll get a beating.'

'I know, Enzo. Jacques has told me a hundred times, but I've got to do your bandages again.'

'It's weird, this thing with you and the nurse.'

'Don't worry about anything, Enzo, he's with us. He knows what he's doing.'

'So? Have you got any news?'

'About what?'

'About the landings, of course! Where have the Americans got to?' demanded Enzo, the way a kid asks when he comes out of a nightmare if all the monsters from his dream have really gone back under the floorboards.

'Listen, the Russians have spared no expense, the Germans are in disarray, people are even saying they might be in the process of liberating Poland.'

'Hey, that's really great.'

'But there's nothing about the landings at the moment.'

I said that in a sad voice and Enzo sensed it; his eyes narrowed, as if death was pulling his sheet towards him, reducing the distance.

And my friend's expression grew fixed as he counted the days.

Enzo raised his head, just a little, enough to shoot me a brief glance.

'You really have to go, Jeannot, if you get caught, you realise?'

'I'd love to leg it, but where am I supposed to go?'

Enzo laughed and it was good to see my friend smile.

'And what about your leg?'

He looked at his leg and shrugged his shoulders.

'Well, I can't tell you that it smells very good!'

'Of course, it'll make it hurt again, but it's better than the worst, isn't it?'

'Don't worry Jeannot, I know; and besides, it will still be less painful than the bullets splintering my bones. Now go, before it's too late.'

His face turns pale, and I feel a kick explode in my back. It's no use him yelling that they're scum, the warders beat me, I'm bent in two, my shoulder is on the ground and they still keep kicking me. My blood spreads out over the flagged floor. Enzo is standing up, his hands clasping the bars of his cell, begging them to leave me alone.

'Well just look at that, you're standing up,' sniggers the warder.

I wish I could faint, no longer feel the blows raining down on my face like an April cloudburst. How far away spring is, on these cold May days.

27

I wake up slowly. My face hurts, and my lips are stuck together with dried blood. My eyes are too swollen to know if the light bulb on the ceiling of the solitary confinement cell is already lit. But I can hear voices through the tiny basement window, so I'm still alive. The friends are exercising in the yard.

A trickle of water flows from the tap fixed to an outside wall. The friends go to it in succession. Frozen fingers can scarcely hold the bar of soap that's used for washing. After they've finished washing, they exchange a few words and go to warm up over where a ray of sunlight stretches over the floor of the yard.

The warders are looking at one of our number. The look in their eyes is the look of a vulture. The kid's legs start to tremble. The prisoners group around him, encircling him as protection.

'You, come with us!' says the chief.

'What do they want?' asks Antoine, the kid, with fear in his face.

'Come on, we've already told you!' orders the screw, pushing his way through to the middle of the detainees.

Hands reach out to seize Antoine's, removing him from life.

'Don't worry,' whispers one of the friends.

'But what do they want with me?' the adolescent repeats endlessly as they drag him by the shoulders.

Everyone here knows very well what the vultures want, and Antoine realises. As he abandons the yard, he looks dumbly at his friends; his goodbye is silent, but the motionless prisoners can hear his farewell.

The warders take him back to his cell. As they enter, they order him to get his things, all his things.

'All my things?' begs Antoine.

'Are you deaf? What did I just say?'

And while Antoine rolls up his straw mattress, it's his life he's packing up; seventeen years of memories, they're soon wrapped up.

Touchin sways from side to side.

'Right, come on,' he says, a disgusting leer on his coarse lips.

Antoine approaches the window, grabs a pencil to scribble a note to those who are still in the yard; he will never see them again.

'That's quite enough,' says the chief, punching him in the back.

They drag Antoine by his hair, which is so fine that they tear it out.

The kid gets up and picks up his bundle, holds it against his belly and follows the two warders.

'Where are we going?' he asks in a frail voice.

'You'll see when you get there!'

And when the chief warder opens the barred door of the condemned cell, Antoine looks up and smiles at the prisoner who welcomes him.

'What the heck are you doing here?' asks Enzo.

'I don't know,' replies Antoine. 'I think they've sent me here so you won't be so alone. What else could it possibly be?'

'Well yes, Antoine,' Enzo replies gently, 'what else could it possibly be?'

Antoine says nothing else. Enzo holds out half of his bread but the kid doesn't want it.

'You have to eat.'

'What's the point?'

Enzo gets up, hops about grimacing and goes to sit on the ground, back to the wall. He lays his hand on Antoine's shoulder and shows him his leg.

'Do you really think I'd go to all this trouble if there wasn't any hope?'

Eyes popping out, Antoine looks at the wound, which is oozing pus.

'So they've succeeded?' he stammers.

'Why yes, as you can see, they've succeeded. I even have news of the landings, if you want to know everything.'

'You, in the condemned cell, have that kind of news?'

'Oh yes! And besides, my little Antoine, you haven't understood anything. Here, it's not the cell you mentioned but the cell belonging to two Resistance fighters, who are still alive. Come here, I have something else to show you.'

Enzo rummages in his pocket and takes out a squashed forty-sous piece.

'I had it in the lining, you know.'

'You've made quite a mess of it,' sighs Antoine.

'First I had to get rid of the portrait of Pétain. Now it's completely smooth, look what I've started to engrave.'

Antoine leans over the coin and reads the first letters. 'What's that you've put?'

'It's not finished yet, but it will say: "There are still Bastilles to capture".'

'You see, Enzo, to be very honest, I don't know if your thing is beautiful or if it's rubbish.'

'It's a citation. It's not from me, it's Jeannot who told it me one day. You're going to help me to finish it, because to be honest with you too, with the fever coming back, I don't have too much strength left, Antoine.'

And while Antoine traces letters with an old nail on

the forty-sous piece, Enzo, stretched out on the boards, makes up news of the war for him.

Emile is a commander, he has raised an army, and now they have cars, mortars and soon guns. The brigade has reformed and they are attacking everywhere.

'You see,' concludes Enzo, 'we're not the ones who are finished, believe me! And what's more, I haven't told you about the landings. They're going to happen soon. When Jeannot gets out of solitary, the English and the Americans will be here, you'll see.'

At night, Antoine doesn't know for sure if Enzo is telling him the truth or if the fever and his delirium are confounding dream and reality.

In the morning, he undoes the bandages, and soaks them in the sanitary bucket before putting them back on. The rest of the day, he watches over Enzo, checks his breathing. When he's not removing his fleas, he works on his coin constantly and each time he engraves a new word, he whispers to Enzo that finally, he's the one who must be right; together, they will see the Liberation.

Every other day, the nurse comes to visit them. The chief warder opens the door and closes it on them, leaving him a quarter of an hour to take care of Enzo, not a moment longer.

Antoine had begun to unwrap the bandages and apologises.

The nurse puts down his treatment box and opens the lid.

'At this rate, we'll have killed him before the firing squad gets around to it.'

He has brought them some aspirin and a little opium.

'Don't give him too much; I won't be back for two days and tomorrow the pain will be even worse.'

'Thank you,' whispers Antoine, as the nurse gets to his feet.

'It's nothing,' says the nurse. 'That's all I have,' he says, sorrowfully.

He thrusts his hands into his pockets and turns towards the cell's iron-barred door.

'Tell me, nurse, what's your first name?' asks Antoine.

'Jules, my name's Jules.'

'Then thank you, Jules.'

And the nurse turns around once more to face Antoine.

'You know, your friend Jeannot has gone back upstairs.'

'Oh! That's good news,' says Antoine. 'And what about the English?'

'What English?'

'The Allies of course, the landings. Don't you keep up with the news?' Antoine asks, stunned.

'I've heard things, but nothing specific.'

'Nothing specific or nothing that wants to be? Because in both our cases, it's not the same, do you understand that, Jules?'

'So what's your first name?' asks the nurse.

'Antoine!'

'Then listen, Antoine, that lad Jeannot I was telling you about just now, well, I lied to him when he came to find me to help your friend with the leg I'd treated too well. I'm not a doctor, just a nurse, and the reason I am here is because I was caught pinching sheets and other odds and ends from the cupboards at the hospital where I worked. I got five years for it; I'm like you, a prisoner. But you're political prisoners, whereas I'm a prisoner through common law, in other words not like you. I'm nothing.'

'Yes you are, you're a good guy,' says Antoine to console him, because he feels keenly that the nurse has a heavy burden of remorse.

'I've failed in everything; I wish I was like you. You're going to tell me that there's nothing to envy about a man who's going to be executed, but I would like to know your pride for a moment, to have your courage. I have met so many lads like you. You know, I was already here when they guillotined Langer. What will I say, after the war? That I was in the nick for pinching sheets?'

'Listen Jules. You can already say that you cared for us, and that's a lot. You can also say that every two days, you took risks to come and redo Enzo's dressings. That's Enzo, the man you're treating, just in case you didn't know. First names are important, Jules. That's how we remember people; even when they are dead, we go on calling them by their first names from time to time; because if we don't, we can't go on. You see Jules, there is a reason for everything, my mother used to say that. You didn't nick your sheets because you're a thief, but because you had to be arrested, in order to be here and help us. There, now that you're feeling better – I can see it in your face, you've got your colour back – tell me, what's happening about the landings?'

Jules walked towards the bars and called for someone to come and fetch him.

'Forgive me, Antoine, but I can't lie any more, I don't have the strength. I haven't heard anything at all about your landings.'

That night, while Enzo is moaning in pain, carried off by fever, Antoine crouches on the floor and finishes engraving the word 'bastilles' on a forty-sous piece.

The next, dismal morning, Antoine recognises the sound of the locks in the next cell being opened and then locked shut again. Footsteps walk into the distance. A few moments later, gripping the window bars, he hears twelve muffled shots striking the execution wall. Antoine lifts his head; in the distance, the 'Partisans' Song' is being sung. It's an immense sound, which passes through the walls of Saint-Michel prison and reaches him, like a hymn to hope.

Enzo opens one eye, and whispers:

'Antoine, do you think that the people will sing when I'm shot, too?'

'Yes, Enzo, they'll sing even louder,' Antoine replies. 'So loudly, even, that their voices will be heard right on the other side of town.'

28

I'm out of solitary and back with my friends. They pooled their resources to offer me some tobacco, enough to roll at least three cigarettes.

In the middle of the night, English bombers fly over our prison. In the distance, we can hear the sirens; I grip the bars and gaze at the sky.

The distant roar of the engines is like the coming of a storm; it takes over the whole space and reaches us.

In the rays of light that sweep the sky, I can see the roofs of our town silhouetted. Toulouse, the rose-coloured city. I think of the war that is being waged on the other side of the walls. I think of the towns in Germany and the towns in England.

'Where are they going?' Claude asks, as he sits on his straw mattress.

I turn around and, in the half-light, look at my friends

and their emaciated bodies. Jacques is sitting with his back against the wall, Claude with his knees drawn up, and curled into a ball. Mess tins are banged against the walls and, from other cells, voices rise up to say to us, 'Can you hear that, lads?'

Yes, we can all hear those sounds of freedom, so near and yet so far, a few thousand metres above our heads.

In the planes up there are guys who are free, with coffee in Thermos flasks, biscuits and plenty of cigarettes; just above us, do you realise? And the pilots, in their leather jackets, pass through the clouds, float amid the stars. Beneath their wings the earth is dark, with not a single light, not even from the prisons, and they fill our hearts with a sudden burst of hope. God but I wish I could be one of them, I would have given my life to be sitting beside them, but I have already given my life to freedom, here, in a stone-walled cell in Saint-Michel prison.

'So where are they going?' repeats my little brother.

'How do I know?!'

'To Italy!' declares one of us.

'No, when they go there they take off from Africa,' answers Samuel.

'Then where?' Claude asks again. 'What are they doing here?'

'I don't know, I don't know, but stay away from the window, you never know.'

'And what about you? You're glued to the bars!'

'I'll watch and tell you what's happening . . .'

Whistling sounds tear through the darkness, the first explosions make Saint-Michel prison tremble and all the prisoners get up and cheer. 'Can you hear that, lads?'

Yes, we can hear. It's Toulouse that is being bombed and the sky reddens in the distance. The anti-aircraft guns begin to respond, but the whistling sounds go on. The others have joined me at the bars. What a firework display!

'But what are they doing?' begs Claude.

'I don't know,' mutters Jacques.

The voice of a comrade chimes in and begins to sing. I recognise Charles's accent, and my mind goes back to the station at Loubers.

My little brother is next to me, Jacques opposite, François and Samuel on their mattresses; below are Enzo and Antoine. The 35th brigade is still in existence.

'If only one of those bombs could bring down the walls of this jail . . .' says Charles.

And tomorrow, when we wake, we will learn that tonight, the planes in the sky stretched out the dawn of the Allied landings beneath their wings.

Jacques was right; spring is returning. Enzo and Antoine may yet be saved.

At dawn on the following day, three men in black entered the yard. A uniformed officer followed them.

The chief warder greets them; even he is stunned.

'Wait for me in the office,' he says, 'I must inform them, we weren't expecting you.'

And while the warder is retracing his steps, a lorry comes through the gateway and twelve helmeted men jump down from it.

This morning, Touchin and Theil are on rest-days. Delzer is on duty.

'It had to fall to me,' grumbles the chief warder's deputy.

He passes through the double-entrance gate and approaches the cell. Antoine hears his footsteps and stands up.

'What are you doing here? It's still dark and it's not time to fill the mess tins.'

'There you go,' says Delzer. 'They're here.'

'What time is it?' asks the young boy.

The warder consults his watch. It's five o'clock.

'Are they here for us?' asks Antoine.

'They haven't said anything.'

'So is somebody going to come and fetch us?'

'In half an hour, I think. They have papers to fill out, and then all the prisoners must be locked up.'

The guard rummages in his pocket and takes out a packet of Gauloises. He passes it through the bars.

'All the same, you'd best wake up your friend.'

'But he can't stand up, they're not going to do that! They have no right, damn them!' rages Antoine.

'I know,' says Delzer, hanging his head. 'I'll leave you. I may be the one who comes back shortly.'

Antoine approaches Enzo's straw mattress. He taps him on the shoulder.

'Wake up.'

Enzo starts and opens his eyes.

'It's going to happen now,' whispers Antoine. 'They're here.'

'For both of us?' asks Enzo, his eyes growing moist.

'No. Not for you, they can't. It would be too disgusting.'

'Don't say that, Antoine. I've become accustomed to us being together. I'll go with you.'

'Shut up, Enzo! You can't walk, and I forbid you to get up, do you hear me? I can go on my own, you know.'

'I know, my friend, I know.'

'Hey, we have two cigarettes, real ones. We're allowed to smoke them.'

Enzo sits up and strikes a match. He takes a long draw and watches the curling smoke.

'So the Allies still haven't landed?'

'Doesn't look like it, old fellow.'

In the dormitory cell, everyone is waiting as usual. This morning, the soup is late. It's six o'clock and the trusted prisoners still haven't entered the building to start their work. Jacques is pacing up and down; you can see from his face that he's worried. Samuel is still prostrate, against the wall. Claude stands at the bars, but the yard is still grey so he comes back to sit down.

'What the hell are they playing at?' ponders Jacques.

'The scumbags!' replies my little brother.

'You think that . . .?'

'Shut up, Jeannot!' orders Jacques, and he goes back to sit down, back to the door, head on his knees.

Delzer has returned to the condemned cell; his face is haggard.

'I'm sorry, lads.'

'And how are they going to get him out there?' begs Antoine.

'He'll be carried on a chair. That's the cause of the delay. I tried to dissuade them, to tell them that these things are not to be done, but they've had enough of waiting for him to get better.'

'The scum!' roars Antoine.

And it's Enzo who comforts him.

'I want to walk out there!'

He stands up, stumbles, and falls. The bandage comes undone; his leg is completely riddled with infection.

'They're going to bring you a chair,' sighs Delzer. 'There's no point in you suffering more pain.'

And behind these words, Enzo hears the footsteps coming for them.

'Did you hear?' says Samuel, standing up.

'Yes,' murmurs Jacques.

The gendarmes' footsteps echo in the yard.

'Go to the window, Jeannot, and tell us what's happening.'

I go up to the bars. Claude gives me a leg up. Behind me, the comrades are waiting for me to tell them the sad story of a world in which two kids lost in the half-light of dawn are led towards death, the one where one of them is swaying on a chair carried by two gendarmes.

The one who can stand is tied to the post; the other placed beside him.

Twelve men line up. Jacques is clenching his hands so tightly that I can hear his fingers cracking, and twelve shots that crack in the dawn of a final day. Jacques roars 'No!' even louder than the songs that are beginning, even longer than the couplets of the 'Marseillaise' that are being thundered out.

Our friends' heads nod and fall, their pierced chests empty of blood; Enzo's leg is still in spasm. It kicks out and the chair falls onto its side.

His face is in the sand, and in the silence of death, I swear to you that he was smiling.

That night, five thousand ships left England and crossed the Channel. At dawn, eighteen thousand parachutists came down from the sky and American, English and Canadian soldiers landed in their thousands on the beaches of France; three thousand lost their lives there in the early hours of that morning; the majority lie in Normandy's cemeteries. We will never forget.

It is 6 June 1944, and the time is six o'clock. At dawn, in the yard of Saint-Michel prison in Toulouse, Enzo and Antoine were executed by firing squad.

29

During the three weeks that followed, the Allies went through hell in Normandy. Each day brought its share of victories and hope; Paris had not yet been freed, but the spring that Jacques had waited for so long was on its way, and even though it was late, nobody held that against it.

Each morning, during our walk, we exchange news of the war with our Spanish comrades. Now, we are certain, we shall soon be freed. But Chief Constable Marty, whose hatred has never left him, has decided otherwise. At the end of the month, he orders the prison administration to hand over all political prisoners to the Nazis.

At dawn, we are gathered together in the gallery, beneath the grey glass roof. We are all carrying our kit, our mess tins and our meagre possessions.

The yard is full of lorries and the Waffen-SS are barking at us to get into rows. The prison is in a state of siege. We are surrounded. The soldiers yell, and make us move forward by hitting us with their rifle butts. In the line I rejoin Jacques, Charles, François, Marc, Samuel, my little brother and all the surviving comrades of the 35th brigade.

Arms behind his back and flanked by several warders, chief warder Theil looks at us, his eyes sparkling with hatred.

I lean towards Jacques' ear and whisper:

'Look at him, he's as white as a sheet. You see, I'm even happier to be in my place than in his.'

'But you do realise where we're going, Jeannot!'

'Yes, but we'll go with our heads held high and he will always live in hushed whispers.'

We had all hoped for freedom, and now we were all leaving in a row, chained once the prison gates opened. We walked through the town, under escort, and the few passers-by, silent on this pale morning, watched the cohort of prisoners being taken away to death.

At Toulouse railway station, where memories came back to me, the goods wagons awaited us.

As we line up on the platform, we can all work out where this train is taking us. It is one of those that, for many months, have been traversing Europe, the ones whose passengers never return.

Terminus at Dachau, Ravensbrück, Auschwitz, Birkenau. We were pushed onto this ghost train like animals.

PART THREE

30

The sun still isn't very high in the sky, but the platform
is already bathed in the day's warmth as the four hundred
prisoners from the Vernet camp wait there. The hundred
and fifty detainees from Saint-Michel prison join them.
A few passenger carriages are coupled between the goods
wagons that are reserved for us. These are for Germans
guilty of minor offences. They are returning home, under
escort. Members of the Gestapo, who have obtained
permission to be repatriated with their families, climb
on next. The Waffen-SS sit on the footboards, their rifles
on their knees. Beside the locomotive, the train
commander, Lieutenant Schuster, gives orders to his
soldiers. At the back of the train, a flat-wagon is attached,
on which an immense searchlight and a machine gun are
mounted. The SS knock us about a bit. One of them
didn't like the face of a particular prisoner. He hits him

with his rifle-butt. The man rolls onto the ground and gets up holding his belly. The doors of the cattle trucks open. I turn around and look for one last time at the colour of the sky. Not a cloud; there's a hot summer's day in prospect, and I'm leaving for Germany.

But the platform is black with people; lines of deportees have formed in front of each wagon, and strangely, I hear not another sound. As we are pushed forward, Claude leans over to whisper in my ear.

'It's the last journey this time.'

'Shut up!'

'How long do you think we'll last in there?'

'As long as we have to. I forbid you to die!'

Claude shrugs his shoulders. It's his turn to get inside. He holds out his hand to me and I follow him. Behind us, the door of the wagon closes.

It takes a little time for my eyes to become accustomed to the darkness. Planks surrounded by barbed wire are nailed to the high windows. There are seventy of us piled into this wagon, perhaps a little more. I realise that in order to rest, we will have to take turns in lying down.

It is soon noon; the heat is unbearable and the train still isn't moving. If we got going, we might have a little air, but nothing happens. An Italian who can't bear his thirst any longer pisses into his cupped hands and drinks his own urine. Here he is, staggering and passing out. Three of us support him beneath the tiny current of air that comes in through the skylight. But while we are bringing him back to life, others lose consciousness and collapse.

'Listen!' whispers my little brother.

We listen hard and all look, doubtfully.

'Shh,' he insists.

It's the rumble of the storm he can hear, and already big drops of rain are bursting on the roof. Meyer rushes forward, stretches out his arms to the barbed wire and hurts himself. What does it matter – a little rainwater mixes with the blood on his skin and he licks it off. Others fight over the space he leaves. Thirsty, exhausted, frightened, the men are in the process of becoming animals; but after all, how can you blame them for losing their reason. Are we not cooped up in animal trucks?

With a jolt, the train sets off. It moves a few metres and then halts.

It's my turn to sit down. Claude is beside me, back to the wall, knees drawn up so as to take up as little space as possible. It's forty degrees and I can tell that his breathing is halting, like the breathing of dogs who take a midday siesta on the hot stone.

The wagon is silent. From time to time, a man coughs before passing out. In death's anteroom, I wonder what the train driver is thinking about; what the German families think, sitting on the comfortable seats in their compartments; I think of those men and women who, two wagons away from us, are eating and drinking their fill. Are there a few among them who imagine these

281

prisoners suffocating, these lifeless adolescents, all these human beings whose dignity is being stolen from them before they are murdered?

'Jeannot, we have to get out of here before it's too late.'

'How?'

'I don't know, but I'd like you to think about it with me.'

I don't know if Claude said that because he really believes escape is possible, or simply because he could sense that I was losing hope. Mother always told us that life hangs solely on the hope we accord it. I wish I could smell her perfume, hear her voice and remember that only a few months ago, I was a child. I see her smile freeze once again, and she says words to me that I don't understand. 'Save the life of your little brother,' her lips say, 'don't give up, Raymond, don't give up!'

'Mother?'

A slap lands on my cheek.

'Jeannot?'

I shake my head and in my grogginess, I see my little brother's confused face.

'I think you were a hair's-breadth from passing out,' he tells me, apologising.

'Stop calling me Jeannot, it doesn't mean anything any more!'

'Until we have won the war, I shall continue to call you Jeannot!'

'As you wish.'

*   *   *

Evening comes. The train hasn't moved all day. Tomorrow, it will change tracks several times, but without ever leaving the station. The soldiers shout, new wagons are coupled on. At the end of the following day, the Germans give everybody some jam and a round rye loaf to last three days, but still no water.

The following day, when the train finally sets off, none of us has the strength to realise immediately.

Alvarez gets up. He observes the lines the light makes on the floor as it passes through the planks nailed to the window. He turns around and looks at us, before tearing his hands by pushing back the strands of barbed wire.

'What are you doing?' asks one man in fright.

'What do you think?'

'You're not going to escape, I hope?'

'What does it matter to you?' replies Alvarez, sucking the blood that's flowing from his fingers.

'It matters to me that if you get caught, they will shoot ten of us by way of reprisals. Didn't you hear that when they said it at the station?'

'Well if you've decided to stay here and they choose you, thank me. I will have shortened your sufferings. Where do you think this train is taking us?'

'I don't know and I don't want to know!' moans the man, clinging to Alvarez's jacket.

'To the death camps! That's where all the ones who haven't already suffocated will end up, the ones killed by the swelling of their own tongues. Do you realise?'

283

roars Alvarez, detaching himself from the deportee's grip.

'Escape and leave him alone,' cuts in Jacques; and he helps Alvarez to remove the planks from the skylight.

Alvarez is at the end of his strength. He's only nineteen and despair mingles with his anger.

The laths are finally brought inside the wagon. Air enters at last, and even if some are afraid of what our friend is about to attempt, everyone appreciates the cool air that enters.

'Bloody hell!' grumbles Alvarez. 'Just look at that bloody moonlight, you'd think it was the middle of the day.'

Jacques looks through the window. In the distance there's a bend, and a forest is visible in the darkness.

'Hurry up, if you want to jump it's now!'

'Who wants to follow me?'

'I do,' replies Titonel.

'So do I,' adds Walter.

'We'll see after that,' orders Jacques. 'Go on, climb up; I'll give you a leg up.'

And so our comrade prepares to carry out the plan he's had in mind ever since the wagon doors closed, two days ago. Two days and two nights, longer than all those in hell.

Alvarez hauls himself up to the window and slides his legs through first before turning around. He'll have to grab hold of the side of the wagon, and slide his body down. The wind slaps his cheeks and gives him back a little strength, unless they are revived by the hope of salvation. All he needs is for the German soldier at the back of the train, the one behind the machine gun, not to see him; all he has to do is not look in his direction. A few seconds only, the time it takes for the little wood to get closer; that's where he'll jump. And if he doesn't break his neck jumping onto the ballast, then he'll find that salvation in the dense forest. A few more seconds, and Alvarez lets go. Immediately, the rattle of machine-gun fire sounds; shooting is coming from everywhere.

'I told you!' shouts the man. 'It was madness.'

'Shut up!' orders Jacques.

Alvarez rolls to the ground. The bullets tear the earth around him. He has broken ribs, but he's alive. And now he's running for his life. Behind him, he hears the train's brakes squeal. A mob is already after him; and while he runs in and out of the trees at a breathless pace, shots ring out around him, striking slivers of bark from the pine trees that surround him.

The forest grows brighter; in front of him stretches out the Garonne, like a long, silver ribbon in the night.

Eight months of prison, eight months deprived of food, plus those terrible days on the train; but Alvarez has a fighter's soul. He has within him the strength that brings freedom. And as he throws himself into the river, Alvarez tells himself that if he succeeds, others will follow; so he won't drown, his friends are worth this journey. No, Alvarez will not die this evening.

Four hundred metres further on, he hauls himself onto the opposite bank. Staggering, he walks towards the only light that shines before him. It's the lighted window of a house that stands beside a field. A man comes to meet him, takes him under his arm and carries him to his home. He had heard the gunshots. He and his daughter offer him hospitality.

Back at the track, the SS who did not find their prey are furious. They kick the wagons and hit them with the butts of their rifles, as if to forbid anyone to make the slightest sound. There will probably be reprisals, but not for the moment. Lieutenant Schuster has decided to get on the move again. The Resistance movement is spreading throughout the region, and it is not a good idea to stay here for too long. The train could be attacked. The soldiers get back on board and the locomotive sets off.

Nuncio Titonel, who was due to jump just after Alvarez, had to give up on the idea. He promises he will make an attempt next time. As soon as he speaks, Marc hangs his head. Nuncio is Damira's brother. After their arrest, Marc and Damira were separated, and he has no idea what has happened to her since they were interrogated. In Saint-Michel prison, he never had any news and he couldn't stop thinking about her. Nuncio looks at him, sighs and comes over to sit down next to him. Never before have they dared to speak of the woman who could have made them brothers if they had been given the freedom to love each other.

'Why didn't you tell me you were together?' asks Nuncio.

'Because she forbade me to.'

'What a strange idea!'

'She was afraid of how you'd take it, Nuncio. I'm not Italian . . .'

'If only you knew how little I care that you're not from our homeland. All I care about is that you love and respect her. We are all foreigners to someone.'

'Yes, we are all foreigners to someone.'

'In any event, I knew about it from the first day.'

'Who told you?

'You should have seen her face when she came back to the house – it must have been the first time you kissed! And whenever she had to go on a mission with you, or go somewhere to meet you, she took an incredibly long time getting ready. I didn't have to be all that smart to work it out.'

'Please, Nuncio, don't talk about her in the past tense.'

'You know, Marc, by this time she must be in Germany, and I'm under no illusion about what happens there.'

'Then why talk to me about her now?'

'Because, before, I thought we were going to get out of this, that we would be freed. I didn't want you to give up.'

'If you escape, I'm coming with you, Nuncio!'

Nuncio looks at Marc. He lays his hand on his shoulder and clasps him tightly to his chest.

'The thing that reassures me is that Osna, Sophie and Marianne are with her; you'll see, they'll stick together. Osna will see that they get out of it, she'll never give up, believe me!'

'Do you think Alvarez has got away?' continues Nuncio.

We did not know if our friend had survived, but in any case, he had succeeded in escaping and for all of us, hope was reborn.

A few hours later, we arrived in Bordeaux.

In the early hours, the doors open. Finally we are given a little water, which we have to drink by first moistening our lips, then taking little sips, before the throat will open up and allow the liquid to pass through. Lieutenant Schuster gives us permission to get out in groups of four or five. Just enough time to relieve ourselves away from the track. Each group is surrounded by armed soldiers; some of them are carrying grenades, to fend off a mass escape. We have to squat down in front of them; it's just one more humiliation, we have to live with it. My little brother looks at me sadly. I give him the best smile I can manage, but I don't think it's a very good one.

31

4 July

The doors are closed once more and the temperature instantly climbs. The train sets off. On board the wagon, the men are lying down on the floor. We, the comrades of the brigade, are sitting with our backs against the wagon's back wall. Looking at us like that, you might think that we are their children, and yet, yet . . .

We discuss the itinerary. Jacques bets on Angoulême, Claude dreams of Paris, Marc is certain that we're travelling towards Poitiers, while the majority agree on Compiègne. There is a transit camp there that serves as a connecting station. We all know that the war is continuing in Normandy, and it appears that there is fighting in the vicinity of Tours. The Allied armies are advancing towards us, and we are advancing towards death.

'You know,' says my little brother, 'I think we're more hostages than prisoners. Perhaps they'll let us go at the border. All these Germans want to go home, and if the train doesn't reach Germany in time, Schuster and his men will be captured. In fact, they fear that the Resistance may slow them down too much by blowing up the tracks. That's why the train isn't moving forward. Schuster is trying to get through the holes in the net. On the one hand, he's caught in a vice by our brothers in the Maquis, and on the other, he's scared stiff of a bombardment by English planes.'

'Where did you get that idea? Did you dream it up all on your own?'

'No,' he admits. 'While we were pissing on the tracks, Meyer heard two soldiers talking.'

'And Meyer understands German?' asks Jacques.

'He speaks Yiddish . . .'

'And where is Meyer, now?'

'In the next wagon,' answers Claude.

And scarcely has he finished speaking when the train comes to a halt once again. Claude hauls himself up to the small opening. In the distance, he can see the platform of a small station; it's Parcoul-Médillac.

It is ten o'clock in the morning, and there's no sign of any travellers or railway workers. Silence envelops the surrounding countryside. The day draws out in unbearable heat. We are suffocating. To help us hang on, Jacques tells us a story. François sits beside him and listens, lost in thought. A man moans at the back of the wagon, and loses consciousness. Three of us carry him to the skylight. There's a little breath of air there. Another spins around in circles; it seems that madness is taking him over. He begins to howl, and his lament is piercing. He too falls. And so the day passes, a few metres from the little railway station, one July 4th, at Parcoul-Médillac.

32

It is four o'clock in the afternoon. Jacques has no more saliva, and has fallen silent. A few whispers disturb the unbearable waiting.

'You're right, we're going to have to think about escaping,' I say, sitting next to Claude.

'We'll only make the attempt when we're sure we can all escape together,' orders Jacques.

'Shh!' whispers my little brother.

'What's the matter?'

'Shut up and listen!'

Claude gets up, and I do likewise. He walks to the window and looks in front of him. Is it once again the sound of the storm that my little brother can hear before anyone else?

The Germans leave the train and run towards the fields, led by Schuster. The members of the Gestapo and their families rush to the shelter of the embankments. There, the soldiers set up machine guns trained on us, as if to prevent any attempt at escape. Claude is now looking at the sky, listening intently.

'Planes! Back away! All back away and lie down on the floor,' he yells.

We hear the humming sound of the approaching planes.

The young squadron leader celebrated his twenty-third birthday yesterday, in the officers' mess at an aerodrome in the south of England. Today, he is gliding through the air. His hand holds the joystick, his thumb on the button that activates the machine guns on the wings. Before him he sees a stationary train on the railway track. The attack will be an easy one. He gives the order to his team members to get into formation, ready for the attack, and his plane dives towards the ground. The wagons are outlined in his visor; there's no doubt this is a goods train transporting German merchandise to supply the front. The order is given to destroy everything. Behind him, his wing-men get into position in the blue sky; they are ready. The train is within range now. The pilot's finger brushes the trigger. In his cockpit too, the heat is stifling.

Now! The wings sputter and the tracer bullets, long as knives, fly thick and fast towards the train as the squadron flies above it, under answering fire from the Germans.

In our wagon, the wooden walls splinter at the repeated

impacts. Projectiles whistle at us from every direction; a man howls and crumples up, another is holding his own entrails, which are pouring out of his torn belly, and a third has a leg torn off; it is carnage. The prisoners try to protect themselves behind their meagre baggage; a derisory hope of surviving the attack. Jacques is thrown on top of François, his body providing him with protection. The four English planes come one after the other, the rhythmic roar of their engines thuds in our temples, but already they are moving away and climbing into the sky. Through the opening, we see them aiming in the distance and coming back towards the train, at a high altitude this time.

I am worried about Claude and I hold him tightly in my arms. His face is so pale.

'Is something wrong?'

'No, but your neck is bleeding,' says my little brother, running his hand across my wound.

It's only a splinter, which has cut into the flesh. All around us, desolation reigns. There are six dead and the same number of wounded in the wagon. Jacques, Charles and François are safe. We don't know anything about the losses in the other wagons. On the embankment, a German soldier lies bathed in his own blood.

We listen for the distant sound of the planes returning.

'They're coming back,' announces Claude.

I looked at the distressed smile on his face, as if he wanted to say farewell to me but didn't dare disobey the order I had given him to stay alive. I don't know what took hold of me. My actions were simply automatic, driven by that other order, which had brought Mother to me in a recent nightmare. 'Save your little brother's life.'

'Pass me your shirt!' I shouted to Claude.

'What?'

'Take it off quickly and give it to me.'

I did the same with mine; it was blue, while my little brother's was vaguely white. And from the body of a man who lay before me, I took the fabric reddened with blood.

With the three pieces of fabric in my hand, I rushed to the opening. Claude gave me a leg up. I stuck my arm out and, watching the planes that were aiming at us, I waved my hand and my makeshift flag.

In his cockpit, the young squadron leader is finding the sunlight uncomfortable. He turns his head slightly to one side, so as not to be dazzled. His thumb strokes the trigger. The train is still out of range, but in a few seconds' time, he will be able to give the order to fire the second salvo. In the distance, smoke is coming from the loco-motive's side. Proof that the bullets have pierced its boiler.

One more pass, perhaps, and this train will never be able to set off again.

The tip of his left wing seems to melt into his wing-man's. He signals to him: the attack is imminent. He looks into his visor and is astonished by a patch of colour that appears on the side of one wagon. It looks as if it's moving. Is it a flash of light off the barrel of a gun? The young pilot knows about light and its strange diffractions. So many times, up here in the sky, he's flown through rainbows that weren't visible from down below, like multicoloured lines linking the clouds together.

The plane begins its dive, and the pilot's hand grips the joystick in readiness. In front of him, the red and blue patch continues to move about. Coloured rifles don't exist, and besides, doesn't that white fabric in the middle complete the appearance of a French flag? His gaze locks onto these pieces of fabric, being shaken from inside a wagon. The English pilot's heart misses a beat; his thumb stops moving.

'*Break, break, break!*' he yells into the on-board radio, and to make sure that his wing-men have heard his order, he pulls the nose up and wiggles his wings, then regains altitude.

Behind him, the planes break formation and attempt to follow him; they look like a squadron of frightened bumblebees climbing into the sky.

From the window, I see the planes flying away. I can feel my little brother's arms giving way beneath my feet, but I cling to the wall of the wagon, to see the aviators keep on flying.

I wish I were one of them; tonight, they will be back in England.

'Well?' begs Claude.

'Well, I think they understood. The way they wiggle their wings is a salute.'

*   *   *

Up above, the planes are regrouping. The young squadron leader informs the other pilots. The train they machine-gunned is not just carrying goods. There are prisoners on board. He saw one of them waving a flag to let them know.

The pilot angles his joystick; the plane leans and makes a turn. Down below, Jeannot sees it make a U-turn and go back the same way to position itself at the rear of the train. And then, here it is again, diving towards the ground; this time, it appears calm. The aeroplane climbs back up along the train's side. It's almost hedge-hopping, only a few metres above the ground.

Along the embankments, the German soldiers can't get over it; not one of them dares move. As for the pilot, his eyes are trained on this makeshift flag, which a prisoner is still waving through the side of a wagon. When he is level with it, he slows down even more, as far as he can go without stalling. His face turns. For the space of two seconds, two pairs of blue eyes lock on to each other: those of a young English officer on a Royal Air Force fighter, and those of a young Jewish prisoner who's being deported to Germany. The pilot's hand rises to his visor and he honours the prisoner, who returns his salute.

Then the plane climbs, accompanying its flight with a final wiggle of its wings.

'They're gone?' asks Claude.
'Yes. Tonight, they'll be in England.'

'One day you'll be a pilot, Raymond, I swear it to you!'

'I thought you wanted to call me Jeannot until . . .'

'The war is almost won, big brother, look at the vapour-trails in the sky. Spring has returned. Jacques was right.'

That day, 4 July 1944, at ten minutes past four in the afternoon, two pairs of eyes met in the middle of the war; for scarcely a few seconds, but for two young men, it lasted for an eternity.

The Germans have got to their feet and are reappearing amid the wild grasses. They come back to the train. Schuster rushes to the locomotive to evaluate the damage. Meanwhile, four men are taken to the wall of a warehouse built next to the railway station. Four prisoners who had attempted to escape, taking advantage of the air attack. They are lined up and immediately executed by machine gun. Stretched out on the platform, their inert bodies bathed in blood, their glassy eyes seem to observe us and say that for them, hell came to an end today, along that railway line.

The door of our wagon opens, and the Feldgendarme retches. He takes a step back and vomits. Two other soldiers join him, one hand in front of their mouths so as not to smell the putrid air in here. The acrid odour of urine mingles with that of excrement, and with the stench of Bastien's entrails: it was he whose stomach was torn open.

An interpreter announces that the dead will be taken out of the wagons within a few hours, and we know that with the prevailing heat, every minute to come will be unbearable.

I wonder if they will bother to bury the four murdered men who still lie a few metres away.

Help is called for from the neighbouring wagons. There are people of all trades on this train. The ghosts occupying it are workmen, lawyers, carpenters, engineers, teachers. A doctor, himself a prisoner, is given permission to tend the numerous wounded. His name is Van Dick, and he is aided by a Spanish surgeon who served as a doctor for three years in the camp at le Vernet. It's all very well spending the hours to come trying everything to save a few lives; it's all pointless. They have no equipment and the unbearable heat will soon finish off those who are still moaning. Some beg for their families to be informed, others seem to smile as they die, as though delivered from their sufferings. Here at Parcoul-Médillac, at nightfall, people are dying by the score.

The locomotive is out of service. The train won't be going anywhere this evening. Schuster orders another one; it will arrive during the night.

Between now and then, the railwaymen will have had the time to sabotage it a little. Its water tank will leak, and the train will have to stop more often to fill it up.

*   *   *

The night is silent. We should rebel but we no longer have the strength. The scorching heat weighs upon us like a lead coating and we all plunge into semi-unconsciousness. Our tongues are beginning to swell, making breathing difficult. Alvarez was right.

33

'Do you think he got away?' asks Jacques.

Alvarez was worthy of the luck that life had given him. The man and his daughter who had sheltered him had suggested that he should remain with them until the Liberation. However, scarcely recovered from his injuries, Alvarez thanked them for looking after him and feeding him, but he must return to the fight. The man did not insist; he knew that Alvarez had made up his mind. So he cut out a map of the region that featured on his post office calendar and gave it to the partisan. He also gave him a knife and invited him to go to Sainte-Bazeille. The stationmaster there belonged to the Resistance. When Alvarez arrived there, he sat on the bench facing the platform. The stationmaster soon spotted him and had him brought into his office immediately. He informed Alvarez that the local SS were still

301

looking for an escaped prisoner. He took him to a shed where a few railwaymen's tools and clothes were kept, gave him a grey jacket, adjusted a cap on his head and handed him a light sledgehammer. After checking that he was correctly dressed, the stationmaster asked Alvarez to follow him along the track. On the way, they encountered two German patrols. The first paid them no attention, the second greeted them.

They reached his guide's house at nightfall. There, Alvarez was welcomed by the stationmaster's wife and his two children. The family did not ask for anything. For three days, he was fed and cared for with infinite love. His saviours were Basques. On the third morning, a black front-wheel-drive car drew up outside the little house, where Alvarez was regaining his strength. Inside were three partisans who had come to fetch him and take him back to the fight.

6 July
At dawn, the train resumes its journey. We soon pass the small station belonging to a village with an odd name. The sign-boards read: 'Charmant'. Given the circumstances, the geographical irony of passing through the charming place makes us laugh. But suddenly, the train halts again. While we are suffocating in our wagons, Schuster fumes over this umpteenth stop and considers a new itinerary. The German lieutenant knows that progress northwards is impossible. The Allies are advancing inexorably and he is increasingly fearful of

operations by the Resistance, which is blowing up the rails to slow down our deportation.

Suddenly the door opens and rolls loudly aside. Dazzled, we see a German soldier framed in the doorway, barking at us. Claude looks at me doubtfully.

'The Red Cross is here, we have to go and fetch a bucket from the platform,' says a deportee who acts as our interpreter.

Jacques designates me. I jump out of the wagon and fall to my knees. It seems my red-headed countenance displeases the Feldgendarme who is standing in front of me: our eyes have only just met, and already he's dealt me a hefty blow to the face with his rifle-butt. I step back and fall on my arse. Groping around, I search for my spectacles. At last here they are, under my hand. I collect up the remains and stuff them in my pocket, and in a thick fog, I keep close behind the soldier who leads me behind a hedge. With the barrel of his rifle, he indicates a bucket of water and a cardboard box, which contains round loaves of black bread to be shared out. This is how food supplies are organised for each wagon. And I realise that we and the people from the Red Cross must never see each other.

When I come back to the wagon, Jacques and Charles rush to the door to help me to get in. All I can see around me is a thick fog, tinted red. Charles washes my face, but the mist doesn't go away. And then I realise what has just happened to me. As I've told you, nature didn't

303

think it was funny enough, just giving me hair the colour of carrots; it also had to make me as blind as a bat. Without my glasses, the world is a blur, I am blind, just about able to tell if it's day or night, scarcely capable of detecting the shapes moving around me. And yet I notice my little brother's presence at my side.

'Good grief, that scumbag really messed you up.'

In my hands I hold what remains of my spectacles. A little piece of glass on the right of the frame, and another, scarcely any larger, dangling on the left side. Claude must be very tired, not to see that his brother isn't wearing anything on his nose. And I know that he doesn't yet realise the scope of the problem. Now, he will have to escape without me; there's no question of him burdening himself with someone infirm. Jacques, on the other hand, has understood everything; he asks Claude to leave us and comes to sit down next to me.

'Don't give up!' he whispers.

'And what am I supposed to do now?'

'We'll find a solution.'

'Jacques, I've always regarded you as an optimist but you've really excelled yourself this time!'

Claude returns and almost pushes me out of the way to make room for him.

'Guess what, I've thought of something for your spectacles. We have to take the bucket back, don't we?'

'And then?'

'Well, as they won't allow any contact between us and

304

the Red Cross, the bucket will have to be put back behind the hedge, once it's empty.'

I was wrong. Not only had Claude understood my situation, he was already in the process of devising a plan. And however impossible it might be, I found myself wondering if from now on, out of the two of us, the little brother would be me.

'I still don't understand what you're getting at.'

'There's still a piece of glass on either side of your frame. Enough for an optician to recognise your degree of myopia.'

With the aid of a splinter of wood and a bit of thread taken from my shirt, I was making efforts to repair the irreparable. Claude put his hands on mine in exasperation.

'Stop trying to fix them! Listen to me, for goodness' sake! You will never be able to jump out of the window, nor take to your heels, with glasses in that state. On the other hand, if we were to put the remains at the bottom of the bucket, perhaps someone would understand and come to our aid.'

My eyes were moist, I must confess. Not only because my brother's solution overflowed with his love, but because at that moment, in the depths of our helplessness and distress, Claude still had enough strength to believe in hope. I was so proud of him that day, I loved him so much that I still wonder if I took the time to tell him so.

'His idea sounds good,' said Jacques.

'It's far from stupid,' added François, and all the others agreed.

I didn't believe it for a second. Imagining the bucket escaping the search before the Red Cross took it back. Dreaming that someone would discover the pieces of my spectacles and take an interest in my fate, in the sight problems of a prisoner being deported to Germany. It was more than unlikely. But even Charles considered my brother's plan 'splendid'.

So, defying my doubts and my pessimism, I agreed to part with the two tiny pieces of glass that would just have enabled me to make out the walls of the wagon.

To give back to my friends a little of the hope they were giving me with such generosity, as Claude had suggested, late that afternoon I placed what was left of my glasses in the empty bucket as it left the wagon. And when the door closed again, I saw the shadow of the departing Red Cross nurse as the darkness of death overwhelmed me.

That night, a storm broke over Charmant. The rain trickled from the roof and ran into the wagon through the holes left by the English aircrafts' bullets. Those who still had the strength stood up, heads in the air, to catch the drops in their wide-open mouths.

34

We've set off again. It's hopeless. I'll never see my spectacles again.

At dawn, we arrive in Angoulême. Around us, all is desolation. The station has been destroyed by the Allied bombing. As the train slows down, we gaze in amazement at the disembowelled buildings, the calcified carcases of wagons, embedded in each other. Locomotives still waste away on the tracks, sometimes lying on their sides. Sinister cranes lie like skeletons. And along the torn-up rails that point to the sky, a few incredulous workmen, spades and pickaxes in hand, watch our train pass by in terror. Seven hundred ghosts, passing through an apocalyptic landscape.

The brakes squeal, and the train halts. The Germans forbid the railwaymen to approach. No one must know what is happening inside these wagons; no one must bear witness to the horror. Schuster is becoming increasingly afraid of an attack. His fear of the Maquis has become obsessive. It has to be said that since we boarded it, the train has never travelled more than fifty kilometres per day, and the front in the battle of Liberation is drawing ever nearer.

We are strictly forbidden to communicate between wagons, but news circulates anyway. Especially news about the war and the Allied advance. Each time a courageous railwayman succeeds in approaching the train, each time a generous civilian comes, under cover of night, to bring us a little comfort, we glean information. And each time, our hope is renewed that Schuster will not succeed in reaching the border.

We are the last train to leave for Germany, the last train containing deportees, and some of us want to believe that we will eventually be freed by the Americans or the Resistance. It's thanks to them that we're not making any progress, and thanks to them that the tracks keep blowing up. In the distance, the Feldgendarmes take two railwaymen to one side; they were attempting to reach us. For this retreating battalion, the enemy is now everywhere. The Nazis see every civilian who wants to come to our aid, and every workman, as terrorists. And yet they are the ones who yell as they brandish their rifles, the ones with grenades in their belts. They are the ones who beat up the weakest among us and brutalise the oldest, just to release the tension that is tormenting them.

*   *   *

Today, we shall not be setting off again. The wagons remain locked and under close guard. And today the heat keeps inexorably increasing, slowly killing us. Outside it is thirty-five degrees; inside nobody can say, since we are almost all unconscious. The only comfort in this horror is to glimpse the familiar faces of my friends. I can picture Charles's smile when I look at him; Jacques always seems to be watching over us. François remains at his side, like a son beside a father he no longer has. As for me, I dream of Sophie and Marianne; I imagine the coolness of the Canal du Midi, and once again I see the little bench where we sat to exchange messages. Opposite me, Marc seems so sad; and yet he is the lucky one. He is thinking of Damira, and I am certain that she is also thinking of him, if she is still alive. No jailer, no torturer can keep prisoners from these thoughts. Feelings pass through the tiniest gap in the bars; they travel without fear of the distance, and know neither the frontiers of language, nor those of religion. They join with each other beyond the prisons invented by mankind.

Marc has this freedom. I would like to believe that wherever Sophie is, she thinks a little about me; a few seconds would be enough, a few thoughts for the friend I was . . . since I couldn't be more to her.

Today, we won't get any water or bread. Some of us can no longer speak; they have no strength left. Claude and I stay together constantly, each of us checking every moment that the other has not passed out, that death is not carrying him off; and from time to time we join hands, just to check . . .

9 July

Schuster has decided to turn back. The Resistance has blown up a bridge, blocking our way. We set off again for Bordeaux. And as the train pulls away from Angoulême and its devastated station, I think again of the bucket that carried away my last chance of seeing clearly. Already two days in the fog, and the night still ahead of me.

We arrive in the early afternoon. Nuncio and his friend Walter think only of escape. That evening, to pass the time, we organise a race using the fleas and lice that gnaw at the little flesh we have left. The parasites live in the seams of our shirts and trousers. It takes a lot of skill to dislodge them, and you've hardly got rid of one colony when another proliferates. We take turns lying down to try and get some rest while the others crouch to make room for them. It's in the middle of this night that an odd question comes to me: if we survive this hell, will we one day be able to forget it? Will we have the right to live again like normal people? Can we rub out the part of our memory that troubles the mind?

Claude is looking at me strangely.
  'What are you thinking about?' my brother asks.
  'About Chahine; do you remember him?'
  'I think so. Why are you thinking about him now?'
  'Because his features will never be erased.'
  'What are you really thinking about, Jeannot?'

'I'm looking for a reason to survive all of this.'

'It's right in front of you, you imbecile! One day we will find freedom again. And then I promised you that you would fly – you do remember that, I hope?'

'What about you? What do you want to do after the war?'

'Tour Corsica on a motorbike, with the most beautiful girl in the world riding pillion.'

My brother leans towards me so that I can make out his face more clearly.

'I knew it! I saw you sniggering. What? Don't you think I'm capable of seducing a girl and taking her travelling?'

I do everything I can to hold back, but it's no good; I can feel laughter taking possession of me, and my brother getting impatient. Now Charles is laughing too; even Marc joins in.

'What on earth has got into you all?' demands Claude, irritably.

'You stink to high heaven, old chap, and if you could see what you look like . . .! In your state, I doubt that even an elderly cockroach would want to follow you anywhere.'

Claude sniffs me, and joins in the absurd giggles that have taken hold of us and won't let go.

10 July

In the early hours of the morning, the heat is already unbearable. And then there's this bloody train, which still isn't moving. Not a single cloud on the horizon, no hope of a drop of rain to ease the prisoners' sufferings. People say that the Spanish sing when things are going badly. A chant strikes up; it's the beautiful language of Catalonia, escaping through the boards of the next wagon.

'Look!' says Claude, who's hauled himself up to the window.

'What can you see?' asks Jacques.

'The soldiers are running about, all along the track. Red Cross vans have arrived. Nurses are getting out. They're carrying water and they're coming towards us.'

They come as far as the platform, but the Feldgendarmes order them to stop, put down their buckets and withdraw. The prisoners will come and fetch them as soon as they have left. No contact with the terrorists is permitted!

The chief nurse pushes away the soldier.

'What terrorists?' she demands, outraged. 'Old men? Women? Starving men inside these cattle trucks?'

She shouts abuse at him and tells him she has had enough of orders. In a while, explanations will have to be given. Her nurses are going to bring the food and water to the wagons, and that's all there is to it! And she adds that the fact he is wearing a uniform does not impress her.

When the lieutenant brandishes his revolver, asking her if that impresses her a little more, the head nurse looks Schuster up and down and asks courteously for a

312

favour. If he has the courage to fire on a woman, and in the back at that, she asks him if he would be kind enough to aim at the centre of the cross she wears on her uniform. She adds that by chance, this cross is sufficiently large that even an imbecile like him is capable of hitting it. That will look good on his service record when he returns home, and even better if he happens to be arrested by the Americans or the Resistance.

Taking advantage of Schuster's stunned amazement, the chief nurse orders her strange troops to advance towards the wagons. On the platform, the soldiers seem amused by her authority. Perhaps they are simply relieved that someone is forcing their commander to display a little humanity.

She is the first one to open the latch on a door, and the others follow suit.

The chief nurse from the Red Cross in Bordeaux thought she had seen everything in her life. Two wars and years spent providing care for the destitute had convinced her that nothing could now surprise her. And yet, as she sees us, her eyes widen, she retches and cannot suppress the exclamation that escapes from her mouth.

Paralysed with fear, the nurses look at us; on their faces we can see the disgust and rebellion that our condition inspires in them. We may have dressed ourselves as best we could, but our emaciated faces betray our condition.

A nurse brings a bucket to each wagon, hands out

some biscuits and exchanges a few words with the prisoners. But Schuster is already yelling that the Red Cross must withdraw and the chief nurse decides that she has relied on luck enough for today. The doors close again.

'Jeannot! Come and see,' says Jacques, who is making sure that everyone gets their biscuits and their ration of water.

'What is it?'

'You'd better hurry!'

Getting up demands a lot of effort and the exercise is even more difficult, given the fog I've been living in for several days. But I can sense a note of urgency that forces me to join my friends. Claude takes me by the shoulder.

'Look!' he says.

You're kidding, Claude! Apart from the tip of my nose, I can't see much: a few silhouettes, among which I recognise that of Charles, and I can guess at Marc and François, who are standing behind him.

I can make out the contours of the bucket that Jacques is lifting up, and suddenly, at the bottom, I glimpse the frame of a pair of new spectacles. I thrust my hand into the water, and seize this thing, which I still can't believe is real.

The others wait silently, holding their breath, as I place the glasses on my nose. And suddenly, my little brother's face becomes clear again, the way it was before; I can see the emotion in Charles's eyes, Jacques' joyful expression and those of Marc and François as they embrace me.

Who could have understood? Who was able to translate the discovery of a pair of broken glasses at the bottom of a bucket into the destiny of a deportee without hope? Who had the kindness and courage to have a new pair made, to follow the train for several days, to work out correctly which wagon they came from, and to do what was necessary for the new pair to find its way there?

'The Red Cross nurse,' answers Claude. 'Who else?'

I want to see the world again, I am no longer blind, the mist has flown away. So I turn my head and look around me. The first surroundings I see are filled with an infinite sadness. Claude leads me over to the opening.

'Look how beautiful it is outside.'

'Yes.' My little brother's right. It is so beautiful outside.

'Do you think she's pretty?'

'Who?' asks Claude.

'The nurse!'

That evening, I tell myself that my destiny is perhaps being traced out at last. The refusals by Sophie, Damira and, to be honest, all the girls in the brigade, to kiss me finally had a meaning. The woman of my life, the real one, was therefore going to be the one who had saved my sight.

When she discovered the spectacles at the bottom of the bucket she had instantly understood the call for help that I had sent out from the depths of my hell. She had hidden the frame in her handkerchief, taking infinite care of the fragments of glass attached to it. She had gone to town to see an optician who sympathised with the Resistance. He had assiduously searched for lenses corresponding to the fragments he had studied. Once the frame had been reconstructed, she had set off again by bike, following the railway lines until she spotted the train. Seeing it heading back towards Bordeaux, she knew that she could successfully deliver her package. With the help of the senior Red Cross nurse, she chose the correct wagon before they arrived, recognising it from the striations left along its side by bullets. And that is how my spectacles came back to me.

That woman's deed had required such compassion, such generosity and courage, that I promised myself, if I got out of this, that I would find her as soon as the war ended and ask her to marry me. I could already see myself, hair flowing in the wind, on a country road, on board a Chrysler convertible, or why not on a bicycle, which would have even more charm. I would knock at the door of her house. I would give two little knocks and when she opened the door to me, I would say, 'I'm the man whose life you saved and my life now belongs to you.' We would have dinner by the open hearth, and we would tell each other about the last few years, all those months of suffering on that long road where, finally, we had met. And together we would close the pages of the past so that, together, we could write the days to come. We would have three children or more if she wanted and we would live happily. I would take flying lessons as Claude had promised me, and when I got my pilot's licence, I would take him up on Sundays, flying over the French countryside. There: everything was logical now. At last life had a meaning for me.

Bearing in mind the part my little brother had played in saving me, and our close relationship, it was entirely normal that I should immediately ask him to be my witness.

Claude looked at me and gave a little cough.

'Listen, old chap. I have nothing in principle against being a witness at your marriage. I'm even honoured. But I must tell you something else before your decision becomes final.'

'The nurse who brought back your spectacles is a thousand times more short-sighted than you, or at least she is, judging from the thickness of her spectacle lenses. You'll tell me that you don't care about that, well, fine; but I must also tell you, since you were still in the fog when she left: she's forty years older than you are, she must already be married and have at least twelve children. I'm not saying that in our state we have the right to expect more, but frankly . . .'

We stayed for three days, crowded into those stationary wagons on a platform at Bordeaux station. We were suffocating. Sometimes one of us got to his feet, in search of a little air, but there wasn't any.

Man becomes accustomed to everything; that's one of his great mysteries. We no longer smell our own stench, nobody cares about the person who's leaning over the minuscule hole in the floor to relieve himself. We'd forgotten about hunger long ago; only our obsessive thirst remained; especially when a new blister appeared on our tongues. The air became rarefied, not only in the wagon but also in our throats; it was harder and harder to swallow. But we had become accustomed to this bodily suffering that no longer left us; we were becoming accustomed to all the privations, including that of sleep. And the only ones who, for short moments, found deliverance, were those who escaped into madness. They stood up, began to moan or to yell, sometimes some wept and then they crumpled up and lay still.

As for those who were still managing to cope, they tried as best they could to reassure the others.

In a neighbouring wagon, Walter was explaining to anyone who would listen that the Nazis would never succeed in taking us to Germany, because the Americans would free us before then. In our wagon, Jacques wore himself out telling us stories to pass the time. When his mouth was too dry to go on speaking, anguish was reborn into the returning silence.

And while those around me were dying in silence, I lived again because I had recovered my sight; and somewhere inside me, I felt guilty.

12 July

It is half-past two in the morning. Suddenly, the doors are unlocked. Bordeaux station is swarming with soldiers. The Gestapo has been despatched here. The soldiers, who are armed to the teeth, yell and order us to take the few things we have left. With kicks and blows from rifle-butts, we are made to get out of our wagons and grouped together again on the platform. Among the prisoners, some are terrified, others content to drink in the air, in great gulps.

Five abreast, we plunge into the dark, silent city. There is not a single star in the sky.

Our footsteps echo on the deserted cobbles where the long procession stretches out. From line to line, information is passed on. Some say we are being taken to the Hâ fort, while others are certain that we are heading for the prison. But those who understand German learn, from the conversations of the soldiers surrounding us, that all the cells in the city are already full.

'So where are we going?' whispers a prisoner.

'*Schnell, schnell!*' roars a Feldgendarme, punching him in the back.

The night march through the silent town ends at rue Laribat, before the immense doors of a temple. This is the first time that I and my little brother have entered a synagogue.

35

There was no furniture left. The floor had been covered with straw and a line of buckets indicated that the Germans had thought of our needs. The three naves could house the six hundred and fifty prisoners from the train. Strangely, all those who came from Saint-Michel prison formed a group, beside the altar. Some women we had never spotted from our wagon were crammed into a neighbouring space, on the other side of a grill.

A few couples are thus reunited through the bars that separate them. For some, it is a very long time since they have seen each other. Many weep when their hands touch again. The majority remain silent; looks can say everything when you love each other. Others barely whisper; what can you say about yourself, about the days that have elapsed, without hurting the other person?

When morning comes, it will take all our jailers' cruelty to separate these couples, sometimes with blows from rifle-butts. For at dawn, the women are taken away to a barracks in the town.

The days pass, and each resembles the previous one. In the evening, we are handed a bowl of hot water in which a cabbage leaf is floating, and sometimes a few bits of pasta. We greet this as though it were a feast. From time to time, the soldiers come to fetch some of us. We never see them again and rumour has it that they are being used as hostages; as soon as the Resistance carries out an operation in the city, they are executed.

Some think of escaping. Here, the prisoners from le Vernet spend time with those from Saint-Michel. They are surprised by our ages. Kids, fighting a war; they can't believe their eyes.

14 July

We are all determined to celebrate today as it should be. Everyone tries to make rosettes out of bits of paper. We attach them to our chests. We sing the 'Marseillaise'. Our jailers close their eyes. Punishment would be too violent.

20 July

Today, three Resistance fighters, whom we met here,

attempted to escape. They were caught by a soldier on duty as they were rummaging in the straw behind the organ, where there is a grille. Quesnel and Damien, whose twentieth birthday is today, succeeded in getting away in time.

Roquemaurel received a good kicking, but when he was being interrogated, he had the presence of mind to claim that he'd been looking for a cigarette-end he'd spotted. The Germans believed him and didn't shoot him. Roquemaurel is one of the founders of the Bir-Hakeim Maquis, who were active in the Languedoc and the Cévennes. Damien is his best friend. Both were condemned to death after their arrest.

Scarcely recovered from their injuries, Roquemaurel and his comrades were constructing a new plan, for another day, which is sure to come.

The standard of hygiene here is no better than on the train, and scabies is rampant. The colonies of parasites proliferate. Together, we've invented a game. First thing in the morning, we each collect up the fleas and lice on our body. The creatures are grouped together in little makeshift boxes. When the Feldgendarmes come to count us, we open them and sprinkle their contents on them.

Even here, we haven't given up, and what may appear a trivial game is for us a way of resisting, armed with the only weapon we have left, and the one that gnaws away at us each day.

Here, we who thought we were alone in resisting meet

those who have never accepted the condition the Germans were trying to impose upon them, have never accepted attacks on the dignity of men. There were so many kinds of courage in that synagogue: bravery that was sometimes submerged by loneliness, but so strong that, some evenings, hope drove away the darkest thoughts that occupied our minds.

At the start, it was impossible for us to have any contact with the outside world. But during the two weeks we have been here, things have been sorted out a little. Each time the chosen prisoners go out into the yard to fetch the cooking pot, an old couple who live in a neighbouring house sing out the information from the front at the tops of their voices. Every evening, an old lady who lives in an apartment overlooking the synagogue writes on a slate in large letters, giving information on the Allied advance, and displays it at her window.

So, Roquemaurel had promised himself that he would make another escape attempt. At the time of day when the Germans allow a few prisoners to go upstairs and fetch toilet requisites (the deportees' meagre baggage had been piled up on the gallery), he rushes out with three of his friends. The opportunity is too good. At the end of the gangway that overlooks the great hall of the synagogue, there is a tiny room. His plan is risky but possible. The boxroom is next to one of the stained-glass windows that decorate the façade. When night comes, all he has to do is break it and escape over the roofs. Roquemaurel and his friends hide there while they wait for nightfall. Two hours pass and hope increases. But suddenly, he hears the sound of boots. The Germans have done their counts and they don't add up. They are searching for them; the footsteps approach, and light enters their hiding place. The delighted expression on the face of the soldier who winkles them out is an indication of what lies in wait for them. The beating is so violent that Roquemaurel lies motionless, bathing in his own blood. When he recovers consciousness the following morning, he is dragged before the lieutenant on duty. Christian, that's his first name, has no doubts about what's going to happen.

And yet, life doesn't hold out the same destiny for him as he assumes.

The officer who interrogates him must be around thirty. He is sitting astride a bench in the courtyard and looks at Roquemaurel in silence. He breathes in deeply, taking plenty of time to weigh up the prisoner.

'I was a prisoner myself,' he says in almost perfect French. 'It was during the Russian campaign. I also escaped, and I covered dozens and dozens of kilometres in the most appalling circumstances. The suffering I underwent, I would not wish upon anyone; I am not a man who delights in torture.'

Christian listens in silence to the young lieutenant who is addressing him. And suddenly, he feels hope that his life may be saved.

'Let us understand each other,' continues the officer, 'and I am sure that you will not have the opportunity to betray the secret I am preparing to confide to you. I consider it normal, almost legitimate, that a soldier should seek to escape. But like me, you will also consider it normal that he who is caught should undergo the punishment that his crime carries in the eyes of his enemy. And I am your enemy!'

Christian listens to the sentence. All day, he must remain motionless, standing to attention, facing a wall. He must never lean his back against it or seek out any other support. He must remain there, arms at his sides, beneath the burning sun, which will soon strike the asphalt in the courtyard.

Each movement will be punished with blows, and if he passes out there will be a sterner punishment.

People say that certain men's humanity is born in the memory of sufferings undergone, in the closeness that suddenly links them with their enemy. These were the two reasons that saved Christian from the firing squad. But it has to be said that this kind of humanity knows its limits.

So the four prisoners who had attempted escape were standing there, facing the wall, separated by a few metres. Throughout the morning, the sun climbs in the sky until it reaches its zenith. The heat is unbearable, their legs stiffen, their arms become heavy as lead, their necks lock.

There is a guard walking behind them. What is he thinking about?

Early in the afternoon, Christian sways, and instantly receives a punch to the back of the neck that throws him against the wall. His jaw broken, he falls and gets up immediately, afraid of undergoing the supreme punishment.

What is lacking in the soul of a soldier who watches and wallows in the suffering he is inflicting on this man?

Then comes tetany: the muscles contract and cannot ever relax. The pain is unbearable. Cramps take over the entire body.

How will water taste as it flows down that lieutenant's throat, while his victims waste away before his eyes?

The question still haunts me sometimes at night, when my memory brings back their swollen faces, their bodies, burned by the heat.

When night falls, their torturers bring them back into the synagogue. We greet them with the cheers usually reserved for the winners of a race, but I doubt they even noticed before they collapsed onto the straw.

24 July

The operations carried out by the Resistance in the city and its surrounding area are making the Germans increasingly edgy. Frequently now, their behaviour borders on hysteria, and they strike us without reason, for having the wrong face, or being in the wrong place at the wrong time. At noon, we are assembled beneath the gallery. A sentry posted in the street claims to have heard the sound of a file inside the synagogue. If the man who is in possession of a tool destined to aid an escape attempt does not hand it over in the next ten minutes, ten prisoners will be shot. Beside the officer, a machine gun aims at us. And while the seconds go by, the man who stands behind the gun's mouth, ready to breathe its carnivorous breath, enjoys taking aim at us. He plays at loading and unloading his weapon. Time passes, and nobody speaks. The soldiers beat prisoners, yell, terrorise; and the ten minutes are over. The commander seizes a prisoner, presses his revolver to his temple, takes off the safety catch and shouts an ultimatum.

And then a deportee takes a step forward, his hand trembling. His open palm reveals a file, one of the kind you use for fingernails. This tool couldn't even make a mark on the thick walls of the synagogue. He's barely able to use this file to sharpen his wooden spoon in order to cut bread, when there is any. It's a trick learned in prisons, as old as the world, ever since men have been imprisoned.

The deportees are afraid. The commandant will probably think he's being made fun of. But the man with the file is taken to the wall and a shot blows half his head away.

We spend the night standing up, in the light from a searchlight, under threat from that machine gun that aims at us and that piece of filth who, in order to keep himself awake, continues to play with his magazine.

7 August

Twenty-eight days have elapsed since we were first detained in the synagogue. Claude, Charles, Jacques, François, Marc and I have formed a group beside the altar.

Jacques has resumed his custom of telling us stories, to kill time and ease our worries.

'Is it true that you and your brother had never entered a synagogue before you came here?' asked Marc.

Claude hangs his head, as though he feels guilty.

I answer for him. 'Yes, it's true, this was the first time.'

'With a name as Jewish as yours, that's pretty unusual. I'm not criticising you,' Marc goes on immediately. 'It's just that I thought . . .'

'Well, you're wrong, we didn't practise at home. Not every Dupont and Durand necessarily goes to church on Sunday.'

'You didn't do anything, not even for the big festivals?' asks Charles.

'If you want to know everything, on Fridays our father celebrated the Sabbath.'

'Yes? And what did he do?' asked François, who was curious.

'Nothing more than on other evenings, except that he

328

recited a prayer in Hebrew and we all shared a glass of wine.'

'Just one?' asks François.

'One, yes. Just one.'

Claude smiles. I can see that he's amused by my account. He nudges me with his elbow.

'Go on, tell them the story, after all it's ancient history now.'

'What story?' asks Jacques.

'Nothing!'

Our friends, ravenous for stories because of their chronic, month-long boredom, all insisted at once.

'Well, each Friday when we went to sit down at table, Papa recited a prayer to us in Hebrew. He was the only one in the family who understood it; nobody spoke or understood Hebrew. We celebrated the Sabbath like that for years and years. One day, our big sister announced that she'd met someone and wanted to marry him. Our parents gave the news a warm reception and were keen that she should invite him to dinner, so they could get to know him. Alice immediately suggested that he should come and join us next Friday, when we could all celebrate the Sabbath together.

'To everyone's surprise, Papa didn't seem at all delighted by this idea. He claimed that this evening was set aside for the family and that any other night of the week would be better.

'It was no use my mother pointing out that as he had won his daughter's heart, their guest was already to some extent part of the family, nothing would change my father's mind. For first introductions, he felt that Monday, Tuesday, Wednesday and Thursday were more suitable. We all rallied to Mother's cause and insisted that the meeting should be on the evening of the Sabbath, when the meal was more copious and the tablecloth nicer. My father raised his arms to the heavens with a moan, and asked why the family was always in league against him. He loved playing the victim.

'He added that he thought it strange, when he was offering with good grace, without asking the slightest question (which proved his immensely open mind), to open the door of his house, every day of the week except one, that his family preferred to welcome this stranger (who was in any case going to take his daughter from him) on the only night that didn't suit him.

'Mother, being naturally stubborn, wanted to know why choosing Friday night posed such a problem for her husband.

'"No reason!" he replied, signalling his defeat.

'My father was never able to say "no" to his wife. Because he loved her more than anything else in the world, more than his own children, I think, and I cannot remember a single wish of my mother's that he did not make efforts to fulfil. In short, the week went by but my father was still not happy. And the more days passed, the more we could sense that he was tense.

'The night of the dinner we were all looking forward

to so much, Papa takes his daughter to one side and asks her, in a whisper, if her fiancé is Jewish. And when Alice replies, "Yes, of course," my father raises his arms to the heavens again and moans, "I knew it!"

'As you can imagine, his reaction stuns my sister, who asks him why this news visibly bothers him.

'"No reason, my darling," he replies, adding with flagrant dishonesty: "What do you mean?"

'Our sister, who's inherited her personality from her mother, seizes him by the arm as he's attempting to slip off into the dining room. She plants herself in front of him.

'"Excuse me, Papa, but I'm more than surprised by your reaction! I was afraid you might display this kind of attitude if I'd told you my fiancé wasn't Jewish, but this!!!"

'Papa tells Alice that it's grotesque of her to imagine such things, and swears that he couldn't care less about the origins, religion or skin colour of the man his daughter has chosen, so long as he is a gentleman and makes her happy, as he has loved her mother. Alice is not convinced, but Papa succeeds in escaping from her and immediately changes the subject of the conversation.

'Friday night arrives at last; we'd never seen Papa so nervous. Mother teased him all the time, reminding him of all the times when he moaned at the smallest pain, the minor attacks of rheumatism when he was sure he would be dead before he could marry off his daughter . . . he was in perfect health and Alice was now in love, so all the reasons to rejoice were gathered together, and there was no reason to worry. Papa swore that he didn't

331

even understand what his wife was talking about.

'Alice and Georges – that's the first name of my sister's fiancé – ring the doorbell at seven o'clock precisely and my father jumps, while Mother lifts her eyes to the heavens and goes off to greet them.

'Georges is a handsome lad with natural elegance; you'd think he was English. Alice and he look so well together that they seem an obvious couple. From the moment he arrives, Georges is accepted by the family. Even my father gives the impression that he's beginning to relax during the aperitifs.

'Mother announces that dinner is ready. Everyone takes their places around the table, waiting religiously for my father to recite the Sabbath prayer. We see him breathe in deeply, his chest swells and . . . then it immediately deflates. Another try; he holds his breath; and . . . his chest goes down again. A third attempt and suddenly, he looks at Georges and announces:

'"Why don't we let our guest recite instead of me? After all, I can clearly see that everyone likes him already and a father must learn to take second place to his children's happiness when the moment comes."

'"What are you saying?" demands Mother. "What moment? And who's asked you to take second place? For twenty years you've made it your duty, every Friday, to recite that prayer, which only you understand, since nobody here speaks Hebrew. You're not going to tell me that you've suddenly got stage-fright in front of your daughter's boyfriend?"

'"I haven't got stage-fright at all," our father assures her, rubbing the lapel of his jacket.

'Georges doesn't say anything, but we all saw him turn white when Papa suggested that he should officiate in his place. Since Mother came to his rescue, he's looking better already.

'"All right, all right," continues my father. "Well perhaps Georges will at least agree to join with me?"

'Papa begins reciting, and Georges stands up and repeats what he's saying, word for word.

'When the prayer has been said, they both sit down again, and the dinner is a wonderfully warm occasion filled with laughter.

'At the end of the meal, Mother suggests to Georges that he should accompany her into the kitchen; it's a chance for them to get to know each other a little.

'Alice reassures him with a knowing smile; everything is going fine. Georges collects up the plates from the table and follows our mother. Once they're in the kitchen, she relieves him of the crockery and invites him to take a seat.

'"Tell me, Georges, you're not Jewish at all!"

'Georges blushes and coughs.

'"I think I am a little, through my father . . . or one of his brothers; Mother was a protestant."

'"You talk of her in the past tense?"

'"She died last year."

'"I'm very sorry," murmurs Mother, sincerely.

'"Does it cause a problem that . . .?"

'"That you're not Jewish? Not a bit,' says Mother with a laugh. "Neither I nor my husband accords any importance to people's differences. On the contrary, we have always thought that difference was exciting and the source of much happiness. The most important thing, when you want to live together for your whole life, is to be sure that you won't be bored together. Boredom is the worst possible thing for a couple; it is what kills love. As long as you make Alice laugh, as long as you give her the desire to come and find you, when you've only just left her to go to work, as long as you're the one whose confidences she shares, and with whom she likes to share her confidences too, as long as you experience your dreams with her, even those you cannot make come true, then I am certain that whatever your origins, the only thing foreign to you as a couple will be the world and its jealous people."

'Mother takes Georges into her arms and welcomes him into the family.

'"Go on, go and find Alice," she says, almost with tears in her eyes. "She'll hate it that her mother is keeping her fiancé hostage. And if she knows that I've uttered the word fiancé, she will kill me!"

'As he's going back into the dining room, Georges turns around in the kitchen doorway and asks Mother how she guessed that he wasn't Jewish.

'"Ah!" exclaims Mother with a smile. "For twenty years, every Friday night, my husband has been reciting a prayer in a language he makes up. He has never known a word of Hebrew! But he is very attached to

334

the moment each week when he stands to speak at the family table. It's a sort of tradition that he carries on despite his ignorance. And even if his words have no meaning, I know that even so they are prayers of love which he formulates and invents for us. So, as you'll suspect, when I heard you just now repeating his nonsense almost identically, it wasn't difficult for me to realise . . . Let all of this remain between you and me. My husband is convinced that nobody suspects his little arrangement with God, but I have loved him for so many years that his God and I no longer have any secrets."

'The moment he got back into the dining room, Georges was drawn aside by our father.

'"Thank you for just now," growls Papa.

'"For what?" asks Georges.

'"Well, for not giving the game away. It's very generous of you. I imagine you must think badly of me. It's not that I derive some kind of pleasure from maintaining this lie; but after twenty years . . . how can I tell them now? Yes, I don't speak Hebrew, that's true. But to me, celebrating the Sabbath means maintaining tradition and tradition is important, do you understand?"

'"I am not Jewish, sir," replies Georges. 'Back there, I just repeated your words without having any idea of what they meant, and I'm the one who wanted to thank you for not giving me away."

'"Oh!" says Papa, and his arms drop to his sides.

'The two men look at each other for a few moments,

then our father lays a hand on Georges' shoulder and says to him:

'"Right, listen to me. I suggest that this little matter remains strictly between the two of us. I say the Sabbath and you're a Jew!"

'"I completely agree," replies Georges.

'"Good, good, good," says Papa, returning to the sitting room. "So, come and see me next Thursday evening at my workshop; we'd better rehearse the words we're going to recite the next day, since now the two of us will be saying the prayer."

'After dinner, Alice accompanies Georges as far as the street, waits until they're hidden by the carriage entrance, and takes her fiancé in her arms.

'"That went really well, and you did amazingly well. I don't know how you did it, but Papa didn't see a thing; he'd never suspect you weren't Jewish in a thousand years."

'"Yes, I think we came out of it rather well," smiles Georges as he walks away.

'So there you are, it's true. Claude and I never had the opportunity to enter a synagogue, before we were locked up here.'

That evening, the soldiers shouted the order to pack up our mess tins and a small suitcase, for those who had one, and to all assemble in the synagogue's main corridor. Anyone who lagged behind was brought back into line with kicks and punches. We had no idea where we were going, but one thing reassured us: when they came to

336

fetch prisoners to execute them, those who were leaving never to return had to leave their possessions behind.

In the early evening, the women who had been transferred to the Hâ fort were brought back and locked up in a neighbouring room. At two o'clock in the morning the temple doors opened. We set off again in a crocodile, and crossed the deserted, silent town, retracing the steps that had brought us here.

We got back on the train. The prisoners from the Hâ fort and all the Resistance fighters captured in recent weeks joined us.

There are now two more wagons containing women, which are at the head of the train. We set off again in the direction of Toulouse, and some of us think we are going home. But Schuster has other plans for us. He swore to himself that the final destination would be Dachau, and nothing is going to stop him, neither the onward progression of the Allied armies, nor the bombing raids that are destroying the villages we pass through, nor efforts by the Resistance to slow down our progress.

Near to Montauban, Walter finally succeeded in escaping. He had noticed that one of the four nuts fastening the bars to the window had been replaced by a bolt. With the little saliva he has and all the strength in his fingers, he makes it turn, and when his mouth is too dry, it's the blood from the wounds that form on his fingers that will perhaps provide sufficient moisture to shift the bolt. After hours and hours of pain, the piece of metal begins to move. Walter wants to believe in his luck; he wants to believe in hope.

His fingers are so swollen that when he achieves his goal, he can't spread them any more. All he has to do now is push the bar and the space in the window will be large enough to squeeze through. Crouching in the wagon's shadows, three comrades are looking at him: Lino, Pipo and Jean, all young 35th Brigade recruits. One is weeping; he can't take any more, he's going to go mad. It has to be said that the heat has never been so intense. We are suffocating and the entire wagon seems to exhale to the rhythm of the stifled prisoners' groans. Jean begs Walter to help them escape. Walter hesitates. But how can he not say anything, how can he not help those who are like brothers to him? So he puts his wounded hands around them and reveals what he has accomplished. They will wait until it's dark to jump – him first, then the others. They go through the procedure in low voices. Hang on to the upright until your whole body is outside, and then jump and run into the distance. If the Germans shoot, it's every man for himself; if they've succeeded, when the red lamp has disappeared, they will go back along the track and regroup.

Daylight is beginning to fade. The moment they've been so eagerly waiting for will soon be here, but destiny seems to have decided otherwise. The train slows down at Montauban station. From the sound of the wheels, we're setting off along the track to an engine shed. And when the Germans take up position on the platform with their machine guns, Walter tells himself that the game's up. With death in their souls, the four accomplices crouch down and retreat into their own solitude.

Walter would like to sleep, and regain a little strength, but the blood is throbbing in his fingers and the pain is just too great. In the wagon, the sound of moaning can be heard.

It is two o'clock in the morning and the train sets off. Walter's heart is no longer beating in his hands but in his chest. He shakes his comrades and together, they wait for the right moment. The night is too clear, and the almost full moon shining in the sky will give them away all too easily. Walter looks out through the opening. The train is moving at a good speed; and in the distance, he can see undergrowth.

Walter and two comrades have escaped from the train. After falling into the ditch, he remained crouching down for a long time. And when the train's red lantern disappeared into the darkness, he raised his arms to the skies and shouted, 'Mother'. He walked for many kilometres, did Walter. Reaching the edge of a field, he happened upon a German soldier who was relieving himself, with his rifle and fixed bayonet by his side. Lying amid the ears of maize, Walter waited for the right moment and threw himself at the soldier. Where did he find such reserves of strength, sufficient to get the upper hand in the scuffle? The bayonet remained fixed, in the soldier's body; as he covered many more kilometres, Walter felt as if he was flying, like a butterfly.

The train didn't stop at Toulouse; we weren't going home. We went past Carcassonne, Béziers and Montpellier.

36

The days pass and thirst has returned. In the villages through which we travel, the people do their best to help us. Bosca, one prisoner among so many others, throws a little note through the opening. A woman finds it close to the track and takes it to the intended recipient. On the scrap of paper, the deportee attempts to reassure his wife. He tells her that he is on board a train that passed through Agen on 10 August and that he is well, but Mme Bosca will never see her husband again.

During a halt near Nîmes, we are give a little water, dry bread and some jam that has gone off. The food is inedible. In the wagons, some prisoners are afflicted with dementia. Foam oozes from the corners of their mouths. They stand up, spin around and howl before crumpling to the floor, shaken by spasms that precede their death. They resemble rabid dogs. The Nazis are going to make us all die like that. Those who have retained their sanity dare not look at them. So the prisoners close their eyes, curl up and stop their ears.

'Do you really think madness is contagious?' asks Claude.

'I have no idea, but make them be quiet,' begs François.

In the distance, bombs are falling on Nîmes. The train stops at Remoulins.

15 August

The train hasn't moved for several days. The body of a prisoner who starved to death is unloaded. The most seriously ill are allowed to go and relieve themselves beside the track. They tear up handfuls of grass, which they distribute on their return. The starving deportees argue over this food.

The Americans and the French have landed at Sainte-Maxime. Schuster is seeking a way of passing between the Allied lines that encircle him. But how is he going to get up the Rhône valley, and before that, cross the river, since all the bridges have been bombed?

18 August

The German lieutenant has possibly found a solution to his problem. The train sets off again. During shunting, a railwayman opened the latch on a wagon. Three prisoners succeeded in escaping, thanks to a tunnel. Others may do so a little later, during the few kilometres that separate us from Roquemaure. Schuster halts the train in the shelter of an opening in the rock; here, he will be protected from bombing; over the past few days, English and American planes have flown over us several times. But, in this opening, the Resistance will not find us either. No train can happen upon us; railway traffic has been interrupted all over the country. War is raging and the Liberation is progressing, like a wave that covers a little more of the country each day. It is impossible to cross the Rhône by train, but what does that matter? Schuster will make us cross it on foot. After all, doesn't he have seven hundred and fifty slaves to transport the goods accompanying the Gestapo families and the soldiers whom he has sworn to bring back home?

On this day, 18 August, we walk in a crocodile formation beneath a blazing sun, which burns the little skin the fleas and lice have left us. Our thin arms carry German suitcases, cases of wine that the Nazis stole in Bordeaux. One further instance of cruelty, for us who are dying of thirst. Those who fall and do not move will not get up again. A bullet in the back of the neck finishes them off as one would kill horses that have lost their usefulness. Those who can, help others to stand upright. When one staggers, his friends surround him to hide his fall and lift him back up as quickly as possible, before a lookout has noticed. Around us, vines stretch out as far as the eye can see. They are laden with bunches of grapes, which the torrid summer has ripened early. We would like to

343

pick them and burst the fruit in our desiccated mouths, but only the soldiers, who yell at us to stay on the road, can fill their helmets with them and enjoy the grapes in front of us.

And we pass, like ghosts, a few metres from the vines.

Then I remember the words of 'La Butte Rouge'. Do you remember? *Those who drink this wine will be drinking our comrades' blood.*

Ten kilometres already. How many lie behind us, dead in ditches? When we walk through villages, the people watch the strange procession in terror. Some want to help us. They run up to us, carrying water, but the Nazis push them away violently. When the shutters of a house open, the soldiers fire at the windows.

One prisoner speeds up. He knows that at the head of the procession his wife is walking, having got out of one of the train's first wagons. His feet bleeding, he succeeds in reaching her and, without a word, he takes the suitcase from her hands and carries it instead.

Here they are together, walking side by side, reunited at last, but without the right to say that they love each other. They barely exchange a smile, for fear of losing their lives. And what remains of their life?

At another village, on a bend, the door of a house opens a little way. The soldiers are also overcome by the heat, and are less vigilant. The prisoner takes his wife's hand and indicates that she should slip into the half-open doorway. He will cover her escape.

'Go,' he says, his voice trembling.

'I am staying with you,' she replies. 'I haven't come all this way to leave you now. We shall go home together, or not at all.'

They both died at Dachau.

Late in the afternoon, we arrive at Sorgues. This time, hundreds of inhabitants see us cross their town and head for the railway station. The Germans are outnumbered. Schuster hadn't foreseen that the population would come out in such numbers. The inhabitants improvise help. The soldiers can't hold them back, they're unable to cope. On the platform, the villagers bring food and wine, which the Nazis seize. Taking advantage of the crush, several help prisoners to escape. They cover them with a railwayman's or peasant's shirt and slip a crate of fruit under their arm, trying to make them pass for one of those who have come to bring help, and they lead them far away from the station before going home and hiding them there.

The Resistance had been informed in advance, and had planned an armed operation to free the prisoners, but there are too many soldiers. It would be carnage. Despairing, they watch us climbing on board the new train, which is waiting at the platform. If, when we climbed into these cattle trucks, we had known that in barely a week, Sorgues would be liberated by the American army . . .

The train sets off under cover of night. A storm breaks, bringing a little coolness and a few drops of rain; they trickle in through the gaps in the roof, and we slake our thirst.

37

19 August

The train is moving along quickly. Suddenly, the brakes squeal and the train skids along the rails, sparks spraying out from beneath its wheels. The Germans jump out of the carriages and rush to the embankments. A deluge of bullets hits our wagons; a ballet of American planes is circling in the sky. Their first pass has caused utter carnage. We rush to the skylights, waving pieces of fabric, but the pilots are too high to see us, and already the engines' noise is growing louder as the planes aim at us.

The moment freezes in time and I can no longer hear anything. Everything happens as if suddenly, time had slowed down every move we made. Claude is looking at me; so is Charles. Facing us, Jacques smiles radiantly, and spits out a mouthful of blood; slowly, he falls to his knees. François rushes over to catch him as he falls. He gathers him up in his arms. Jacques has a gaping hole in his back; he would like to say something to us, but no sound comes out of his mouth. His eyes mist over. It's no use François holding up his head, it slips to one side, now that Jacques is dead.

His cheek stained with the blood of his best friend, the one who has never left him throughout this long journey, François yells, 'NO!' and the sound fills the space. We are unable to hold him back as he hurls himself at the skylight, ripping away the barbed wire with his bare hands. A German bullet whistles past, taking off his ear. This time it's his own blood that trickles down his neck, but that doesn't matter. He holds onto the wagon wall and slides out. The minute he lands on his feet, he stands up, rushes to the wagon's door and lifts the latch to let us out.

I can still see François, silhouetted against the sunlight. Behind him, in the sky, the planes circle and come back towards us; and right behind his back, a German soldier aims and fires. François' body is projected forward and half of his face spreads out over my shirt. His body jerks, gives a final quiver, and François joins Jacques in death.

On 19 August, at Pierrelatte, among so many others, we lost two friends.

The locomotive is smoking all over. Steam is escaping from its pierced sides. The train will not be setting off again. There are many wounded. A Feldgendarme goes to fetch a doctor from the village. What can this man do, helpless before these prostrate prisoners, some with their entrails exposed, some with gaping wounds in their limbs? The planes come back. Taking advantage of the soldiers' panic, Titonel does a bunk. The Nazis open fire on him and a bullet goes right through him, but he continues running across the fields. A peasant finds him and takes him to the hospital at Montélimar.

The sky has grown calm again. Beside the track, the country doctor is begging Schuster to entrust him with the wounded he can still save, but the lieutenant will have none of it. That night, they are loaded into the wagons, just as a new locomotive arrives at Montélimar.

For almost a week now, the Free French and Resistance forces have been on the offensive. The Nazis have been put to flight, and their retreat has begun. The railway lines, like the *Route Nationale* 7, are at the centre of violent battles. The American armies, and the armoured division commanded by Général de Lattre de Tassigny, landed in Provence and are progressing northwards. The Rhône valley is an impasse for Schuster. But the French forces fall back to support the Americans, whose target is Grenoble; they are already in Sisteron. Even yesterday, we would have stood no chance of crossing the valley, but momentarily the French have loosened the vice. The lieutenant takes advantage of this; it is now or never. In Montélimar, the train stops at the station, on the track used by trains that are going down to the south.

Schuster wants to get rid of the dead as quickly as possible and abandon them to the Red Cross.

Richter, head of the Gestapo in Montélimar, is on the spot. When the Red Cross representative asks him to hand over the wounded as well, he refuses categorically.

So she turns her back on him and walks away. He asks her why she is doing so.

'If you do not allow me to take the wounded with me, you can cope with your corpses yourselves.'

Richter and Schuster discuss the matter, and end up giving in. They swear that they will come back and fetch these prisoners as soon as they have recovered.

From the openings of our cattle trucks, we watch our comrades leaving on stretchers: those who moan, and those who no longer say anything. The corpses are lined up on the floor in the waiting room A group of railwaymen is contemplating them sadly. They take off their caps and pay them a final homage. The Red Cross evacuates the wounded to the hospital, and to ensure that the Nazis – who still occupy the town – have no appetite for coming to finish them off, the Red Cross representative lies and says they are all infected with typhus, a terribly contagious illness.

As the Red Cross vans move away into the distance, the dead are taken to the cemetery.

Among the bodies laid out in the trench, the earth closes over the faces of Jacques and François.

20 *August*

We are heading towards Valence. The train stops in a tunnel to avoid a squadron of aircraft. The air becomes rarefied, to the point where we all lose consciousness. When the train enters the station, a woman takes advantage of a Feldgendarme's distraction and brandishes a sign from the window of her flat. It reads: 'Paris is surrounded, have courage.'

21 *August*

We pass through Lyon. A few hours afterwards, the Resistance forces burn down the fuel depot at Bron airport. The German general staff abandons the town. The front is getting closer to us, but the train continues on its way. We stop again at Chalon, where the railway station is in ruins. We encounter elements of the Luftwaffe who are heading back to the east. A German colonel very nearly saved the lives of a few prisoners. He demands two wagons from Schuster. His soldiers and weapons are much more important than the ragged human wreckage that the lieutenant is keeping on board. The two men almost come to blows, but Schuster is a determined man. He is going to transport all these Jews, wops and terrorists to Dachau. Not one of us is to be freed. The train sets off again.

The door of my wagon opens. Three young German soldiers with unknown faces hand us some cheese and the door shuts again immediately. We have received neither food nor water for thirty-six hours. We organise a fair distribution.

At Beaune, the population and the Red Cross come to our aid. We are brought a little something to perk us up. The soldiers seize the cases of Burgundy. They get drunk, and when the train departs again, they play at firing the machine gun at the fronts of houses bordering the railway track.

Barely thirty kilometres have been covered; we are now in Dijon. The railway station is in a terrible state of confusion. No trains can head north. The battle for the railway is raging. The railwaymen try to prevent the train from leaving. The bombing raids are incessant. But Schuster will not give up and, despite the protests by the French workmen, the locomotive whistles, its connecting rods start to move, and off it goes, hauling its terrible procession.

It won't go very far; the rails have been removed. The soldiers make us get down and set us to work. Once deportees, we are now convicts doing hard labour. Beneath a burning sun, in front of Feldgendarmes who point their rifles at us, we replace the rails that the Resistance removed. We will be deprived of water until the repairs are complete, yells Schuster, standing on the footplate of the locomotive.

Dijon is behind us. At nightfall, we try to keep believing that we will get out of this. The Maquis attack the train,

352

not without precautions so as not to hurt us, and immediately the German soldiers retaliate from the platform at the rear of the train, driving back the adversary. But the fight recommences. The Maquis are following us in this infernal race which is bringing us inexorably closer to the German border; once we have crossed it, we know we shall never return. And with each kilometre that disappears beneath the wheels of the train, we wonder how many still separate us from Germany.

From time to time, the soldiers machine-gun the countryside. Have they seen a shadow that worries them?

23 August

Never has the journey been so unbearable. These last few days have been burning hot. We have no more food, no more water. The landscapes we are passing through have been laid waste. It will soon be two months since we left the yard of Saint-Michel prison, two months since the journey began, and on our emaciated faces, our sunken eyes can see our bones mapping out our skeletons in detail, all the way down our fleshless bodies. Those who have resisted madness sink into a profound silence. My little brother, with his hollow cheeks, looks like an old man; but each time I look at him, he smiles at me.

25 August

Yesterday, some prisoners escaped. Nitti and a few of his friends succeeded in removing some planks. They jumped down onto the rails under cover of night. The train had just passed Lécourt station. They found the body of one, cut in two; another had his leg cut off. In all, six are dead. But Nitti and a few others succeeded in escaping. We have gathered around Charles. At the speed the train is travelling, it is now only a question of hours before we cross the border. No matter how often the planes fly over, they can't free us.

'We can only count on ourselves now,' grumbles Charles.

'Are we going to try?' asks Claude.

Charles looks at me and I agree with a nod. What have we to lose?

Charles sets out his plan. If we succeed in opening a few floorboards, we will slide down into the hole. In turn, the comrades will hold onto the one who is sliding out. At the signal, they will let go of him. Then he must let himself fall, with arms by the sides so they don't get cut off under the wheels. Above all he mustn't raise his head, or he risks being decapitated by the fast-moving axles. It's important to count the wagons that pass above us: twelve, thirteen perhaps? Then wait, motionless, until the train's red light has disappeared, before getting up. To avoid crying out and alerting the soldiers on the platform, the one who is jumping will stuff a piece of fabric into his mouth. And as Charles makes us repeat the manoeuvre, a man gets up and sets to work. With all his strength, he pulls on a nail. His fingers slip under the metal and keep on trying to make it turn. Time is pressing; are we even still in France?

The nail yields. His hands covered in blood, the man takes it and digs into the hard wood; he pulls on the planks, which barely move, and digs away again. His palms are pierced all over, but he ignores the pain and continues his task. We want to help him but he rejects us. He is creating the door to freedom on the floor of this ghost train, and he insists on being allowed to get on with it. The man doesn't mind dying, but not for nothing. If he can at least save some lives that deserve it, then his life will have been of some use. He wasn't arrested for acts of resistance, just for a few thefts; it's only by chance that he found himself in the 35th brigade's wagon. So he begs us to let him do this; he owes it to us, he says, digging again and again.

Now his hands are no more than shreds of flesh, but the plank moves at last. Armand rushes over and we all help him to pull out a first plank, then another. The hole is big enough to slide through. The din of the wheels fills the wagon, the sleepers shooting past at top speed as we watch. Charles decides the order in which we will jump.

'You, Jeannot, you'll go first, then Claude, then Marc, Samuel . . .'

'Why are we first?'

'Because you're the youngest.'

Exhausted, Marc indicates that we're to obey him. Claude doesn't argue.

We must get dressed. Putting our clothes on over our abscess-covered skin is torture. Armand, who is jumping

355

ninth, offers the man who made the hole a chance to escape with us.

'No,' he says, 'I'll be the one who supports the last one of you to jump. There has to be someone, doesn't there?'

'You can't go now,' says another man sitting with his back to the wall. 'I know the distance that separates the poles, I've counted the seconds between them. We're travelling at least at sixty kilometres per hour; you'd all break your necks at that speed. You'll have to wait until the train slows down. Forty per hour, that's the maximum.'

The man knows what he's talking about: before the war, he put down railway lines.

'What if the loco was at the back of the train and not at the front?' asks Claude.

'Then you'll all get through,' replies the man. 'There's also the risk that the Germans have fixed a bar to the end of the final wagon, but that's a risk you have to run.'

'Why would they have done that?'

'Precisely so that nobody could jump down onto the rails!'

And suddenly, as we're weighing the pros and cons, the train loses speed.

'It's now or never,' says the man who put down tracks when the country was at peace.

'Go!' says Claude. 'You know what's waiting for us when we arrive, anyway.'

356

He and Charles support me by the arms. I stuff the piece of fabric into my mouth and my legs slide through the gaping hole. I must prevent my feet touching the ground before my friends give me the signal, otherwise my body will turn over and be cut into pieces in seconds. My belly hurts; there's no muscle there now to help me keep this position.

'Now!' Claude shouts to me.

I fall. The ground hits my back. Don't move. The din is deafening. A few centimetres away, on either side, the wheels are whistling past on the rails. Each connecting rod brushes against me. I can feel the air it displaces and smell the metal. Must count the wagons. My heart is beating so hard in my chest. Another three, perhaps four? Has Claude already jumped? I want to be able to embrace him one more time, tell him that he's my brother, that without him I never would have survived, I could never have fought this battle.

The din stops and I hear the train moving into the distance. The darkness surrounds me. Am I at last breathing the air of freedom?

In the distance, the train's red lamp fades and disappears around a bend in the rails. I am alive; in the sky, the moon is full.

'Your turn,' orders Charles.

Claude stuffs the handkerchief into his mouth and his legs slide between the planks. But the others pull him up straight away. The train sways; is it about to stop? False alarm. It was passing over a small bridge in poor

357

condition. We start again and this time, Claude's face disappears.

Armand turns around. Marc is too exhausted to jump.

'Get your strength back. I'll help the others and then we'll go after.'

Marc nods. Samuel jumps, then Armand is the last to be engulfed by the hole. Marc didn't want to go. The man who made the hole in the floor carries him.

'Go on what have you to lose?'

So Marc decides at last. He lets go and in turn he slides down. The train brakes suddenly. The Feldgendarmes disembark immediately. Huddled between two sleepers, he sees them coming towards him. His legs no longer have the strength to help him run away and the soldiers catch him. They bring him back to a wagon. On the way, they beat him up so badly that he loses consciousness.

Armand remained hanging onto the axles so as to escape the soldiers' lamps as they do the rounds, searching for other escapees. Time passes. He can feel his arms about to give way. So close to the goal, it's impossible, so he resists; I've told you before, we've never given up. And suddenly, the train sets off. He waits until it gathers a little speed and then lets himself fall onto the track. And he is the last to see the red lantern fade into the distance.

It's about half an hour since the train disappeared. As we agreed, I walk back up the railway line, looking for my comrades. Has Claude survived? Are we in Germany?

Before me I make out a little bridge, guarded by a German sentry. It's the one where my brother almost jumped, just before Charles held him back. The soldier in question is humming 'Lili Marlene'. This seems to answer one of the two questions that haunt me; the other concerns my brother. The only way to get past this obstacle is to slide along one of the posts that support the bridge's roadway. Suspended in emptiness, I advance in the clear night, fearing that I will be caught any second.

I've walked so long that I can no longer count my steps, nor the sleepers on the track I'm walking along. And in front of me there's still this silence, and not a living soul. Am I the only one to have survived? Are all my friends dead? 'You've got a one in five chance of coming through,' the former track-layer had said. And what about my brother, for goodness' sake? Not that! Kill me instantly but not him. Nothing must happen to him, I will bring him back, I promised Mother, in the worst of my dreams. I thought I had no more tears, no more reasons to weep, and yet, kneeling in the middle of the track, alone in that deserted countryside, I confess to you that I cried like a kid. Without my little brother, what use was freedom? The track stretches out into the far distance and Claude is nowhere.

*   *   *

359

A rustle in a bush makes me turn my head.

'Right, are you going to stop blubbering and come and give me a hand? These thorns hurt like hell.'

Head down, Claude is caught in a thicket of brambles. How on earth did he manage to get into this situation?

'Get me out first and then I'll explain!' he moans.

And while I extricate him from the imprisoning branches, I see the silhouette of Charles, walking unsteadily towards us.

The train had disappeared for good. Charles was weeping a little, and hugging us. Claude was trying to pull the thorns out of his thighs as best he could. Samuel was holding the back of his neck, hiding a nasty wound he'd acquired when he jumped. We still didn't know if we were in France or already on German soil.

Charles points out to us that we are out in the open and that it's time to get out of here. We make our way to a small wood, carrying Samuel whose strength has left him, and hide behind the trees, waiting for daylight to come.

38

26 August
Dawn is breaking. Samuel has lost a lot of blood during the course of the night.

While the others are still sleeping, I hear him moaning. He calls to me, and I come over to him. His face is white as a sheet.

'How stupid, so close to the goal!' he murmurs.

'What are you talking about?'

'Don't pretend to be stupid, Jeannot, I'm going to die. Already I can't feel my legs any more, and I'm so cold.'

His lips are violet, and he's shivering. So I take him in my arms to warm him up the best I can.

'It was one hell of an escape though, wasn't it?'

'Yes Samuel, it was one hell of an escape.'

'Can you smell how good the air is?'

'Keep your strength, old fellow.'

'What for? It's only a question of hours for me now. Jeannot, one day you have to tell our story. It mustn't die like me.'

'Shut up, Samuel, you're talking nonsense and I don't know how to tell stories.'

'Listen to me, Jeannot, if you don't manage to do it, then your children will do it in your place. You have to ask them. Swear it to me.'

'What children?'

'You'll see,' Samuel went on, in a hallucinatory delirium. 'Later you'll have them, one, two or more I don't know, I don't really have the time to count now. Then you'll have to ask them something for me, and you have to tell them that it means a lot to me. It's a little as if they were keeping a promise that their father made in a past that won't exist any more. Because that wartime past won't exist any more, you'll see. You'll tell them to tell our story, in their free world. That we fought for them. You will teach them that nothing is worth more on this earth than that whore freedom, who is capable of offering herself to the highest bidder. You'll tell them too that this big slut loves the love of men, and that she will always escape from those who want to take her prisoner, that she will always grant victory to the one who respects her without ever hoping to keep her in his bed. Tell them, Jeannot. Tell them to recount all this on my behalf, in their own words, the words of their own era. Mine are just made up of the accents of my country, and the blood that's in my mouth and on my hands.'

'Stop, Samuel, you're exhausting yourself for nothing.'

'Jeannot, promise me this: swear that one day you will love. I would really like to have been able to do it, to be able to love. Promise me that you'll carry a child in your arms and that into the first look of life that you give it, in that fatherly look, you will put a little of my freedom. Then, if you do it, a little of me will still remain on this damned earth.'

I promised and Samuel died at daybreak. He breathed in very hard, blood flowed from his mouth, and then I saw his jaw clench because the pain was so violent. The wound on his neck had turned violet. And so it remained. I believe that beneath the earth that covers him, in that field in Haute-Marne, a little of that purple has resisted time, and the absurdity of men.

In the middle of the day, we spotted a peasant in the distance, walking towards us across his field. In our state, starving and wounded, we could not hold out for long. After a discussion, we decided that I would go out and meet him. If he was German, I would put my hands up, and the others would remain hidden in the little wood.

As I walked towards him, I wondered which of us would terrify the other one more. I, in rags, in the clothes of a ghost, or the peasant: I still didn't know what language he would use to speak to me.

'I am a prisoner who escaped from a deportation train and I need help,' I cried, reaching out my hand to him.

'You are alone?' he asked me.

'Are you French, then?'

'Of course I'm French, dammit! What a question! Come along, I'll take you to the farm,' said the alarmed farmer. 'You're in a terrible state!'

I signalled to the others, who immediately came running up.

It was 26 August 1944, and we were saved.

39

Marc regained consciousness three days after our escape. The train commanded by Schuster entered the death camp at Dachau, its final destination, which it reached on 28 August 1944.

Yet out of the seven hundred prisoners who had survived the terrible journey, barely a handful escaped death.

As the Allied troops were retaking control of the country, Claude and I retrieved a car abandoned by the Germans. We went back up the lines and left for Montélimar, to find the bodies of Jacques and François, so that we could bring them back to their families.

Ten months later, on a spring morning in 1945, behind the gates of Ravensbrück camp, Osna, Damira, Marianne and Sophie saw the American troops arrive to free them.

A short time before, in Dachau, Marc – who had survived – had also been freed.

Claude and I never saw our parents again.

We had jumped from the ghost train on 25 August 1944, the same day that Paris was liberated.

In the days that followed, the farmer and his family lavished care upon us. I remember the evening when they made us an omelette. Charles looked at us in silence, as we recalled the faces of our comrades, sitting around the table at the little station in Loubers.

One morning, my brother woke me up.

'Come with me,' he said, dragging me out of bed.

I followed him outside the barn where Charles and the others were still sleeping.

We walked like that, side by side, not speaking, until we reached the middle of a large field of stubble.

'Look,' said Claude, holding my hand.

In the distance, the lines of American tanks, and those belonging to the Leclerc division, were converging, heading east. France was free.

Jacques was right, spring had returned . . . and I felt my little brother's hand gripping mine tightly.

In that field of stubble, my little brother and I were, and would forever remain, two children of freedom, who had lost our way amid sixty million dead.

366

Epilogue

One morning in September 1983, when I was almost eighteen years old, Mother came into my room. The sun was barely up and she announced that I would not be going to school.

I sat up in my bed. That year, I was preparing for my baccalaureate and I was astonished that Mother was suggesting I skip lessons. She was going out with Father for the day and wanted me and my sister to come with them. I asked where we were going. Mother looked at me with that smile that never left her.

'If you ask him, perhaps on the way your father will tell a story that he never wanted to tell you.'

We arrived in Toulouse around midday. A car was waiting for us at the railway station and took us to the town's large stadium.

As my sister and I were taking our places on the almost deserted seats, my father and his brother walked down the steps, accompanied by a few men and women, and headed for a platform, which had been erected in the middle of the pitch. There, they lined up; then a minister came towards them and gave a speech:

'In November 1942, the immigrant workforce in the South-West formed a military Resistance movement, creating the 35th FTP-MOI Brigade.

'Jews, manual workers, peasants, for the most part Hungarian, Czech, Polish, Romanian, Italian and Yugoslav immigrants, several hundred of them took part in the liberation of Toulouse, Montauban and Agen; they fought in all the battles to drive the enemy out of Haute-Garonne, Tarn, Tarn-et-Garonne, Ariège, Gers, and the Low and High Pyrenees.

'A number of them were deported or lost their lives, as did their leader Marcel Langer . . .

'Hunted down, destitute, emerging from oblivion, they were the symbol of the brotherhood forged in the torment born out of division, but also the symbol of the commitment shown by women, children and men who contributed to the fact that our country, which had been delivered up as a hostage to the Nazis, could emerge slowly from its silence and at last come back to life . . .

'This fight, although condemned by the laws then in force, was glorious. It was a time when the individual exceeded his own capabilities, showing contempt for wounds, torture, deportation and death.

'It is our duty to teach our children that this fight was the bearer of essential values, and, because of the heavy tribute paid to freedom, how much it deserves to be engraved in the French Republic's memory.'

The minister pinned a medal on the lapels of their jackets. When it was time to decorate one of them, who was notable for his red hair, a man climbed up onto the platform. He wore the blue uniform of the Royal Air Force and a white cap. He approached the man who, in another time, had been known as Jeannot, and saluted him slowly as one might salute a soldier. And so the eyes of a former pilot and those of a former deportee had met once more.

As soon as he came down from the platform, my father took off his medal and stuffed it into his jacket pocket. He came to me, put his arm around me and said quietly, 'Come with me, let's introduce you to my friends, and then we'll go back home.'

That evening, on the train that was taking us back to Paris, I caught him gazing out of the window as the countryside rolled by, locked up in his silence. His hand was resting on the small table that separated us. I covered it with mine, which was quite something; he and I rarely touched. He didn't turn his head, but I caught the reflection of his smile in the window. I asked him why he hadn't told me all of this earlier, why he had waited all this time.

He shrugged his shoulders.

'What did you want me to tell you?'

Personally, I thought that I would have liked to know that he was Jeannot; I would have liked to wear his story under my school uniform.

'Many friends died on these rails; and we ourselves had to kill. Later on, I just want you to remember that I was your father.'

And, a great deal later, I realised that he had wanted to fill my childhood with something other than his own.

Mother didn't take her eyes off him. She placed a kiss upon his lips. From the looks they exchanged, my sister and I could guess how much they had loved each other from the very first day.

Samuel's last words come back to me.

Jeannot has kept his promise.

There you are, my love. That man with his elbows on the counter of the café des Tourneurs, the one who's giving you the elegant smile, that's my father.

Under this French soil lie his friends, the freedom fighters, his fellow foreigners.

Each time I'm here or there and I hear someone expressing his ideas in the middle of a free world, I think of them.

Then I remember that the word 'Foreigner' is one of the most beautiful promises in the world, a colourful promise, as beautiful as Freedom.

371

I could never have written this book without the testimonies and accounts collected in *Une histoire vraie* (Claude et Raymond Levy, Les Editeurs Français Reunis), *La Vie des Français sous l'Occupation* (Henri Amouroux, Fayard), *Les Parias de la Résistance* (Claude Levy, Calmann-Lévy), *Ni travail, ni famille, ni patrie – Journal d'une brigade FTP-MOI, Toulouse, 1942–1944* (Gérard de Verbizier, Calmann-Lévy), *L'Odysée du train fantôme, 3 juillet 1944 : une page de notre histoire* (Jürg Altwegg, Robert Laffont), *Schwarzenmurtz ou l'Esprit de parti* (Raymond Levy, Albin Michel) and *Le Train fantôme – Toulouse-Bordeaux, Sorgues-Dachau* (Etudes Sorguaises).

The speech on pages 368 and 369 was delivered by M. Charles Hernu, the Army Minister, in Toulouse on 24 September 1983.

Marc Levy was born in 1961 in France. He spent six years with the Red Cross and then went on to found several companies, the last of which became one of the leading architectural firms in France. When the film rights of his first novel, *If Only it Were True* were sold to DreamWorks, Marc Levy left his architectural practice and moved to London to dedicate himself to writing. Marc Levy's books have been translated into thirty-eight languages.

Visit www.AuthorTracker.com for exclusive information about Marc Levy.

www.marclevy.info